U L

D 13

TRANSVESTISM AND THE ONNAGATA TRADITIONS IN SHAKESPEARE AND KABUKI

TRANSVESTISM AND THE ONNAGATA TRADITIONS IN SHAKESPEARE AND KABUKI

EDITED BY

MINORU FUJITA
AND
MICHAEL SHAPIRO

GLOBAL
ORIENTAL

TRANSVESTISM AND THE ONNAGATA TRADITIONS
IN SHAKESPEARE AND KABUKI

Edited by Minoru Fujita and Michael Shapiro

First published 2006 by
GLOBAL ORIENTAL LTD
PO Box 219
Folkestone
Kent CT20 2WP
UK

www.globaloriental.co.uk

© Global Oriental 2006

ISBN 1-901903-31-1
ISBN 978-1-901903-31-7 [13-digit]

British Library Cataloguing in Publication Data
A CIP catalogue entry for this book is available
from the British Library

Set in Garamond 11 on 12 point by Bookman, Langley, Berks
Printed and bound in England by Antony Rowe Ltd., Chippenham, Wilts

CONTENTS

[*Plate section faces page 114*]

INTRODUCTION

J ust before daybreak, I felt a thunderous roar welling up from deep in the ground and almost simultaneously the earth itself began shuddering and quaking; I do not know how long this terrifying experience lasted. A devastating earthquake measuring 7 on the Richter scale had struck the city of Kobe and its vicinity, from which my own residence was but a distance of 30 kilometres. In the disaster, houses were torn apart and burnt down; thousands of people died; huge concrete buildings crumbled; an elevated highway lay on the ground like a dead earthworm; railway tracks were mangled and shredded, and the greater part of the city of Kobe was rendered into a river of debris like Pompey and Herculaneum in the wake of the Vesuvian eruption. This happened on 17 January 1995. A women's college had been chosen for the site of an international conference on Shakespeare and kabuki, which was scheduled to be held during the summer of the same year. It was soon known that the college, located in the remoter suburbs of the devastated city, had narrowly escaped the destructive effects of the earthquake, but nobody could be optimistic about the possibility of opening the proposed conference about half a year later.

The planning committee for the Shakespeare-kabuki conference met on numerous occasions only to recognize the virtual impossibility of making any further preparations for the conference. What was it, then, that finally made us decide to open the conference on 8 August that year, as scheduled? The day after the conference ended, Professor Shapiro and I were given a ride in a press car, which had special permission to enter the centre of Kobe city, where we found the greater portion of the urban destruction was still left virtually untouched or unrestored – such was the extent of destruction caused by the earthquake. Nevertheless, the scale of the destruction was, in fact, the very reason and the impetus which impelled us to decide to proceed with our initial plan. We believed it was encumbent on us to attempt to inspire and invigorate the discouraged minds of the citizens in the damaged areas of Kobe by letting them know that an international meeting was going to take place despite the great physical devastation caused by the natural disaster and also that Shakespeare and kabuki were also great survivors and spiritual invigorators of people. This episode will, I believe, demonstrate that theatre, symbolized by kabuki and Shakespeare, is mightier than any natural catastrophe!

The essays included in this volume more or less represent the discussions and arguments that featured in the three-day international conference on Shakespeare and kabuki, with the theme of 'Traditions of Cross-dressing and Cross-gender Casting', held in Nishinomiya city, near Kobe, from 8 to 10 August 1995. The essays by Professors Ann Thomson, Michael Shapiro and Bunzō Torigoe were originally lectures given in plenary sessions, and discussions by Professors Yumiko Yamada and Yoseharu Ozaki are here selected from among those given during the paper sessions and seminars and more or less revised afterwards. Though it was not possible to include Samuel Leiter's original paper, I am delighted that he was able to provide the essay published here which speaks directly to our central theme.

These discussions cover the themes of feminism, transvestism, cross-dressing, cross-gender casting, Elizabethan boy actors and kabuki onnagata – all of them featuring the course and the development of the histories of Shakespeare and kabuki. Comparative approaches to Shakespearean drama and kabuki plays were of course most typical of the kinds of studies that comprised the conference, and this direction of approach reached its acme in the forum session that marked the finale of the memorable three-day meeting. The forum entitled 'Shakespeare and Kabuki' was joined by professors from abroad – Leonardo Pronko, Ann Thompson, and Michael Shapiro, and also by Japanese professors, Tetsuo Anzai and Mitsuo Hirata, and a kabuki critic Tamotsu Watanabe; the discussion was chaired by Professor Tetsuo Kishi.

The idea of Japanese 'onnagata', which may be well-known but often only understood by a limited number of theatre connoisseurs, continues today in kabuki as a living tradition. In the course of the conference seminars, it was variously compared and contrasted with the historicized notion of the 'boy actor' that featured on Shakespeare's own stage, and the acme of this direction of discussion was found in the forum session. The comments and discussions exchanged in the forum were informative and penetrating, and the final chapter of this book is devoted to the rerunning of all the forum exchanges. No marked agreement in opinions about kabuki onnagata and Elizabethan boy actors seemed to have been achieved, and readers will find more disagreements than agreements in the observations made by the various participants; but they are sure to elicit valuable fragments of opinion, which it is hoped will help expand and deepen their own insight into what the kabuki onnagata truly is and in what respects Shakespearean transvestism shares its essence with the traditional female impersonation in kabuki. In this regard, I think that Professor Paul Schalow's iconographical and phenomenological approach to the audience response to kabuki onnagata is most illuminating.

Another great item in the conference programme that strongly interested its participants was the informative report made by Mr Kōji Orita about his kabuki adaptation of Shakespeare's *Hamlet*. The adapted version of this Shakespearean tragedy was based on one of the earliest Japanese translations (1886). Being at the time one of the most senior members of the staff managing the National Theatre in Tokyo (today he is its artistic director) and a most experienced and learned director of traditional kabuki plays in the theatre, Mr Orita's Japanese version of *Hamlet* and the production of it on the stage of the Tokyo Globe theatre in kabuki style with kabuki actors playing the parts of Hamlet, Ophelia and Claudius, may be said to have been one of the greatest phenomena in the Japanese theatre world in the past few decades. This kabuki version of *Hamlet* was brought to England in 1991 and proved to be a great success when it was produced in Dublin, Newcastle and London. Most attractive and miraculous about this version of *Hamlet* is, of course, the female impersonation of the kabuki actor in kimono, and one actor's performance of the two parts of Hamlet and Ophelia. Mr Orita's detailed account of this adapted tragedy, combined with the attached photographs of some of its scenes, will surely capture the interest of the readers of this book. Professor Scott Johnson's supporting explanatory notes are invaluable.

Needless to say, we may trace a strong parallelism between the two traditions, one associated with kabuki in Japan and the other with Shakespeare in England; but there seems to have been a new aspect in the keen interest in the similarities and correspondences between the two theatre traditions. In 1989, the Tokyo Globe theatre was constructed under the supervision of the architect Arata Isozaki. He seemed to have derived his basic architectural concept of the Elizabethan Globe partly from Frances Yates's view of Shakespeare's Globe theatre. Yates had been interested in the Vitruvian idea of the Roman theatre, and as a Shakespearean I was interested in the influence of Classical thought on Renaissance culture and literature, and in the possibility of Classical influence on Shakespeare's Globe theatre. Earlier, in 1978, I translated Yates's book, *Theatre of the World*, into Japanese, and in the late 1980s I was asked to be an adviser to the construction of the Tokyo Globe. In London, I became acquainted with Sam Wanamaker when he was still very well and actively making tremendous efforts to raise funds for the reconstruction of the Globe, on the south bank of the Thames. The opportunity of becoming acquainted with the nature of a rectangular 'open platform stage' set in a circular building, first in Tokyo and then in London, awakened me to the nature of the prototypical rectangular open stage in relation to the Japanese classical *nō* drama and kabuki plays which had evolved their rectangular shape in the same time-frame as the Elizabethan public theatre.

The rectangular open platform stage placed in the centre of the circular Elizabethan amphitheatre was exactly where Shakespeare's drama attained its growth. The year 2000 saw the completion of the building of the Globe theatre in London, and its artistic director Mark Rylance consciously started to revive or recreate the tradition of female impersonation in his productions of Shakespearean plays on the Globe stage. When he played the role of the Egyptian queen in *Antony and Cleopatra* in 2003 and performed the part of Lady Olivia in the 2004 production of *Twelfth Night*, it was evident that he was, in earnest, making efforts to create a new type of female impersonation under the influence of or under the impact of kabuki's tradition of the onnagata performance. This and other similar varieties of circumstances surrounding Shakespeare and kabuki have impacted on the imagination of those interested in Shakespeare and kabuki and have given fresh impetus to their efforts to clarify the meaning and significance of these two theatre traditions. My own essay included in this volume is but a mere precursor of the kind of study concerning the female impersonation on the new Globe's stage as contrasted with that of the traditional kabuki stage. Other kinds of research can be found in this volume that will serve to make the reader more knowledgeable about what Elizabethan boy actors were and why Japanese onnagata came into being and about how actors performed on their stages in Shakespearean and kabuki dramas.

MINORU FUJITA

ACKNOWLEDGEMENTS

Thanks are due, first of all, to all of those who contributed to the success of the international conference on Shakespeare and Kabuki held in Kobe in 1995. I owe particular gratitude to the late Professor Yasunari Takahashi, who first asked me to organize the international conference and then rendered invaluable help and support in every way towards the accomplishment of the various ends and purposes of the meeting. To Professor Michael Shapiro, who filled the crucial role of organizing the conference programme and editing the present volume, I feel infinitely indebted. I am indeed thankful to Mr Paul Norbury who earlier published my volume of essays *Shakespeare East and West* and again was generous enough to offer kindness to me and was patient enough to sustain his endurance for my sake in making careful preparation for the publication of this book. Thanks are also due to Professor Scott Johnson for proofreading and providing significant editorial support in the final stages of the book's make-up and organization.

M.F.

LIST OF CONTRIBUTORS

Tetsuo **Anzai**, Professor Emeritus at Sophia University (Tokyo), is author of *Shakespeare, Man of the Theatre* (1994) and numerous other books; he has translated and professionally directed Shakespeare as well as other Elizabethan plays, including *Hamlet Q1, King Lear, The Jew of Malta*, and *The Alchemist*.

Minoru **Fujita**, Professor Emeritus at Osaka University, has been a life-long student of Shakespeare and his theatre, was an adviser to the construction of the Tokyo Globe, and co-edited (with Pronko) *Shakespeare East and West* (1996).

Mitsuo **Hirata** is Emeritus Professor at Tohoku University (Sendai), who is interested in early English stages and has written essays on medieval and Renaissance drama, both religious and secular, and is a connoisseur of kabuki theatre arts.

Scott **Johnson**, a Professor at Kansai University, has a doctorate in theatre studies, but has written more about book illustration. His introduction to the translation of Orita's talk combines both these interests.

Izumi **Kadono** is Professor of English at Seisen University. She is the co-author of *Shakespeare in Japan for One Hundred Years* (1989) and other books on Shakespeare, and also has written essays on kabuki. She is currently studying Victorian theatre, especially Sir Henry Irving.

Tetsuo **Kishi** is Professor Emeritus of English at Kyoto University. He is co-author (with Graham Bradshaw) of *Shakespeare in Japan* (2005) and has written numerous other books and articles on Shakespeare. Currently he is Vice-chair, International Shakespeare Association.

Samuel L. **Leiter** is Distinguished Professor of Theater at Brooklyn College and the Graduate Center, CUNY. He was the editor of *Asian Theatre Journal* from 1992-2004 and has published nearly two dozen books, including *New Kabuki Encyclopedia* and *A Kabuki Reader*.

Kōji **Orita** is Artistic Director of the National Theatre of Japan, and has produced and directed numerous kabuki plays there. 1991 saw his production and direction of the 1886 Japanese kabuki adaptation of *Hamlet* which is the subject of his contribution to this book.

Yoseharu **Ozaki** is Professor Emeritus at Nara Women's University, who has published books and articles with the themes ranging from Shakespearean drama, text and language, to kabuki onnagata.

Leonard **Pronko** is Professor of Theatre Arts at Pomona College in Claremont, California, where he has directed numbers of kabuki productions in English and was decorated by the Japanese government with the Order of the Sacred Treasure.

Paul G. **Schalow** is Asso. Prof. at Rutgers University. A specialist in Japanese literature and gender studies, he has translated and introduced Ihara Saikaku's *The Great Mirror of Male Love* (1990).

Michael **Shapiro** is Professor Emeritus of English at the University of Illinois. He is the author of *Children of the Revels: The Boy Companies of Shakespeare's Time and Their Plays* (1976) and *Gender in Play on the Shakespearean Stage* (1994).

Ann **Thompson** is Professor of English and Head of the School of Humanities at King's College London. She is a General Editor of the Arden Shakespeare (third series). She has published widely on Shakespeare, mainly in feminist criticism, editing and language studies.

Bunzō **Torigoe**, a leading scholar of Japanese theatre history, is Professor Emeritus at Waseda University and the former director of the Tsubouchi Memorial Theatre Museum at Waseda University.

Tamotsu **Watanabe**, a distinguished dramatic critic, has written *The Destiny of Onnagata* (in Japanese) and other prize-winning books on kabuki, and was awarded the Purple Ribbon Medal by the Japanese government.

Yumiko **Yamada** is a Professor at Kobe College. She is the author of *Ben Jonson and Cervantes: Tilting against Chivalric Romances* (English, 2000) and other writings, including studies of Shakespeare, Chapman, Inigo Jones, Aristotle, and Richard Strauss.

1

A NOTE ON THE GENESIS OF ONNAGATA

BUNZŌ TORIGOE

I n Japanese theatre, male actors specializing in female roles are
called onnagata; in the period when women were still allowed to
act in female roles, the term 'onnagata' did not exist. Only after
1629, the year female performers were banned from the stage, did
the term come into use for male actors in female roles.

Here, I wish to explain the background as to why female
performers were prohibited and then why there were no attempts to
revive female performers in kabuki.

First, let me offer a brief account of the historical circumstances
which led to the creation of the onnagata in kabuki.

In 1603, the name of the woman Izumo no Okuni, the so-called
founder of kabuki, was widely known. Her performances and
reputation gave rise to many successors, thus establishing the period
of *onna* kabuki, or women's kabuki. This is now accepted as
common knowledge in kabuki history. However, I would like to
stress two points. First, there exists the false impression that in
women's kabuki there were only women on stage. Indeed, the stars
were all female, but the supporting roles were, of course, also
performed by male actors. Second, we need to understand that the
fact men and women performed together was indeed epoch-
making.

Beginning with Okuni, women performed in both female and
male parts, wearing men's costumes. The popularity of the

performances – especially the male parts played by women – reflected the new ideas of those days, with the period of civil war having just ended.

In contrast to art forms older than kabuki, in which masks were used, in kabuki make-up is used instead. So it is easy to understand that audiences were very enthusiastic about this new type of performance with enticing women not hiding, but showing their faces openly. However, because of the enormous popularity of kabuki, the government issued a decree that banned kabuki performances. In kabuki history this is considered to have ended women's kabuki. This prohibition, in fact, applied to all activities of female performers. Therefore, kabuki continued with young male actors who, at a glance, looked like women. Eventually, these performances were also banned, thus triggering the beginning of mature male kabuki or *yarō* kabuki in 1653.

The period of young male kabuki stars is called *wakashū* kabuki, and it was during this period that the first onnagata occurred. But it was not until the end of the 1660s that there was a real need of onnagata.

By the end of the seventeenth century the differentiation of role types in kabuki was completed. Different from male role types, there were only two female role types, distinguished according to the age of the woman to be played, namely young women, *wakaonnagata*, and older women, *kashagata*. The male role types were not just differentiated according to age, but also classified according to the character of the person to be played, namely into comic roles, *dōkegata*, and evil men, *katakiyaku*. I would like to stress that such classification did not exist among onnagata role types. Later, numerous kabuki plays were written, leading to the appearance of comic and evil female characters on stage, for example Akuba. Nevertheless, the basic differentiation of onnagata role types was made according to age.

The kabuki of today requires onnagata and needs successors. In kabuki, onnagata have always been highly valued and as kabuki history shows, times of prospering kabuki were always times of famous onnagata, too. Kabuki, with its focus on onnagata, might be considered a strange form of performing art. But let us take a look at the *nō* theatre first. *Nō* matured some three hundred years prior to kabuki and is performed by men only . Among its numerous plays, those with the main actor playing a female role are considered the most important. So, against this background, it is evident that kabuki's female impersonators are not that special.

Switching to ancient Japanese folk-performing art forms, the first entertainer to appear in history is a woman, *Ame no Uzume no Mikoto*. Later records do mention female performers, too, but as a matter of fact, in the course of the history of folk-performing arts in Japan, all genres were generally performed by men. If they were done by women at all, the genre itself was determined by the term *onna*, 'female' like *onna mai, onna gaku, onna kusemai, onna dengaku, onna sarugaku*, etc. It was tacitly understood that all entertainment forms with no gender specified were performed by men.

In ancient times, the term for performer was *wazaogi*. As *waza* means 'technique' and *ogi* 'to attract' the term implies that a performer had a special technique to attract.

The one who was to be attracted was the god or *kami*. In Japan the gender of *kami* is generally understood to be male. Therefore, women were considered to be the most suitable persons to attract these male gods. Not only in Japan, but also on the Korean Peninsula, the term '*miko*' means woman in the service of the gods. The business of attracting the gods is still considered a divine service. The most suitable performers to entertain the women that called in the gods, were men. The way these men entertained, their extraordinary action, is regarded as *geinō* or folk-performing art. Assuming that there is the scheme god = male, the one attracting the god = female, the one entertaining them = male, then performers have to be male.

Against the background of this spiritual structure in Japan, nobody was really concerned about the prohibition of female entertainers in the seventeenth century. Rather, in the long pre-modern history of Japanese performing art forms, the early period of kabuki, thus women's kabuki, could be considered to be exceptional.

This concludes my 'personal view'. During the oral presentation of this paper, I included many more examples, which I have omitted here, because this text has to be translated into English. So there might be some points not easy to understand.

2

SHAKESPEARE AND KABUKI

YOSEHARU OZAKI

K abuki has lately become a favourite subject for comparative studies. It was taken up for one or two of the seminars of the Fifth World Shakespeare Congress held at Tokyo in 1991, and again in the International Conference on Kabuki and Shakespeare held at Seiwa College, Kobe, in 1996. Three months later, in November 1996, there was a study meeting with the theme of 'Vicissitudes in and Prospects for Kabuki' as a cultural heritage.

Indeed, Shakespeare and kabuki have one thing in common, with this difference: they both have female impersonators (or a substitute for a woman), but in the case of Shakespeare, it is not a man but a boy who plays a woman, usually a young girl (not forgetting Lady Macbeth, Volumnia, Cleopatra, etc.), while in kabuki, a grown-up man plays a female, whether young or old. The tradition of Shakespeare's boy-actress (or the boy-actor who specializes in female impersonation) has long been lost since the actress first appeared at about the time of the Restoration (1660-85), while that of kabuki's onnagata has been kept and is still cherished. On Japanese stages, too, actresses entered at about the time of the Meiji Restoration (1868) but not on the kabuki stage. But both types of drama – roughly speaking, one, a literature (a play to hear, as Hamlet says),[1] and the other, a performing art (an entertainment to see, as strongly opposed by Ben Jonson, who wished his audience 'were come to hear, not to see, a play'[2]) – for them to be a drama, required roles of women and players who enact such roles: that is, female impersonation and the female impersonator, which is the original meaning of onnagata, to be transcribed in Chinese characters as (女方) (one in charge of a woman('s) part). But we have in mind something different and somewhat more than a mere substitute for a woman, when we use the term onnagata, which indeed sounds the same, but means something different and when written, written in such different Chinese characters as (女形). This onnagata literally means the female shape or form (as against formless), i.e. the ideal feminine form, and also one who embodies that ideal, i.e. not simply an imitator of a living woman but a creator of the woman in ideal form both physically and spiritually; ideal, that is, from the viewpoint of a man in the particular society of the particular time, in which the necessity of this female impersonation first came into being, that is, when neither a woman nor a youth, but an adult actor had to play a woman. And the history of onnagata is, in a way, a progress from onnagata (女方) to onnagata (女形), from mere substitution for a woman, through female impersonation, to the creation of an ideal feminine form in body and spirit: -*gata* (方) (from -*kara*) means 'one in charge', whereas the meaning of -*gata* (形) is probably the same as that in *hito-gata* (人形) (human shape, or puppet) or *hana-gata* (花形) (floral shape or luminary, i.e. star). This evolution has taken as much as four centuries' assiduous elaboration on the part of adult kabuki actors.

Here is another difference between kabuki and Shakespeare: the actions of onnagata were entirely left to the invention of the individual actor, with hardly any help from play scripts, while Shakespeare helped his boy-actresses considerably with his texts, taking advantage of this stage convention that a boy plays female parts. For kabuki was primarily an entertainment to watch depending more on the actor's personal charms originally, than on his dancing (and later, acting) ability than on the script itself, while with Shakespeare, 'the play's the thing' and he set down every single word in the text, as Hamlet warns the players to 'let those that play your clowns speak no more than is set down for them' (*Hamlet* III.ii.38-40). Actually, there were originally no scripts in kabuki, nor were they necessary at first, for kabuki's chief attraction was dancing and this hardly needed any texts (one early text that remains is suggestive of *nōh-kyōgen*). As this shows kabuki came to have plots and became more complicated than what had been an improvised performance – based on a plot established by word of mouth by the leading actor (i.e. *kuchi-daté* (口立て), with dialogues made up by individual performers on the scene (this is still a method used in kabuki) – came to be a play to be studied by means of the *kashiragaki* (頭書き) method, i.e. by jotting down only the head (or first) part of each speech. Then whole speeches came to be written down and published at about the time of the Meiji Restoration. Until then, playwrights had been subservient to actors, and were considered immodest, if they put their names to their own plays. People actually didn't care who wrote the plays. Indeed, kabuki plays had always been written with the actor at their core, the chief point being to show off the actor's art and his charm to best advantage. So one of the chief duties on the part of a playwright attached to a theatre (as all of them were) was to rewrite old plays to adjust them to the new circumstances and the particular actor's skill so as to enhance their art. Thus, kabuki play scripts underwent changes so frequently that they couldn't afford to settle into standard texts.

Consider one extreme example, which incidentally also shows how, although kabuki is not a play to listen to (like Shakespeare), it is something in which to enjoy the actor's voice and his art of elocution. *Shibaraku* (Wait a Moment) is one of 'The 18 Representative Kabuki Plays' (the famous Ichikawa family's collection), though not much of a literary work; its title is taken from a shout delivered from offstage by the hero just before he enters on the *hanamichi* (literally 'flower path', a raised passageway that joins the stage and passes straight through the auditorium), to save the innocent victims. For many years, this chief character had a different name (depending on which background was chosen for the play) whenever the play was revived. In recent times, however, he has been known as Kamakura Gongorō Kagémasa. He speaks at great length about his name on the *hanamichi*, half way to the main stage (according to the *tsurané* convention in which *aragoto* (rough business) heroes deliver, in sonorous tones, long speeches about their names, intentions, origins and virtues). It was once part of the Ichikawa family tradition to have each actor write his own *tsurané* for this play, but the task eventually fell to the house playwrights, who then considered the particular actor's skill and the particular occasion on which the play was revived, invented the appropriate speech, and handed that to the actor each time he took on the role. More than fifty versions of this speech still remain today, each differing according to the situation, so that it is impossible for the play to settle into *the* text. But that couldn't be helped, for kabuki was, first and foremost, an actor-centred entertainment. People came to the theatre, primarily to see and hear their favourite actors, not the plays.

Therefore, Sakata Tōjūrō (1647-1709), by far the best actor of *Kamigata* (the Kyoto and Osaka area), was exceptional in remarking, when told regrettably that he had nothing much to act in a certain play, that the purpose of his theatre is not to present himself, but to present a play; and also in asking the playwright to invent the best lines he could, when improvisation by actors was in fashion. And the playwright that Tōjūrō finally came to work with was the great Chikamatsu Monzaémon (1653-1724), who had been writing for the puppet theatre, and had to write down everything – narration, dialogues and all (since puppets cannot speak for themselves) – for the *shamisen* (three-stringed instrument) accompanist to compose music for the reciter to recite to. Chikamatsu is said to have had a sort of disagreement later with the great female impersonator, Yoshizawa Ayamé, and eventually returned to the puppet theatre that aimed at the realistic representation of human nature. Anyway, he had put his name to his works for the puppet theatre (and then for kabuki theatre), four years before Tominaga Heibei, an actor, who turned to writing in the 1670s, printed his name for the first time as a playwright in the 1680 *kaömisé* (all-star cast) production programme, which was quite unusual then and brought public censure upon him.

Thus, roughly, kabuki's essence (like that of ballet or opera) is in actors and their acting on the stage, while Shakespeare's is in the text of his dramatic poetry on the printed page. As kabuki was founded by a woman called Okuni and her troupe, women first played men dashingly in fashionable and gorgeous attire to enhance their sex appeal, and men presumably played women with a gesture of grotesquerie to add a touch of comic effect. These can also be called onnagata, but not the onnagata we have in mind.

The art of onnagata came to be seriously considered when

mature actors of *yarō*-kabuki (adult men's kabuki) had to play female parts. In 1652, when *wakashū*-kabuki (young men's kabuki) was officially banned in Edo and Osaka, and four years later in Kyoto, for much the same reason as *onna*-kabuki (women's kabuki) or *yūjo*-kabuki (courtesans' kabuki) after Okuni, had been prohibited in 1629 for reasons of having given moral offence. Although women's parts had been played by men in women's kabuki, it was for comic effect, and young men played women to enhance their sex appeal. Indeed, young men's kabuki had their own female impersonators among the company of charming, handsome boys. During this period of young men's kabuki (ca. 1629-52), Murayama Sakon, born in Sakai, Osaka, went down from Kyoto to Edo in 1638 or 1642, and made his debut there in 1642, dancing in a rich glossed-silk costume, his head covered with a long coloured piece of cloth (*oki-tenugui*), and a twig of artificial cherry flowers in his hand. He looked so charmingly like a woman that it was difficult to distinguish man from woman. Moreover, when women's kabuki had been banned, some actresses surreptitiously joined young men's kabuki and performed with them dressed in female attire, so that in August 1642, Sakai Tadakatsu, a member of the Shōgun's Council of State, suggested the prohibition of men from playing women.

Saruwaka Kanzaburō and six other theatre managers appealed the matter in February of the following year and were permitted in April to have an actor act as a woman on the condition that they should thereafter present in advance a list of actors, specifying who and how many would respectively play male and female parts, so as to make sure that there would be no women there (1643). Hence, the term onnagata (one who plays a woman's part) came to be used. Thus, individual actors had to limit themselves to one role and were expected to devote themselves assiduously to their specialized role, without interfering with each other. Now, it would be easy for young men to play women, for 'boys and women are for the most part cattle of this colour' (*As You Like It*, III.ii.414-15), says Ganymede/ Rosalind, and Stephen Orgel mentions 'practical similarities between boys and women' recognized in Elizabethan times.[3] The same similarities were also acknowledged in the Edo period in Japan, and homosexuality, which then was called 'the way of male love', spread even among the townsfolk. And the onnagata in young men's kabuki could easily be substitutes for women, and relied more on their sex appeal (as boys as well as female disguises) than on their acting ability. Hence the final banning of this type of kabuki in 1652 (in Edo and Osaka) and in 1656 (in Kyoto). In Edo and Osaka, however, actors by appeal were allowed to perform again the next year, and in Kyoto the same year, on two conditions: first, all actors had to shave the young men's attractive forelocks, which were actually the symbol of *wakashū* (boys usually of eleven to sixteen years of age, when they had the ceremony of assuming manhood by way of changing their hairstyle), and have their heads bald in front (*yarō-gashira*, i.e. adult men's coiffure); and second, what they were to act should be '*monomané-kyōgen-zukushi*' (all-imitation pieces, i.e. 'not mimicking of voices and mannerisms of particular persons, but of people, young and old, male and female, high and low, sacred and secular', plays, that is, instead of mere singing and dancing. This is called *yarō*-kabuki (adult men's kabuki); though at first played by young men in the adult hairstyle, until about 1673, when it simply came to be called kabuki.

The frequently attempted official oppressions, therefore, turned out to be an enormous gain for kabuki: now, the actors had to rely more on their acting talent than on their sex appeal to earn a living. Kabuki for the first time was given a chance to become a regular performing art. Since the actors had to imitate life, they also had to impersonate women of various types and ages, i.e. not only courtesans, who were then admired as ideal women of culture, but samurai (soldiers) and citizens' wives and daughters. Hence the emergence of the various role-types of women, the invention of wigs (*oki-tenugui*) (see Murayama Sakon above) would have been enough for dancing, but not for plays, and the need for legitimate plays to represent life.

It is, indeed, unnatural for a man to act as a woman, but art, by definition, is unnatural, and is opposed to nature. It is not art for a woman to be on the stage as a woman. This is not acting; she merely is. She acts only when she becomes somebody other than herself. She must therefore first obliterate the woman within herself, as onnagata must do the man within himself, before she becomes the woman for the theatre. It does not matter, therefore, whether it be a man or a woman who plays the woman's part. What matters is how best to play a woman, or to be more precise, how best to represent such a character as the audience willingly takes to be a woman. A player, whether male or female, is a shadow, to use Shakespeare's favourite word, or a code, which itself should ideally be nothing, but exist only to represent something else. It is quite possible, therefore, that an actress can fail more easily to become a woman for the stage, as she generally tends to be over-confident of her own femininity, without thinking what it really is. A woman *can* be attractive even as she is, but *is* not always so even in real life, much less so on the stage. What really matters is not whether the actor *is* beautiful, but whether he *looks* beautiful on the stage. Arashi Sangorō was a very ugly actor, but when he played a role (in character) of a fisherman called Red-Faced Konohei, he doubled as a handsome and unrivalled beau named Ariwara-no-Yukihira in *Hama-Matsukaze*, and he is said to have looked the handsomest man in the world, for he danced so well. What made him look so enchantingly handsome was, of course, his dancing skill.

The onnagata first tries to observe and imitate living women but selectively and creatively, exaggerating and stylizing what are (physically as well as morally) good about them, as the onnagata originally tried to grasp them as the pattern of beauty both in body and spirit, and create an ideal woman of them. Bad women were not played by onnagata, but by *tachiyaku* (one who takes a man's part, and impersonated wicked characters, either male or female). Thus, turning their own disadvantages to advantages, onnagata later came to contrive such varieties of female characters as real women are incapable of.

Even today, some actresses have adopted the acting style of onnagata. Companies which started in the 1890s and were called *shimpa* to distinguish their New School from the Old School or kabuki, still included onnagata; some of the favourite plays for their repertoire were, and still are, by Izumi Kyōka (1873-1939), which couldn't possibly be satisfactorily staged with actresses, but only with onnagata. It seems that Mizutani Yaéko I (1905-79), a veteran actress of *shimpa* and Taïchi Kiwako (?-1992), also an actress from *shingéki* (New Drama), when acting, first became onnagata, then played their female roles in the onnagata style.

Indeed, most onnagata parts in kabuki and in *shimpa* would be too much for women. The onnagata first becomes a woman for the stage (without obliterating his manhood completely), and then plays 'her' part; therefore, the art of onnagata is more of an art than that of an actress. Not only onnagata, but kabuki performance as a whole is a fiction; it is the very acting that makes a papier-mâché teacup look as heavy and fragile as a real one. Indeed, it is not proper in kabuki to use real objects on the stage. The art of onnagata, too, is sometimes jokingly called *ninsan bakéshichi* (人三化七), 30% person, 70% transformation: in other words, 30% of the actor's representation may involve his personal charms, but the rest turns on his art of impersonation. Formalization and stylization by dancing is indeed a great help, though the first great onnagata Yoshizawa Ayamé (1673-1729) tried to imitate a living woman and live a daily life as a woman, making much of *jigei* (realist art) as opposed to *shosagoto* (dancing) in which his rival, Mizuki Tatsunosuké (1673-1745) excelled. It is indeed impossible for a man to become a woman; an actor can only hope to cultivate the art of impersonating a woman as closely as possible, and this can be achieved more easily by stylized acting than by realistic acting. There are two schools of onnagata: one, realistic (by way of 'living as the woman') and the other, formalistic (by way of 'acting as the woman'), both being equally arts, as opposed to nature. Segawa Kikunojō I (1691-1749), one of the second generation of onnagata, brought Ayamé's subtle and elaborate art to its culmination not only by living his daily life as a woman but by achieving the way of female impersonation as esoteric transformation. While Ayamé, thus by living as a woman, acted naturally as a woman, Kikunojō calculated how to impress the audience with his beauty on the stage, exploiting aesthetic distance so that they applauded him enthusiastically, saying he was a perfect *onna-gata* without *gata*, which was unnecessary. Then came the third generation of onnagata, who saw the limits of a man trying to 'live naturally (and act naturally) as the woman'; the art of onnagata then became a system of techniques to be learned deliberately and handed down, at about the time when the whole acting method of kabuki came to be accomplished as a system of techniques. Nakamura Tomijūrō (1721-86), the third son of Ayamé, who was versatile in acting talent, was particularly skilful at *onna-budō* (female martial arts), that is, performing the roles of women who are strong both in martial arts and in spirit, and even went so far as to play a role of *aragoto* (rough business). He, therefore, acted against his father's principles as onnagata, but the contemporary audience welcomed his playing roles outside his original specialty. As the boundary between male and female impersonators was disappearing, people found it interesting to see them fuse and exchange each other's roles. The strict role-type system (i.e. one actor for one role-type) was being broken down, as social demoralization increased and outlaws in various fields came out. On the stage, too, an entirely new type of woman, a pert tomboy, with charms of boyish naughtiness, turned up, fresh from the contemporary underworld. Thus, such classifications as onnagata, *wakashūgata*, *dōkégata*, *tachiyaku* and others were now applied to the roles, not to the actors themselves. As Ichikawa Danjūrō IX (1839-1903) said much later, although he had no physique fit for onnagata, he could play women's parts, first because dancing helped him, and second because he strictly observed the disciplines of onnagata. In this way, onnagata became a matter of discipline and acting technique, which, once mastered, allowed the male impersonator to play women's parts as well.

Kabuki does not have as many disguised heroines as Shakespeare, but it employs, on the other hand, what is called *hayagawari* ('quick-change technique', used when an actor playing more than one role in the same scene make quick changes of costume and make-up from one role to another), and also, as we have seen, it is not unusual in kabuki for two or more parts to be taken by one actor, so that the actor is given a chance to show his versatility. One famous example, among others, is *Osomé Hisamatsu Ukina no Yomiuri* (Hawking Ballad of Osomé and Hisamatsu's Love Affair) (1813), in which rapid changes are required of the one actor who plays as many as seven roles: Osomé (heroine), Hisamatsu (her lover), Takékawa (Hisamatsu's elder sister), Téishōni (Osomé's mother), Oroku (*akuba*, or a wicked maid), Omitsu (a country girl, in love with Hisamatsu) and Osaku (a peasant's wife). All these seven roles were first played by Iwai Hanshirō V, the most popular female impersonator of the time; the wildly acclaimed wicked maid Oroku was that entirely new type of woman fresh from the underworld of contemporary Edo, whom onnagata had never before represented. In June 1991, a *Kabuki Version of Hamlet – Hamuretto Yamato-Nishikié* (Hamlet in Ancient Colour Print) (adapted originally by Kanagaki Robun in 1886) – was performed for the first time. In this version. Ichikawa Somégorō doubled the parts of Hamuramaru (Hamlet) and Mikariya-himé (Ophelia). Who could think of Gielgud or Olivier playing both Hamlet and Ophelia in the Nunnery Scene? But kabuki is entertainment of a kind unfamiliar in Western drama, and the kabuki audience sometimes likes to see an actor in as many parts as possible.

Presumably, Shakespeare's audience also liked to see his boys both in boys' and girls' parts. It seems rather natural and also easier for boys playing women to play boys in disguise. Actually, however, it is not so easy as it seems for a boy-actress to play a girl's part and then disguise himself as a boy, without reverting to himself, but still retaining some femininity of the girl in disguise as the boy. Indeed, an Elizabethan boy who was brought up in female attire until five or six years of age, would have been more at ease in a girl's disguise than in a boy's with some femininity left about him. A well experienced female impersonator of kabuki could do this, like Nakamura Senjaku (later Ganjirō III) in *Ōishi Saïgo-no-Hi* (The Last Day of Ōishi's Life; see Appendix), but possibly the boy-actress could hardly ever cope with this. So Shakespeare seems to have helped his boy-actress with his words, in case they couldn't act well enough: indeed, his audience's eye, with Oliver's, could well profit by his tongue (Orlando's description):

> If that an eye may profit by a tongue,
> Then should I know you by description –
> Such garments and such years: 'The boy is fair,
> Of female favour, and bestows himself
> Like a ripe sister: the woman low
> And browner than her brother.'

(As You Like It, IV.iii.83-87)

Although Rosalind has disguised herself as Ganymede, Orlando sees the woman under her male attire and says so in his description. And strange, isn't it, that he says nothing much about Celia, even if he is the lover of Rosalind who, however, is not supposed to be there. But Celia should be attractive enough for Oliver to fall in love with at first sight. All this seems to be Shakespeare's special consideration for Rosalind. Not only her lover, but Phebe, a wild shepherdess in love with 'him', sees more of the woman in 'him' and finds that attractive, as the 'damask cheek' was a traditional epithet to apply to the beautiful woman:

> The best thing in him
> Is his complexion; and faster than his tongue
> Did make offence, his eye did heal it up.
> . . . . . .
> There was a pretty redness in his lip,
> A little riper and more lusty red
> Than that mix'd in his cheek; 'twas just the difference
> Betwixt the constant red and mingled damask.
>
> (III.v.115-23)

Boys are universally acknowledged as akin to women, as the charming hero Wakamatsu in the Okinawan version of the *Dōjōji* legend looks to be quite a woman with feminine make-up and feminine costume; boys were not supposed to be full men (nor, of course, women) before the initiation rite of assuming manhood (*genpuku*) at fifteen or sixteen years of age, and served at the Okinawan Court wearing the same hairstyle as a woman's, the only difference being in the way of wearing *kanzashi* (ornamental hairpin). And youth is often associated with a woman; thus Coriolanus, when young enough to play the woman in the theatre, proved the bravest warrior in the battlefield:

> When he might *act the woman* in the scene,
> He prov'd best man i'th'field, . . .
>
> (*Coriolanus*, II.ii.96-97)

But what about an elderly woman, and how to act her part? Here may be a difference between the onnagata played by a grown-up actor and Shakespeare's boy-actress. Both use a *kata* (style of acting) and both begin by observing and imitating a living woman, of which both make a *kata* but with a difference: an adult actor cannot end with this realistic *kata*, but has to create, and still improve, the *kata* of the woman as the ideal pattern of female beauty, both physical and spiritual, which he can continue to act however old he becomes, thus attaining what Zéami called *makoto-no-hana* (true flower); whereas the boy-actress can still go on mimicking, taking advantage of youth, and enjoy Zéami's *jibun-no-hana* (flower of the time, i.e. of youth, and therefore temporary). The art of onnagata is how to make the old look youthful or the plain look beautiful, whereas the art of the boy-actress seems to be how best to imitate or 'usurp the grace,/ Voice, gait, and action of a gentlewoman' (*The Taming of the Shrew*, Ind.i.131-32), or of any woman (which indeed is the starting point for both boy-actress and onnagata). 'If the boy have not a woman's gift', says the Lord, 'To rain a shower of commanded tears, An onion will do for such a shift' (*The Taming of the Shrew*, Ind.i.124-26). But Shakespeare's lines will do more. 'I am pale, Charmian' (*Antony and Cleopatra*, II.v.59), says Cleopatra. This is, presumably, a stage direction for Cleopatra to turn pale, but what if she couldn't? Well, the 'onion' of words, especially prepared by Shakespeare has already accomplished that shift, and 'an [audience's] eye may profit by a [player's] tongue'; while the onnagata, left on his own, contrives to *look like* weeping, if not really to weep, which indeed is what matters on stage.

Thus, Shakespeare keeps reminding the audience of the boy in their sight being actually a girl in disguise by making other characters observe her femininity in disguise:

> For they shall yet belie thy happy years,
> That say thou art a man. Diana's lip
> Is not more smooth and rubious; thy small pipe
> Is as the maiden's organ, shrill and sound,
> And all is semblative a woman's part.

> (*Twelfth Night*, I.iv.30-34)

Orsino sees in Cesario both man and woman – a man rightly (though he says Cesario is not old enough to be a man, yet a male at any rate) – and a woman rightly and wrongly (as Cesario is a woman in disguise and that woman impersonated by a boy, as the audience was well aware). Was Orsino attracted by the woman (Viola) in the man (Cesario) or by the man (Cesario or/and the boy-actress) in the woman (Viola) or both? Was he 'the master mistress' of Orsino's passion? Was the audience who knew better also attracted in much the same way? The boy has impersonated Viola, who then impersonates Cesario without apparently reverting to himself nor losing Viola's feminine charm (the above lines are helping him there, reminding the audience of his female part). Also Shakespeare has helped his boy enacting his female part when he again disguises himself as a boy by making 'her' ashamed of her transformation as monstrosity (e.g. *Twelfth Night*, II.ii.34: 'poor monster'; also *ibid.*, I.27; *The Two Gentlemen of Verona*, V.iv.104-7), or by making her crack a bawdy joke to cover her embarrassment when she turns to a man (*The Merchant of Venice*, III.iv.60-80). Indeed, transvestism was prohibited by the Bible, but *Hic Mulier*, or masculine women, were rampant in early seventeenth-century London, as Juliet Dusinberre remarks.[4] But Jessica, who is going to elope in man's attire, is not of the sort:

> I am glad 'tis night, you do not look on me,
> For I am much asham'd of my exchange.
> But love is blind, and lovers cannot see
> The pretty follies that themselves commit,
> For if they could, Cupid himself would blush
> To see me thus transformed to a boy.

> (*The Merchant of Venice*, II.vi.34-39)

And Lucetta teases Julia who is going to pursue Proteus, with a bawdy jest:

> *Luc.* Why then your ladyship must cut your hair.
> *Jul.* No, girl, I'll knit it up in silken strings,
>   With twenty odd-conceited true-love knots:
>   To be fantastic may become a youth
>   Of neater time than I shall show to be.
> *Luc.* What fashion, madam, shall I make your breeches?
> *Jul.* That fits as well as 'Tell me, good my lord,
>   What compass will you wear your farthingale?'
>   Why, e'vn what fashion thou best likes, Lucetta.
> *Luc.* You must needs have them with a codpiece, madam.
> *Jul.* Out, out, Lucetta, that will be ill-favor'd.
> *Luc.* A round hose, madam, now's not worth a pin,
>   Unless you have a codpiece to stick pins on. . . .

> (*The Two Gentlemen of Verona*, II.vii.45-56)

To Julia, a codpiece is, indeed, not only ill-favor'd but useless, but to the boy impersonating Julia, a codpiece comes in more than handy. This kind of bawdy joke, which had usually been made by a servant in Shakespeare's early plays, came to be cracked by heroines later on, as he became confident that the audience, far from blaming them for being immodest, would rather enjoy it. So it is now Portia who confides to Nerissa her plan of going to their husbands 'in such a habit/That they shall think we are accomplished/With that we lack' (*The Merchant of Venice*, III.iv.60-62), and Nerissa, her waiting-gentlewoman, who is surprised to ask, 'Why, shall we turn to men?' (*The Merchant of Venice*, III.iv.78), which Portia wittingly distorts, 'Fie, what a question's that,/If thou went near a lewd interpreter!' (*The Merchant of Venice*, ibid., 79-80).

Now, this convention of a boy playing a woman's part, disguising himself as a girl offstage and of a disguised girl again disguising herself as a boy onstage seems to have been so well established with the English public that they were offended with the mixed French troupe when they came to play in London. Not only that, but also the convention was reversed with great success in *Epicoene* where fiction (a silent 'woman') turns out to be reality (a boy) on the stage. Yet, it was still considered ungainly (or monstrous) for a man, if not a boy, to disguise himself as a woman onstage. One passage from The Introduction to *Antonio and Mellida* is well known:

ANTONIO. I was never worse fitted since the nativity of
     my actorship; I shall be hiss'd at, on my life now.
FELICHE. Why, what must you play?
ANTONIO. Faith, I know not what, an hermaphrodite,
     two parts in one; my true person being Antonio son
     to the Duke of Genoa, though for the love of Mellida,
     Piero's daughter, I take this feigned presence of an
     Amazon, calling myself Florizel and I know not what.
     I a voice to play a lady! I shall ne'er do it.
ALBERTO. O, an Amazon should have such a voice,
     virago-like. Not play two parts in one? away, away; 'tis
     common fashion. Nay, if you cannot bear two subtle
     fronts under one hood, idiot go by, go by, off this
     world's stage. O time's impurity!

(Ll.65-76; G. K. Hunter's edition)

All this, of course, is a self-conscious joke, to prevent the audience's unfavourable reaction, gibing in passing at the times' fashion. And that is understandable, since we know how Falstaff disguised himself as 'the old woman of Brainford' (*The Merry Wives of Windsor*, IV.ii.86-86) and how village boys of Windsor disguised themselves as brides in its final scene.

How, then, did the page Bartholomew disguise himself as a drunken tinker's (Sly's) wife? He is supposed to:

> bear himself with honorable action,
> Such as he hath observ'd in noble ladies
> Unto their lords, by them accomplished;

> (*The Taming of the Shrew*, The Induction, i.110-12)

and the Lord seems well sure that:

> the boy will usurp the grace,
> Voice, gait, and action of a gentlewoman.

> (The Induction, 11.131-32)

It seems therefore that the actor who plays the part of the page is a boy-actress, who specializes in disguising himself as a lady, and will presumably play the part well – at least well enough to take in the drunken Sly, since the actor had not appeared on the stage as himself (a page). When he enters, he enters playing the part he plays in the play-within-the-play improvised by the Lord, but the page and the Lord are also the parts they play in this play of *The Taming of the Shrew*, which, indeed, is the play-within-the-play played before the drunken Sly by the players who again had not appeared on the stage as themselves. So Sly (reality on the stage) as the Lord (fiction on the stage) watches the play-within-the-play (fiction on the stage), as the Lord (reality) watches Sly as the Lord (fiction) watching the-play-within-the-play ('The Taming of the Shrew') (fiction). As 'The Taming of the Shrew' goes on, the onstage audience – Sly, the Lord, his page and others – disappears, and when the play-within-the-play ends, the play itself ends, and 'The Taming of the Shrew' has become *The Taming of the Shrew*, the fiction thus becoming the reality on the stage. But the reality on the stage is, indeed, the fiction, and Sly, the Lord and Bartholomew are really actors offstage, that is, on 'this world's stage'. In this way Shakespeare presents reality in the fiction and fiction in the reality on his stage.

Nakamura Tomijūrō I (1721-86), in his sixties, wanted to revive a dance play of his own creation, called *Kyōkanoko Musumé Dōjōji*, in which he was to play the part of a young girl of seventeen or eighteen. When his wife told him to give up the idea, saying he couldn't conceal his age, Tomijūrō left home, saying nothing. When he returned, he asked his wife if anyone had visited him in his absence. She answered somewhat jealously that a pretty girl of seventeen or eighteen had come to see him, but told of his absence, left reluctantly. Tomijūrō laughed and said: 'That girl was me! Now you see that I can put on *Dōjōji* still.' And most probably he did: a man of sixty could well present a girl of sixteen at an aesthetic distance on the theatrical stage, but not on 'this world's stage'. However dark it may have been in the inside of an old Japanese house, it is really incredible to mistake the kabuki's thick make-up and the onnagata's feigned voice for a natural, and that by his own wife in real life!

When the Rosalind actor speaking the Epilogue on the theatrical stage says, 'It is not the fashion to see the lady in the epilogue. . .', Rosalind (fiction) is speaking, but when 'she' goes on to say, 'If I were a woman. . .', the boy-actress (reality) is speaking, but when she curtsies and exits, it is Rosalind (fiction) again who is asking the audience to bid her farewell by applauding. Thus, the Rosalind actor plays fiction (the part), then reality (himself), and finally fiction (the part) into which the actor disappears. The boy-actress is really 'boying' here, changing the grammatical function from that of the noun to that of the verb and again back to that of the noun, changing accordingly himself to the fictitious person and then back again to himself, but still on the theatrical stage and rightly. For the art of onnagata or of boy-actress or any art to have its magical effect, aesthetic distance from the audience will be absolutely necessary.

APPENDIX

In *The Last Day of Ōishi's Life*, a pretty young page comes stealthily into a room, from which he can clearly see one *rōnin* after another going to the execution ground. The page, Shizuma, is then caught by Ōïshi, the leader of the forty-seven *rōnin* (lordless samurai), who is also going to be executed that day, and exposes his identity. The page proves no page at all but a girl Omino who has fallen in love with one of the *rōnin* about to be executed that day. In order to see her beloved once again before he is executed, she comes in male disguise and gets caught. Ōïshi has suspected at once that the page is a woman in disguise, but an ordinary spectator might not have. To me at any rate, he looked an extraordinary pretty, graceful young page, who, however, once his identity having been revealed, looked convincingly a woman, acted by Nakamura Senjaku (later Ganjirō III). Apart from Ōïshi, I saw no man on the stage but Omino in male disguise, the physical 'man' in Senjaku having completely disappeared into the roles, i.e. a disguised man (Shizuma) and a woman in disguise (Omino). The actor, having impersonated Omino, did not revert to being himself when Omino disguised herself as a page, but created an entirely new male role. This indeed takes a high level of acting skill, and Shakespeare's lines would have helped his boy-actress a great deal, if the boy when in male disguise should revert to being himself.

NOTES

1. See *Hamlet* II.ii.535, passim.
2. *The Staple of News*, the prologue for the stage, I.2; also the prologue for the court, ll. 5-8.
3. See his essay on 'Why in England did boys play women?' included in Japanese translation in *Current Shakespeare Criticism*, Tokyo: *Kenkyūsha*, 1993, p. 287.
4. See *Shakespeare and the Nature of Women*, London: The Macmillan Press Ltd, 1975, p. 239. Also p. 255, ibid.

3

PERFORMING GENDER:
THE CONSTRUCTION OF
FEMININITY IN
SHAKESPEARE AND KABUKI

ANN THOMPSON

I n London in 1845, theatre-goers had a choice between two
performers in the role of Romeo in Shakespeare's *Romeo and
Juliet*: Samuel Phelps and Charlotte Cushman. Phelps was in his
mid-forties and Cushman was in her late twenties; neither would
seem the ideal choice for the part in the context of a modern
Western tradition of naturalistic casting – Phelps on account of his
age, Cushman on account of her gender – yet both were celebrated
in the role. One of the 'hottest' (hardest to obtain) theatre tickets in
London 150 years later, in August 1995, is for Deborah Warner's
production of *Richard II* at the National Theatre with Fiona Shaw in
the title role. The National Theatre has also recently cast Virginia
Radcliffe as 'Prospero, deposed Duchess of Milan', in a version of
The Tempest directed by Brigid Larmour of the Education
Department as a performance project for schools, and we have
seen the return to London after a successful international tour of
the Cheek by Jowl company's all-male *As You Like It* (directed by
Declan Donnellan, first performed in 1991) in which Rosalind,
played by Adrian Lester, was not only male but black.

Cross-race casting has become so common in England at the

National Theatre and the Royal Shakespeare Company that I could not find a reviewer who even thought it worth commenting on the fact that the RSC had cast a black actor, Hugh Quarshie, as Loveless, the philandering husband and object of desire in this season's production of Vanbrugh's *The Relapse*, though such a casting decision would have drawn adverse comments ten or even five years ago. On the other hand, reviewers *were* puzzled what to make of the casting of the same black actor as Mephistopheles in *Faust*, so it seems that blackness can mean different things in different contexts: sometimes audiences are required to ignore race, but at other times they may be required to focus on it as a deliberate and meaningful decision.

Cross-gender casting is rather more conspicuous, though this depends of course on how it is employed. Many play-goers at *As You Like It* remarked that they simply stopped noticing after a while that the entire cast was male (though someone behind me during the first run refused to believe that Audrey was acted by a man on account of what he termed the performer's 'terrific' legs). The same thing seems to have happened when the Women's One World (WOW) collective put on an all-female version of Sheridan's *The School for Scandal* directed by Alice Forrester and Heidi Griffiths in New York in 1989, according to Kate Davy (1994, p. 132). This can also occur when only one part is cross-cast: it was possible for some viewers of *Richard II* to forget that the King was being played by a woman, perhaps because Fiona Shaw dressed and behaved like a man, albeit an effeminate one at times. In *The Tempest*, however, Virginia Radcliffe dressed and behaved like a woman – indeed a mother – and Brigid Larmour's production encouraged the audience to think about her gender rather than to overlook it. A similarly explicit focus on the cross-casting of the central character seems to have produced mixed reactions in audiences of Robert Wilson's production of *King Lear* in Frankfurt in 1990, which starred Marianne Hoppe in the title role, according to Erika Fischer-Lichte (1992).

These recent productions raise a large number of issues in relation to contemporary gender politics as well as performance conventions. They need to be discussed in the context of the growing empowerment of female directors and performers (amongst whom one would want to include the extraordinarily versatile Kathryn Hunter who has performed an astonishing range of roles, male and female, young and old, in her work with Theatre de Complicite and the National Theatre). I am mentioning them now (obviously enough) as a way into our discussion of cross-gender casting in Shakespearean drama and kabuki, two theatrical traditions which share the practice of regularly and uniformly casting men in women's roles. I want to explore the notion that this is not, in either tradition, merely a question of costume, though recent studies of English Renaissance Drama have focused productively on issues of 'cross-dressing'. I am thinking here of books such as Marjorie Garber's *Vested Interests: Cross-Dressing and Cultural Anxiety* (1992), Jonathan Dollimore's *Sexual Dissidence*, which has a chapter on 'Cross-Dressing in Early Modern England' (1991) and Laura Levine's *Men in Women's Clothing* (1994).

Cross-dressing is of course an important element in what is going on, but 'Femininity' – and indeed 'Masculinity' – are constructed through voice, gesture and other performative codes which relate to (but may not be identical to) real-life gender stereotyping and real-life behaviour. Gender itself, one might say, *is* performance: a cultural construct or system of learned codes. We all project and perceive signals about gender all the time in standard social situations, as analysts such as Erving Goffman have shown. (*The Presentation of Self in Everyday Life*, 1959. See also Marianne Wex, 1980 and Judith Butler, 1990.) Are the theatrical codes simply more exaggerated, more graphic, more abstract than the real-life codes? We have to learn gendered behaviour in real life: I remember being told by one of the nuns at the convent school, where I spent two years, that I should smile more, because the proper expression for a girl's or woman's face in repose is a smile, whereas a boy or man can look serious. I was dismayed by this and failed to learn it. Can performers learn (or fail to learn) the theatrical codes in the same way? Is learning to perform as someone of a different gender comparable to learning to perform as someone of a different age or class? I think we also need to ask, in the context of Shakespearean theatre and kabuki, how far the male performers in each tradition are directly *imitating* women and how far they are *performing* women, and what this distinction means. (I should add at this point that I speak with much more knowledge of Shakespeare than of kabuki; I defer to other contributors with more expertise on the latter.)

To begin with, why are women not allowed to perform on the stage in the first place? Why the need for impersonation of women by men? The proscription against female performers is usually represented as a moral one. In Japan, although the conventional account of the origins of kabuki in the early seventeenth century attributes it to female dancers, notably Okuni of Kyoto, women were forbidden to perform in 1629, apparently because of the association of the performances with prostitution. Young male actors began to play women's parts but this, too, caused problems and accusations of homosexual practices and from the 1650s only adult males were allowed to perform. In Renaissance England the all-male acting tradition is assumed to have grown out of the guild-based medieval drama. It was also of course the object of sustained moral opprobrium – again associated with homosexuality – and the 1662 prohibition of men acting women's parts was presented as a moral reform – ironically in the light of the exploitation of the female body which followed immediately on the Restoration stage. (See Elizabeth Howe, *The First English Actresses*, 1992.)

While actual women were prevented from appearing on either stage, the notion of performance could simultaneously be considered as something belonging to a female sphere; male actors were (and still are) seen as effeminate, and the process of acting or impersonation can constitute a threat to male identity. The association with prostitution has not gone away; for a man to act or to dance can still mean signalling a 'feminine' kind of sexual availability. And there are several other asymmetries at work. What of the audience? Even in the naturalistically-cast Hollywood cinema it has been maintained that the privileged spectator is a man – women in the audience must adopt the so-called 'male gaze' – so who is supposed to be watching the men performing as women in the cross-cast theatre? Are men performing as women for the gratification of other men? What is being said about women in such a case, and what is happening to or for the women in the audience? One might make use here of Laura Mulvey's very influential essay on 'Visual Pleasure and Narrative Cinema', first published in *Screen* in 1975, and of the subsequent debate in film theory and criticism.

Valerie Traub, writing as a lesbian critic, has in *Desire and Anxiety* (1992), applied this approach to the audience of Shakespearean comedy, arguing for a less simple or binary view of the 'identification' between spectator and spectacle.

Further, how does cross-dressing on the stage relate to cross-dressing in the street? The Elizabethan and Jacobean Puritans condemned women dressing as men on the street at the same time as they condemned men dressing as women on the stage. In the West today, women 'normally' dress as men on the street, wearing trousers without exciting notice and without in any way pretending to be men. For a woman to make a public statement that she is cross-dressing, she has to go to some trouble, for example by buying her clothes only in men's clothing stores, or by adopting the stylized male evening dress associated with Weimar cabaret, Marlene Dietrich and female drag. Western men do not 'normally' dress as women on the street; a man wearing a skirt or dress is definitely noticeable, unless he is pretending to be a woman so successfully as to be 'invisible'. In the past, kabuki actors who specialized in female roles apparently maintained their stage gender in real life; this was certainly recommended by the celebrated performer Yoshizawa Ayame (1673-1729) (see Shively, 1978, p. 41 ff.), and it also occurred, and became a cause of scandal, in the Takarazuka Revue in the 1920s and 30s, when members of the all-female acting company undertook to learn 'secondary genders' according to the Western Stanislavski method and continued to behave as men outside the theatre (Robertson, 1992). I am informed by Japanese friends that to this day some of the older onnagata give television interviews as women. Charlotte Cushman, one might add, wore masculine dress offstage as well as on. After seeing her as Romeo a female spectator recorded with significant ambiguity in her diary 'Miss Cushman is a very dangerous young man (see Joseph Leach, 1970, p. 175).

The standard gender hierarchy is also a factor to be taken into account. In most societies until very recently to be human meant to be male; women were seen as an inferior sub-species. Hence for a woman to dress as a man is to dress 'up' in hierarchical terms, while for a man to dress as a woman is to dress 'down'. And of course 'masculinity' and 'femininity' have very different connotations; an 'effeminate' man can be stigmatized in a different way from a 'masculine' woman. (Significantly, there is no 'opposite' or pair word for 'effeminate' in polite English, though the slang term 'butch' carries some of the meaning.) As Alan Sinfield explains in *Cultural Politics: Queer Reading* (p. 15):

> Effeminacy is founded in misogyny: the root idea is of a male falling away from the purposeful reasonableness that is supposed to constitute manliness, into the laxity and weakness conventionally attributed to women . . . . The effeminate male is (1) 'wrong' and (2) inferior (female); the 'masculine' woman, conversely, is (1) 'wrong' and (2) impertinent (aspiring to manliness).

There is a long tradition of female impersonation (that is, men impersonating women) from the very classical theatres we are discussing to gay camp performers and pub drag queens, but there is no such historically and socially sanctioned tradition of male impersonation (that is, women impersonating men). The female impersonator can be presented/imagined as powerful and subversive, while the male impersonator is not, according to Peter Ackroyd who writes in his book *Dressing Up: Transvestism and Drag: The History of an Obsession* (p. 102):

> The male impersonator, the actress in trousers, seems . . . to lack depth and resonance . . . [and] is never anything more than what she pretends to be: a feminine, noble mind in a boy's body. It is a peculiarly sentimental and therefore harmless reversal.

The belittling vocabulary ('actress', 'boy', 'sentimental', 'harmless') loads the argument here but the basic contrast is difficult to deny.

Because of these asymmetries I do not think it is actually possible to make a direct and simple comparison between a woman playing Romeo and a man playing Rosalind, or between an all-female *School for Scandal* and an all-male *As You Like It*. In an ideal world we might want to experiment with an 'open' system of casting which would allow performers to take on any role; Richard Schechner and the editorial staff of *The Drama Review* have argued in favour of 'Race Free, Gender Free, Body-Type Free, Age-Free Casting' (1989, p. 4) and questioned what this might mean:

If body type, age, race and gender are set aside what then would the criteria be for playing a character or dancing a role? Is training plus insight into a role sufficient? If so, should we assemble 'mixed' casts where the gender, race, age and body type of the performers are, as it were, not perceived? Or should we make productions where some kind of social and/or aesthetic comment, framed by the world of the artwork, is expressed by means of the casting? These two approaches are very different.

Citing kabuki as an example of an acting style which puts the stress on the abstract qualities of the role rather than on the close fit between the representer and the represented, Schechner and his colleagues advocate a widening of that gap in Western performing styles, and a higher degree of awareness of it – 'it is more delightful to see the gap than to mask it' (p. 7) – but optimum flexibility of casting would involve a much greater codification of systems of representation than Western audiences are used to and, perhaps, a wilful blindness to social and historical contexts.

In addition, it might operate as a way of maintaining the differential between stage acting and screen acting, the former possessing a prestige which comes precisely from what is perceived as a more demanding level of impersonation; screen actors, in the popular view, simply 'play themselves' with the gap between performer and role seen as minimal. A screen actor such as Robert Mitchum has colluded in this view by his famous practice of marking pages of his scripts 'NAR' standing for 'No Acting Required'. The notion of 'age free' and 'body-type free' casting is of interest here: in the live theatre a man of 'four score years and upward' would simply not have the physical stamina to play King Lear, any more than a genuinely obese man would be able to play Falstaff, so it becomes part of the actor's job to impersonate age or obesity. But on screen it is possible, indeed almost obligatory, to cast a person of the 'right' age and body type, even though this can lead to other problems: the frail and elderly Yuri Yarvet playing Lear in Grigori Kozintsev's 1971 film was clearly incapable of carrying the body of Cordelia, and Laurence Olivier at seventy-seven in the Granada television version of *Lear*, directed by Michael Elliott in 1984, had enormous difficulty learning his lines and could not sustain the part for more than quite short takes.

Shakespeare's texts of *Hamlet* (the Second Quarto and the Folio, though not the First Quarto) insist that the prince is thirty, though many readers prefer to imagine him younger. Viewers apparently found Mel Gibson at thirty-six acceptable in Franco Zeffirelli's 1992 film, but many critics objected to the casting of Glenn Close (aged forty-seven) as his mother. It is extraordinary to imagine Thomas Betterton playing Hamlet at seventy-four as he did in 1709, though we can still see the sixty-year-old Johnston Forbes-Robertson tackling the part in the 1913 film directed by E. Hay Plumb. As for body type, we have had in England recently the saga of Simon Russell Beale and Hamlet: after he publicly declared his ambition to play the part and his regret that his tendency to corpulence prevented him from being cast (most people insist that Hamlet is *not* 'fat' in the modern sense despite Gertrude's use of the word in the final scene). A production starring him did in fact take place in 2000 at the National Theatre to general acclaim and favourable reviews.

Finally, I shall return to two more specific issues. I asked earlier, to what extent were/are the male actors on the Shakespearean and kabuki stages imitating women and to what extent were/are they performing women? In his essay on 'The Social Environment of Tokugawa Kabuki', Donald H. Shively traces a shift from imitation to performance in the development of the onnagata, the kabuki performers specializing in women's roles, as the adult actors had to use their acting resources rather than their physical attractions (p. 40):

> Most of the onnagata had, of course, been kabuki youths. Yet as they grew older, they relied increasingly on a more subtle skill in playing women's roles. They could not merely mimic for, aging and wrinkled, their lantern chins and heavy noses more pronounced, their voices more gravelly, they could hardly be mistaken in appearance for women. A more abstract method of interpretation was required. Thus they singled out the most essential traits of a woman's gestures and speech and gave to these a special emphasis in much the same way that puppets exaggerate human gestures to appear alive.

This stylization is seen as the essence of kabuki acting to the point that real women would be unconvincing in the roles. Shively claims that attempts by women to play these parts have in fact been unsatisfactory. He continues:

> The beauty of onnagata acting lies in its formalized grace. Women in these roles appear too natural, too realistic. Furthermore, since male roles are played in a strong, sometimes exaggerated manner, women lack the physical strength to project an equal stage presence. And again, women do not exude the peculiar eroticism with its homosexual overtones which has become an inherent characteristic of kabuki. Actresses become plausible only when they play their parts, not by miming women, but by imitating onnagata.

There seems to be something paradoxical here: surely the rather grotesque old men evoked by Shively, 'aging and wrinkled', with their 'lantern chins', 'heavy noses' and 'gravelly' voices, would not have as much physical strength to project into their stage roles as so many fit young women? (I am inclined to question Shively's assumptions, although I would of course defer to those who have more experience of kabuki than I have.) One is reminded of the conservative Restoration critics who maintained that the actresses did not play the women's parts as well as the men had done, but it is remarkable how quickly the women established themselves on the London stage after 1662 and how a man still acting women's parts in the early 1660s like Edward Kynaston became seen as something of a freak, as Colley Cibber recalls (*Apology*, p. 71):

> *Kynaston* at that time was so beautiful a Youth that the Ladies of Quality prided themselves in taking him with them in their Coaches to Hyde Park, in his Theatrical Habit, after the Play.

It is clear in any case that the cross-casting tradition before 1642 in England aimed rather more towards naturalism than the kabuki tradition. On the rare occasions when Shakespeare actually stages men impersonating women within the diegesis of his plays the need for some degree of plausible imitation is stressed. In the Induction of *The Taming of the Shrew*, for example, the Lord is confident that his page Barthol'mew, will not just be dressed as Sly's wife, but will 'well usurp the grace, / Voice, gait and action of a gentlewoman'.

(*Riverside Shakespeare*, ed. G. Blakemore Evans, Induction 2.131-2.) I shall end with a brief discussion of the question of voice which was clearly an important marker in this theatre in which, unlike the later kabuki theatre, boys rather than men played women's parts and it seems that they ceased to play them when their voices broke. (At least two scholars, Juliet Dusinberre and Stephen Orgel, have written books in which the use of boy actors is discussed; we certainly need more information about their training, their lives and their careers.) The comparatively high voice is often mentioned by Shakespeare as a characteristic shared by boys and women as well as being a distinction between boys and men, as when Scroope emphasizes the scale of the popular defection to Richard II by telling him (3.2.113-5):

> boys, with women's voices,
> Strive to speak big, and clap their female joints
> In stiff unwieldy arms against thy crown.

Femininity, on the other hand, is simply defined in relation to Anne Page in *The Merry Wives of Windsor* who according to Slender 'has brown hair and speaks small like a woman' (1.1.47-8). (Editors gloss 'small' as meaning 'high' or 'treble'.) When Francis Flute is reluctant to play Thisbe in the Mechanicals' play in *A Midsummer Night's Dream* because he has a beard coming, Peter Quince rejects that excuse – 'That's all one; you shall play it in a mask' – but emphasizes the need for the performer to be vocally convincing: 'you may speak as small as you will'. Bottom immediately volunteers to do it speaking in 'a monstrous little voice' (1.2.49-52).

Conversely, when Portia and Nerissa are about to undertake male impersonation in *The Merchant of Venice* Portia says they must 'speak between the change of man and boy / With a reed voice' (3.5.66-7). Orsino in *Twelfth Night* stresses the voice when listing the 'feminine' physical features of Cesario (Viola) (1.4.30-34):

> For they shall yet belie thy happy years
> That say thou art a man. Diana's lip
> Is not more smooth and rubious; thy small pipe
> Is as the maiden's organ, shrill and sound,
> And all is semblative a woman's part.

Malvolio gives a more hostile view of the apparently ambiguous or 'liminal' nature of Cesario's gender in the next scene, also mentioning the voice. Orsino's new messenger is, he reports (1.5.156-62):

> Not yet old enough for a man, nor young enough for a boy; as a squash is before 'tis a peascod, or a codling when 'tis almost an apple. 'Tis with him in standing water, between boy and man. He is very well-favored, and he speaks very shrewishly. One would think his mother's milk were scarce out of him.

Viola's first plan had of course been to present herself as a eunuch to Orsino (1.2.56) – presumably another way of reconciling a masculine appearance and a feminine voice.

Coriolanus sees the possibility of being 'unmanned' in terms of exchanging his man's voice for that of a eunuch or a woman (3.2.111-15):

> Away, my disposition, and possess me
> Some harlot's spirit! My throat of war be turn'd
> Which quier'd with my drum, into a pipe
> Small as an eunuch, or the virgin voice
> That babies lull asleep!

Interestingly, he associates this vocal transformation with the whole idea of acting a role, asking his mother 'Would you have me / False to my nature? Rather say, I play / The man I am' (3.2.14-16) and predicting accurately enough 'You have put me now to such a part which never / I shall discharge to th'life' (3.2.105-6). So, finally, we are back with the apparently inescapable association between acting and effeminacy. While real women are banished from both the Shakespearean and the kabuki stages, performance itself is gendered female. I find this rather mysterious, and larger questions remain: what if anything does the construction of femininity in these theatres have to say about women, and what, if anything, does it say to women in today's audiences? I hope our seminar will address these issues.

REFERENCES

Ackroyd, Peter, *Dressing Up: Transvestism and Drag: The History of an Obsession*. New York: Simon and Schuster, 1979.

Butler, Judith, *Gender Trouble: Feminism and the Subversion of Identity.* New York: Routledge, 1990.

Cibber, Colley, *An Apology for the Life of Mr. Colley Cibber.* London, 1740.

Davy, Kate, 'Fe/male Impersonation: The Discourse of Camp'. In Senelick, 130-48, 1994.

Dollimore, Jonathan, *Sexual Dissidence.* Oxford: Clarendon Press, 1991.

Evans, G. Blakemore (ed.), *The Riverside Shakespeare.* Boston: Houghton Mifflin, 1974.

Fischer-Lichte, Erika, 'Between Difference and Indifference: Marianne Hoppe in Robert Wilson's *Lear*'. In Senelick, 101-16, 1992.

Garber, Marjorie, *Vested Interests; Cross-Dressing and Cultural Anxiety.* New York: Harpers, 1992.

Goffman, Erving, *The Presentation of Self in Everyday Life.* New York: Doubleday, 1959.

Howe, Elizabeth, *The First English Actresses.* Cambridge: Cambridge University Press, 1992.

Leach, Joseph, *Bright Particular Star: The Life and Times of Charlotte Cushman.* New Haven: Yale University Press, 1970.

Levine, Laura, *Men in Women's Clothing: Anti-theatricality and Effeminization, 1579-1642.* Cambridge: Cambridge University Press, 1994.

Mulvey, Laura, 'Visual Pleasure and Narrative Cinema'. In *Screen* 16.3, 6-18, 1975.

Robertson, Jennifer, 'The "Magic If": Conflicting Performances of Gender in the Takarazuka Revue of Japan'. In Senelick, 46-67, 1992.

Schechner, Richard, 'Race Free, Gender Free, Body-Type Free, Age Free Casting'. In *The Drama Review* 33, 4-12, 1989.

Senelick, Laurence, *Gender in Performance: The Presentation of Difference in the Performing Arts.* Hanover and London: The University of New England Press, 1992.

Shively, Donald H., 'The Social Environment of Tokugawa Kabuki'. In James R. Brandon, William P. Malm and Donald H. Shively, *Studies in Kabuki.* Honolulu: University of Hawaii Press, 1-61, 1978.

Sinfield, Alan, *Cultural Politics: Queer Reading.* London: Routledge, 1994.

Traub, Valerie, *Desire and Anxiety: Circulations of Sexuality in Shakespearean Drama.* London: Routledge, 1992.

Wex, Marianne, *'Weibliche' und 'mannliche' Korpersprache als Folge patriarchalischer Machtverhaltnisse.* Frankfurt: Frauenliteraturvertrieb Hermine Fees, 1980.

4

THE INTRODUCTION OF ACTRESSES IN ENGLAND: DELAY OR DEFENSIVENESS?

MICHAEL SHAPIRO

I n the past several decades, English-speaking audiences on both sides of the Atlantic have seen all-male productions of *As You Like It*. Clifford Williams directed one for the National Theatre in 1967, which he revived in 1974 with a different cast for a North American tour. Cheek by Jowl, a British company, which had taken its production on a world tour, performed at the Brooklyn Academy of Music in October and December of 1994. Neither company attempted to replicate the particular pattern of all-male casting used in the original production of c. 1600. On Shakespeare's stage, female roles were customarily taken by 'play-boys', i.e. youths in late adolescence, who were younger and probably slighter in build than adult male performers. As apprentices and hirelings rather than fully-fledged actors or sharers in the company, 'play-boys' probably occupied a lower social status than the adult male actors playing adult male characters. In the two recent all-male productions, however, Rosalind was played by very experienced adult performers – Ronald Pickup and Gregory Floy for the National, Ronnie Lester for Cheek by Jowl.[1] Even with play-boys, the effects of such cross-gender casting for modern audiences would be different from what they were for Elizabethan spectators. For us it is a novelty; for them it was the norm.

For centuries, in fact, the use of male actors in female roles had been normative not only in England but throughout the West. Stephen Orgel has recently characterized the retention of cross-gender casting in England as 'a uniquely English solution to the universal European disapproval of actresses'.[2] Orgel makes the additional point that retention *per se* of tradition is not an adequate explanation for a continuing cultural practice, especially one being abandoned in neighbouring countries. Whereas Orgel sees the English commercial stage as unique in its use of female impersonators, I would describe it as late in introducing actresses.

In this chapter I want to explore some of the possible reasons for that lateness. I have not found explanations based on English sexual attitudes to be fully convincing, especially when those attitudes occur in other European societies which find different ways to come to terms with the employment of actresses during the same period. The first task then is to question the uniqueness of the English solution and to interrogate explanations based on the assumptions of that uniqueness. Second, although I have nothing in the way of fresh evidence to offer in support of some alternative explanations for the late introduction of actresses on the English stage, I want to direct the inquiry away from cultural attitudes towards gender and towards the economics of the English commercial theatre, specifically towards the training of actors and demands of touring. Perhaps such a shift in the way we approach the problem may lead to the discovery of new documentary evidence.

ENGLISH ACTING TROUPES AND THE ALL-MALE TRADITION OF EUROPEAN THEATRE

Acting had been an all-male activity in ancient Greece as well as in the official theatres of Rome, although the popular Roman festival of Floralia featured a farcical and bawdy style of mime which included female performers.[3] In Medieval Europe, most officially-sanctioned theatrical activity took place under the auspices of all-male ecclesiastical institutions, despite some evidence of performances in nunneries and of limited participation by girls or young women in French and English biblical plays or cycles put on by craft guilds.[4] There are also traces of women appearing all over Europe as itinerant entertainers, probably as singers, dancers and acrobats, under such names as *joculatores*, or *jongleurs*.

Nowhere in Europe did women act in plays performed by professional theatre troupes until Italian popular touring companies, the *commedia dell'arte*, employed actresses in the 1560s: 'the first record . . . is the appearance in a troupe list of 1564 of a certain Lucrezia Senese'.[5] In the four centuries since the introduction of actresses, audiences have come to accept the use of women in female roles as natural, when in fact it is merely conventional and at one time was considered innovative. Perhaps the appropriate question is not why the English theatre resisted the use of actresses until 1660, but rather why real women replaced female impersonators.

Glynne Wickham answers this question in terms of decorum: a growing demand for verisimilitude in the theatres of Italy, first largely in regard to scenic design, led to an equivalent demand for verisimilitude in the casting of female roles.[6] However, the productions which first used scenic design to suggest domestic interiors or realistic street facades were those mounted by private academies, in which men continued to play female roles long after actresses appeared in plays performed by the popular troupes. The popular troupes themselves were slower to adopt verisimilitude in scenic design, for as itinerant companies they used trestle-and-board stages easily set up in market-places or halls.

The kind of aesthetic inconsistency Wickham describes was evidently not perceived as a problem. As Michael Anderson remarks about a drawing of the celebrated actress Isabella Andreini performing on a crude stage: 'It may seem strange that the foremost actress of her day should appear on a stage which, in scenic terms, is no better equipped than that of the Zanni performing in the *piazza* or the most modest of *stanze*.'[7] Casting practices also undermined verisimilitude: while the Isabellas and other chaste upper-class romantic heroines were played by the earliest actresses, who were often relatives of the male members of the company, the low comic roles of female servants, who often engaged in raucous and bawdy farce, were played by men. In two cast lists, that of I Comici Uniti from Padua in 1584 and that of Uniti from Genoa in 1614, the character of Francesquina is assigned to a man. One suspects that the families involved, no less than the civic authorities, had no wish to see their female relatives engage in coarsely eroticized slapstick, such as the scene from the *Recueil Fossard* collection in which Pantalon is spying on Harlequine through the curtains as the latter reaches his right hand under the skirt and between the thighs of Francesquina.[8]

A more obvious explanation than Wickham's for the introduction of actresses is commercial: popular troupes exploited the appeal of actresses when and where civic and ecclesiastical authorities did not stop them from doing so. The innovation was not welcomed everywhere, for public performances by women were seen as too provocative by those in power, who sometimes feared that actresses were engaging in prostitution. Despite such resistance, the use of actresses spread throughout Europe, although not in any simple linear fashion, as a rapid overview will indicate.

Even in Italy, women were forbidden to act in public in certain localities. In Rome in 1588, a troupe known as the Deosisi (also known as Company of Diana because of its association with an actress named Diana Ponti) was ordered by Pope Sixtus V to replace their actresses with boys. He subsequently banned women from performing publicly throughout the Papal States, a decree which held (with some exceptions) until late in the eighteenth century. This Papal ban included singers as well as actresses, so that in Rome, as elsewhere in Italy, voices in the upper registers were supplied by castrati.[9]

In Spain, actresses, as opposed to dancers and singers, probably did not appear until an Italian troupe petitioned the authorities for permission to use its women in 1587. The practice was subsequently adopted by competing Spanish companies, not without clerical opposition, although some of that opposition was bought off by the promise to donate a portion of playhouse profits to orphanages, hospitals and poor houses maintained by the religious confraternities which controlled the Madrid theatres.[10] Even after actresses were permitted on the Spanish stage in 1587, they were outlawed between 1596 and 1600 and carefully regulated thereafter: they had to be married women, accompanied by their husbands, not visited more than twice backstage by male spectators, and they were forbidden to wear costumes considered too revealing. Ursula Heise notes that Spanish authorities were troubled by female characters adopting male disguise and tried to curtail if not forbid it in a series of edicts, fearful that male attire revealed women's bodies and thus accentuated rather than veiled female sexuality. Spanish clerics were apparently divided over whether the danger of using men in female roles was more acute than that of using women. Heise links objections to female impersonation to an intense and violent wave of persecution of homosexuals which swept over Spain in the sixteenth century, although the reissuing of edicts outlawing such cross-gender casting suggests that companies continued the practice, perhaps using both men and women in female roles.[11]

In France, there is evidence of actresses even before the arrival of Italian popular troupes. An actress named Marie Fairet and her manager signed a contract at Bourges in 1545, but the use of actresses on a regular basis followed the arrival of the Italian popular companies, which played at court and publicly in Paris in the early 1570s. A French troupe introduced actresses in Bordeaux in 1598 and shortly thereafter in Paris.[12]

What emerges from this admittedly rough and schematic survey of the introduction of actresses in Italy, France and Spain is a steady, if non-linear, increase in their use on the commercial stage, but with important countercurrents. (Throughout Europe, non-commercial productions such as those under the auspices of all-male institutions like academies, schools and universities, of course, remained all-male.) In the Protestant countries of northern Europe, theatrical representation of women is no less complicated than in the Catholic countries to the south. In Geneva in 1546, for example, a local troupe applied to the town council for permission to perform a dramatization of *The Acts of the Apostles.* E. K. Chambers summarizes the case:

> The council ordered the book of the piece to be submitted to Calvin, and agreed that it should be performed, should his report be favourable. Calvin and the other ministers did not much like the proposal, more particularly as the players declined to give alms to the poor out of the profits of the

enterprise. It so happened, however, that one of the ministers, Abel Poupin, was himself the author of the play and partly because of this, and partly because he was not sure that an attempt to prevent the performance would be successful, Calvin seems to have persuaded his colleagues to offer no objection. . . . A preacher of fiery temper, Michel Cop, got into the pulpit and denounced the play, accusing the women performers of a shameless desire to display themselves in public and thereby ensnare the eyes of men.[13]

Although Calvin agreed with Cop's objection, invoking Tertullian's anti-theatrical authority, he justified his earlier decision to permit the play on grounds of expediency. The following year, the council refused to permit a performance by a troupe evidently consisting of Richard Chaultemps and his wife and children, although other plays on classical and religious subjects were permitted. In 1572, the Synod of Nimes outlawed the performance of all but strictly educational plays within the French reformed church.[14]

If women playing female characters caused a problem for Calvin and his followers, so did the casting of young men or boys in such roles. In a sermon in 1556, Calvin cited the prohibition of cross-dressing in Deuteronomy 22:5 as an absolute rule. By contrast, his successor at Geneva, Theodore Beza, author of Christian humanist plays such as *Abraham's Sacrifice*, fully supported cross-gender casting. According to Richard Braithwait, Beza 'constantly affirmed, that it was not only lawful for them to set forth and act those *Playes*, but for Boyes to put on women's apparell for the time'.[15] Puritan opinion, at least in Geneva, could waver in regard to the representation of women by actresses or male performers, for either women or the images of women could, from their point of view, stir the erotic imagination; some English anti-theatrical writings also grant such evocative power to male performers themselves.

In Holland, the picture is also mixed. Touring troupes in the sixteenth century may have used actresses, but productions by the Chambers of Rhetoric were all-male affairs. Female roles were taken not only by boys but according to some accounts by older men as well. The first actresses did not appear in Dutch commercial theatres until 1655, and even then they often shared female roles with male performers.[16]

The retention of cross-gender casting by the English commercial companies must be judged against this variegated history of female representation by both men and women in early modern Europe. Whether Catholic or Protestant, religious and some civic officials feared that any display of women could be disruptive to social order, whether the display was by real women exhibiting their own bodies or by female impersonators creating theatrical representations of women. In England, productions at the universities often evoked considerable anxiety over the issue of female impersonation.[17] On the continent, the Jesuits, who were as strongly influenced by Deuteronomy 22:5 as the English anti-theatricalists, initially prohibited female characters or female costumes in their school productions (*nec persona ulla muliebris vel habitus introducatur*), but eventually relaxed this rule in order to produce plays based on heroines such as Judith.[18] English anti-theatrical tracts, some written by and for puritans, denounce cross-gender casting as a violation of the biblical injunction against cross-dressing. They would probably have objected to women on stage with equal vigour, as Nashe slyly suggests in his defence of the English system of cross-gender casting: 'Our Players are not as the players beyond sea, a sort of squirting baudie Comedians, that have whores and common Curtizens to playe womens partes, and forbeare no immodest speech or unchast action that may procure laughter.'[19] In fact, although instances of social cross-dressing such as the *Hic Mulier* movement evoked considerable anxiety in the period, especially when women wore male attire, I tend to agree with Alan Nelson's conclusion that for most of the English anti-theatricalists the real target was drama *per se*, and the biblical injunction against cross-dressing was simply a handy weapon in that campaign.[20]

There was throughout early modern Europe a pervasive impulse to control women's freedom of movement and association in order to restrict their sexual activity. Ironically, English women enjoyed relatively greater freedom of movement in their daily lives than did most women on the continent, especially in Spain. All over Europe, theatrical displays of female sexuality aroused intense fears and invited rigid forms of regulation if not outright prohibition. Such fears were expressed by anti-theatricalist writers in both Catholic and Protestant countries, and they seem as agitated when women performers displayed their own bodies, faces and voices, as when skilled male performers created theatrical illusions of women. Some societies preferred male performers as the lesser of two evils, although this solution raised two other fears. One was that the erotic allure of the cross-dressed male actor might be sexually arousing to male spectators.[21] A second fear was the effeminization of male spectators through their enthralment either by the cross-dressed male performer *per se* or by the character he portrayed. Thus, Heise concludes her comparison of English and Spanish anti-theatrical writings by noting that both movements construct the theatre, regardless of whether women or men play female roles, as an essentially 'female' spectacle which threatens to sap the virility of male spectators, the dominant and most significant faction of the audience, rendering them unfit for positions of military or civic leadership and robbing the nation of economic vitality. Despite her indebtedness to Orgel's work, Heise finally expresses doubt that English 'cultural anxieties about the nature of male identity' were 'due to the convention of *male* cross-dressing in particular' (my emphasis) and concludes that 'the same dynamic would have asserted itself had women been admitted to the stage'.[22]

The reasons why English troupes preserved the practice of cross-gender casting might more readily be linked to such factors as protection of male employment, the maintenance of recruitment and training systems already in place, the lack of a pool of potential actresses, and the relative advantages or disadvantages of touring with women.

THE TRAINING OF ACTORS IN EARLY MODERN ENGLAND

As throughout Western Europe, one strand of English theatrical activity grew out of all-male institutions – grammar schools, universities and chapel choirs. Another strand grew out of the work of small travelling troupes which toured throughout England and whose activities are now being chronicled in *Records of Early English Drama* (REED) volumes. Extant casting lists from the latter half of the sixteenth century indicate that most companies comprised six or eight men and two boys who usually doubled in any number of female and juvenile roles.[23] The larger London companies, like Shakespeare's, typically comprised twelve full-time adult members, or sharers, and three or four younger male performers to take female and juvenile roles. At about the age of nineteen, as in the case of Ezekiel Fenn, the play-boys were ready to assume adult male roles, and, one presumes, to relinquish female roles to younger boys. There is no evidence that any female roles were played by grown men in the London commercial theatres before 1642.[24]

Play-boys entered the adult acting companies either as apprentices or as 'covenant servants'. Those described as apprentices were bound to an individual adult actor rather than to a company. In return for fees paid by a parent or guardian, the actor housed the boy and undertook to teach him the profession of acting. Starting ages for apprentice actors could vary from about the age of ten to sixteen, and the length of service from three to ten years. By contrast, most apprenticeships in the craft guilds started around the age of twenty and lasted about seven years, only occasionally ending before the age of twenty-four. Acting apprenticeships probably began earlier so that, once trained, the play-boys could perform for several years in female roles before the onset of puberty, which occurred later than it does now, made them better suited to adult male roles.[25]

Two pieces of literary evidence suggest that young male actors were leased by the week. Captain Tucca, a character in Ben Jonson's *Poetaster* (1601) considers offering his two 'pyrgi', or boy servants, to the actor, Histrio: 'What wilt thou give mee a weeke, for my brace of beagles, here, my little point-trussers?' Tucca has the boys demonstrate their skill in a variety of roles, until Histrio seems ready to make a deal – 'what will you aske for 'hem a weeke, Captaine?' – only to have Tucca refuse on the grounds that the player would peddle them as catamites ('sell 'em for enghles'). Venus, the deaf Tire-woman in Jonson's *Christmas, His Masque* (1616) brags about the acting abilities of her son, a 'Prentise in Lovelane with a Bugle-maker', who will play Cupid in the masque:

I forsooth, he'le say his part, I warrant him, as well as ere a

> Play boy of 'em all: I could ha' had money enough for him,
> an I would ha' beene tempted, and ha' let him out by the
> weeke, to the Kings Players: Master *Burbadge* has beene
> about and about with me; and so has old Mr. *Hemings* too,
> they ha' need of him.[26]

The passage is rich in self-reflexive irony because in all likelihood Venus herself was represented by a 'play-boy'.

Fragments of documentary evidence suggest that boy actors were sometimes leased and sometimes apprenticed, but to individuals rather than companies. On 19 December 1597, Henslowe recorded the purchase of a boy named James Bristowe for eight pounds from the actor William Augusten and subsequently records payments of three shillings per week he received from the company for the use of Bristowe's services. Decades later, in 1633, John Shank testified that he paid 40 pounds for a boy named John Thompson. Susan Baskervil received seven shillings per week from a troupe playing at the Red Bull for the services of a boy who had previously been apprenticed to her late son, William Browne, an actor, who died in 1634.[27]

The apprenticeship system continued into the Caroline periods, even as it blended into another system, that of the training or nursery company. Earlier in the seventeenth century, members of grammar school and chorister troupes such as Nathan Field eventually found employment in adult companies. In 1629, efforts were made to create a juvenile or nursery company, when Richard Gunnell and William Blagrave established the Children of the Revels at the Salisbury Court Theatre 'to train and bring up certain boys in the quality of playing with intent to be a supply of able actors to your Majesty's Servants of the Blackfriars', i.e. the King's Men.[28] But Blagrave acquired at least one member of that troupe, Stephen Hammerton, by buying the remaining nine years of his apprenticeship from a merchant tailor. Similarly, in 1636-37, Christopher Beeston founded another juvenile company, 'Beeston's Boys', or the King's and Queen's Young Company, to play at the Cockpit, perhaps on the model of the Salisbury Court Company of a few years earlier. After Beeston's death in 1637, his son William managed the troupe until it was dissolved in 1642. Even during the interregnum, when the London theatres were officially closed,

William Beeston tried to establish a clandestine troupe of youthful actors at the Cockpit. As Beeston testified in a lawsuit a year or so later, he laid out a substantial sum in 1650 to repair the theatre after acquiring it 'and after that took prentices and covenant servants to instruct them in the quality of acting and fitting for the stage'.[29]

The phrase 'covenant servants' suggests an alternative to apprenticeships as a method of recruiting; evidently the boys were regarded as personal property, to be sold or rented for theatrical performers. The price of boys, as of everything else, had risen since Henslowe had bought and leased James Bristowe, perhaps through general inflation and perhaps because talented or trained young male actors had become an increasingly valued commodity as the London theatrical industry expanded. In a legal document dated 1635, the Burbage family recalled that the King's Men acquired some of the actors from the Children of the Queen's Revels when they took over Henry Evans's lease of the Blackfriars theatre in 1608, evidently to replenish their own supply of young male actors, 'the boys daily wearing out'.[30] In the Caroline period, training companies were started, as we have seen, presumably to augment the supply of youthful male performers, but some adult troupes might still have recruited their own play-boys to take juvenile and female roles.

However the play-boys were recruited, there is testimony to their skill in acting. Writing about a performance of *Othello* by the King's Men at Oxford in 1610, Henry Jackson commented on the power of the young male playing Desdemona: 'she always acted the matter very well, in her death moved us still more greatly; when lying in bed she implored the pity of those watching with her countenance alone'.[31] Some post-Restoration accounts of the earlier female impersonators strike a different note: Colley Cibber disparaged these 'Boys, or young Men of the most effeminate Aspect' as 'ungain Hoydens',[32] but one suspects that he is denigrating the theatre of the previous age to praise that of his own.

Perhaps the strongest reason for the continued exclusion of women from the stage was a desire on the part of male actors to preserve the profession of acting as a site for male employment. The apprenticeship system itself need not have prevented English troupes from bringing young women into their ranks, for some crafts did take female apprentices.[33] In any case, there was no actors' guild in England, and although many actors maintained active membership in craft guilds, only three recorded cases of theatrical apprenticeship were channelled through those institutions.

Even if women were theoretically eligible for theatrical apprenticeships, the economic climate for female employment outside of the home or family business was deteriorating. For most of the sixteenth century, women were being pushed out of economic niches they had occupied earlier. Modifying a time-honoured practice of female impersonation in order to include women in acting troupes would probably have seemed threatening to male performers accustomed to all-male companies (one composed of sharers in the case of the King's Men) in which many had learned the craft by starting with juvenile female roles, the very roles women would usurp should they enter the profession.

Shortly after the Restoration, one group of actors had to be compelled by economic and legal pressure to act alongside women. This was a troupe of veteran performers, all of them professionally active before 1642, whom Michael Mohun led at the Red Bull in defiance of the monopolies granted to companies led by Killigrew and Davenant, as well as of the efforts of Sir Henry Herbert, Master of the Revels, to assert his authority over the renewed commercial theatrical life of London by taxing the companies. Mohun's group evidently revived theatrical practices from the Caroline period. In a petition to the king, the troupe complained that it owed Herbert no fees as he was unable to protect them from Killigrew, who pressured them to join his company and forced them to accept a set of new theatrical practices:

> Mr. Killegrew, having your Majesties former grante, supprest us, until wee had by convenant obliged ourselves to act with woemen, a new theatre, and habitts according to our sceanes.[34]

Mohun, incidentally, was remembered by James Wright in *Historia Histrionica* as having performed the female role of Belimente in Shirley's *Love's Cruelty* (1631) both before and after the Restoration.[35] Although actresses were already a great attraction, Mohun and his group apparently revived the theatre as they had known it, and were reluctant to admit women to the fraternal order of stage players and perhaps even to share roles with them. The bias continued even after women became established on the London stage, for no actress ever became a full sharer of a company until 1695.[36]

THE FIRST ENGLISH ACTRESSES

In 1660, when the theatres reopened, the few available trained female impersonators were eighteen years older than they had been when the theatres closed in 1642. Evidently some, such as Michael Mohun, resumed earlier female roles, and it is possible that Thomas Jordan was alluding to just such superannuated 'boy actresses' in his barb: 'men act that are between / Forty and Fifty, wenches of fifteen.'[37] Other, younger performers, such as Edward Kynaston (born in 1643), William Betterton (born in 1644) and James Nokes (birthdate unknown), were initially great successes in female roles, and for a brief time, female roles were taken by both men and women, but very quickly the use of actresses became standard. Pepys mentions 'the first time that ever I saw women come upon the stage' in his entry for 3 January 1661, but Andrew Newport had already written two weeks earlier to Sir Richard Leveson on 15 December 1660, that 'Upon our stages we have women actors, as beyond seas.'[38] When Charles II authorized the resumption of playing by chartering two companies, he issued patents in May and August 1660, but the clause specifically permitting actresses first appeared in a revised patent dated 15 January 1662. The inserted passage notes that in 'many plays, formerly acted . . . the womens parts therein have been acted by men in the habits of women, at which some have taken offence'. The revised patent then proposes to remedy that situation, although by 1662 actresses had already been performing on the London stage for over two years:

> And we do likewise permit and give leave that all the womens parts to be acted in either of the two said companies for the time to come, may be performed by women, so long as these recreations, which, by reason of the aforesaid, were scandalous and offensive, may by such reformation be esteemed not only harmless delights, but

> useful and instructive representations of humane life, to
> such of our good subjects as shall resort to see the same.[39]

Despite the king's high moral tone, the display of women's bodies, accentuated by theatrical costume – especially the display of legs made possible by the donning of doublet and hose in the disguised heroine plays – was a powerful playhouse attraction.[40]

Why, we must ask again, did England's commercial theatres wait until 1660 to adopt a practice which had for some decades been commonplace in many areas on the continent? There was never, so far as I know, any legal statute prohibiting the appearance of women on stage, and indeed aristocratic women, like their male counterparts, often appeared as nonspeaking dancers in masques performed in the Jacobean court, an elite setting where any moral objections to the display of female bodies were overpowered by the desire of the Queen and her ladies to perform. Italian companies, presumably with female performers, occasionally visited England, playing largely but not entirely at court. There is evidence of widespread familiarity with their work, although not always with their use of female performers.[41]

French troupes employing actresses played in London in 1629 and 1635.[42] The former attracted significant audiences, for Prynne refers to 'French women Actors in a play not long since personated in Black friars Playhouse to which there was great resort,' adding a note which gives the date as Michaelmas 1629.[43]

The place to see women on stage was abroad, and Englishmen travelling on the continent often reported on this novelty. Thomas Coryate, who visited Venice in 1610, is typical:

> Here I observed certaine things that I never saw before. For I saw women acte, a thing that I never saw before, though I have heard that it hath beene sometimes used in London, and they performed it with as good a grace, action, gesture, and whatsoever convenient for a Player as ever I saw any masculine Actor.[44]

Coryate sought out all manner of exotica during his travels – e.g. Jewish circumcisions and Venetian courtesans, so that one would think that he of all people would have taken advantage of any available opportunity to see women perform in London playhouses.

Perhaps he is referring to touring Italian troupes, possibly to the appearance of Queen Anne and several aristocratic women in Jacobean court masques. Scholars are puzzled.

In the Caroline court, Aurelian Townshend's masque, *Tempe Restor'd*, featured two female singers, a Mme Coniacke and a Mrs Shepherd, while other women appeared in masque-like pastorelles.[45] By the 1630s, playhouse audiences seemed receptive to the idea of female performers. A character in James Shirley's *The Ball* (1639) comments that women actors are 'a thing much desir'd in England', while a character in Richard Brome's *The Court Beggar* (1640) refers both to the current practice of female impersonation and the current interest in actresses: 'If you have a short speech or two, the boy's a pretty actor, and his mother can play her part – women actors now grow in request.'[46] Nevertheless, up to the time the theatres closed in 1642, we know of no actresses who appeared in the commercial theatres of London nor in productions by itinerant troupes outside of London. For the average English theatre-goer (and many women went to plays too) all-male casting was, and was accepted as, standard practice. Still, one wonders why some shrewd English theatrical entrepreneur like Philip Henslowe did not attempt to gain a commercial advantage over his competitors by adapting the new continental fashion of employing actresses.

Perhaps the delay in introducing actresses on the English stage may have been caused by the difficulty of finding women with the kind of education and training who would be willing to enter a field traditionally seen as one remove from prostitution. Moll Frith, the model for Moll Cutpurse in Dekker and Middleton's *The Roaring Girl*, once made a kind of guest appearance on the stage of the Fortune in 1611. She did so not as an actress but as an eccentric celebrity of marginal social status and ambiguous gender who represented a version of herself. She was not someone amenable to the rigorous training needed to gain steady employment as an actress. In the years before the closing of the theatres it is not clear that there was a class of women who might have entered the acting profession were it possible to do so. It is hard to imagine many literate girls or young women whose families would have allowed them to become apprentices (which would have meant leaving home and moving into the master's house) at an age probably even earlier than the usual one for other crafts or for entering domestic service.

Although biographical information is scanty and of dubious accuracy, most early Restoration actresses came from the ranks of 'dowerless daughters of the genteel poor', i.e. from impoverished middle-class families, and in some cases from royalist families ruined by the civil war.[47] When actresses did finally appear on the English stage, only one – Susannah Mountfort – was the daughter of an actor, and one or two others were said to have been raised in theatrical families. By 1660, the commercial stage had made some gains in social stature: the two London companies were chartered by the king and relied heavily on an élite clientele. Whether the primary task of the actress was to represent the behaviour of upper-class heroines or to advertise her own beauty and charm before male playgoers, the theatre, having no young men trained to play female roles, came to rely on a class of young women who by virtue of their family's social backgrounds would require a minimum of training in order to represent dramatic heroines on the Restoration stage. Such a class of women may not have been as readily available or desperate for livelihood before 1642, nor was there a class of literate courtesans with expertise in, say, music and dance, who might also have furnished acting troupes with a supply of female performers.

Restoration actresses, while not recruited from the ranks of courtesans, often became involved in sexual liaisons of varying degrees of permanence with male spectators, and in a few cases became prostitutes after leaving the stage. While some actresses signalled their availability, others, like Anne Bracegirdle, were praised for keeping admirers at bay. There was considerable discussion over the family backgrounds of Restoration actresses, largely a coded discourse about whether particular female performers were of a class and descent that made them sexually available to male playgoers or whether their social origins might somehow help them deflect unwanted sexual advances.

In Italy, most of the earliest actresses were wives and sisters of actors, and presumably entered family businesses under the protection of male relatives. One of the most famous, Isabella Andreini, was held in respectful adulation during her lifetime: 'her admirers [went] to great length to stress her virtue and high moral tone'.[48] Although suspected of prostitution, actresses on the continent seem to have been related by marriage or blood to male performers, and thus worked in what amounted to family businesses. In England, the obvious economic advantages to such an arrangement may have been thwarted by the resistance of male actors, as has been suggested, or may have been outweighed by economic liabilities.

ACTRESSES AS LIABILITIES FOR ITINERANT ACTING TROUPES

The REED archives and forthcoming volumes may contain evidence about the presence of women in provincial touring companies, but thus far none has come to my attention. To judge from Edward Alleyn' s letters to his wife back home, English actors of the seventeenth century did not take their wives and families with them when they went on provincial tours. Italian touring companies, which were as we have seen essentially family businesses, did include female relatives, but it is not clear why English troupes were not organized around family units. The economic advantages of such a *modus operandi* are obvious, to say nothing of the possible drawing power of female performers. What factors might then have rendered so obvious an innovation ineffective from the economic point of view?

Scholars are only now realizing the importance of touring to the theatrical industry of early modern England, in part because of the extensive documentation in the REED volumes of theatrical activity outside of London. Andrew Gurr puts it succinctly: 'Travelling dictated all the early playing practices. The habits that went with it lasted through much of the early Stuart period when London playing became secure.'[49]

To gain an audience, a travelling company had to secure permission from a lord mayor or magistrate or some other local authority. Companies with women might have found it hard to secure such permission, not only because of the association of actresses with prostitution or promiscuity, a common assumption throughout Western Europe in the late-medieval and early-modern periods, but because of a series of laws beginning in the 1570s making parishes responsible for any illegitimate children born there. There was great pressure to force the fathers of such children to marry the women they had impregnated but when it was not possible to identify, locate or coerce such fathers, responsibility fell upon local communities.[50]

At the same time, there was great social upheaval and displacement in rural England, owing to the enclosure of common grazing lands and other changes in the agrarian economy, as well as to overpopulation and inflation. These displacements produced large numbers of homeless, most of them gravitating towards London in search of employment but some wandering without so clear a purpose. The Vagabond Acts of Tudor England attempted to curtail the movement of impoverished vagrants, while another series of laws, known as the Poor Laws, endeavoured to set forth the charitable responsibilities of local communities and to give them power to prevent 'sturdy beggars' from elsewhere from draining communal resources designated for their own deserving poor. In earlier forms of Vagabond Laws, common players of interludes were grouped with other categories of undesirable vagrants, but after 1572 exception was made for actors who could show that they were in the employ of someone of the rank of baron or above. To distinguish themselves from 'masterless men' and other indigent wanderers, itinerant acting troupes were required to show local authorities patents or licences identifying themselves as servants of some master before they were given permission to perform in a given community.[51] The local constables who enforced such laws, constituting a rotating volunteer police force such as the one caricatured in *Much Ado About Nothing*, might have kept an eye out for women late in pregnancy and so prevented any actress with child from entering the town, delivering her baby, and abandoning it to the charge of the local citizens.[52] In practice, companies with women might have aroused the suspicion of local officials that the actresses were either prostitutes when not on stage or might leave bastard children behind when the troupe left town to resume its travels.

Recently discovered diary entries belonging to Sir Henry Herbert, Master of the Revels, indicate that wives in some branches of the entertainment industry accompanied their husbands, or were licensed to do so in the early Stuart period. On 20 August 1622, Herbert thus records the payment of 10 shillings for the granting of 'a license to Thommas Barrell with one man his wife & children to toss a pike for a year'. Exactly one year to the day later, he granted 'a license to Marke Bradley with his wife to make shewe of a Ramme with 4 horns for a year'. On 25 August 1624, he granted a license to William Smith & Jane his wife with two assistants 'to shewe *a birde called a Starr'* for six months.[53] Wives like those referred to in these entries were not actresses but there does seem to have been a niche for family businesses, at least at the lower end of the itinerant entertainment industry.

In a few recorded cases, such women, or the family troupe they toured with, received a less than cordial welcome, evoking the kind of suspicion which theatre companies employing actresses might well have elicited. Thomas Wyatt and his wife Joan, who had been licensed by Herbert's predecessor as Master of the Revels, Sir George Buc, 'for the shewynge of one Peter Williams a man monstrously deformed', were thus brought before a magistrate in Norwich on 16 June 1618, and told 'to shew him this present day & no longer'. On 27 September 1614, Ciprian de Roson with 'his wife & two assistantes', who had been licensed by Buc 'to shewe feates of actitity together with A Beast Called an Elke [were] nowe enjoyned to depart the Cytty [of Norwich] this present day upon payne of whippyng'.[54]

It is not clear that these troupes were sent packing because of the presence of women, or suspicions or accusations attending on their presence although one is tempted to draw such an inference after reading the following extract from the Constables' Accounts of Manchester for 1624-25 involving a blind fiddler and his wife, where the distinction between itinerant entertainer and beggar might have easily become blurred in the eyes of the arresting constable(s), perhaps because the wife was pregnant:

> Robert Cowbornne beeinge a blind man A ffiddler and his wiffe beeinge Taken beggine shee beeinge verye great with Child and beeinge putt in the Dungeon whilest the passe was makeinge beeinge not past halffe ane howere was delivered of a Child which was christned and they were

both kept o the townes chardges till shee was churched
whiche was xiiii[teen] dayes.[55]

Given the large numbers of wayfaring homeless, the ancient and
prejudicial ambiguities between actors and vagabonds, and between
actresses and prostitutes, plus a fear of being burdened with some
other parish's bastards, provincial theatrical troupes may have
anticipated that travelling with women would jeopardize their ability
to secure the permission they needed from local authorities in order
to perform. If so, even the London troupes may have felt it would
be uneconomical to train women to play female roles for their own
playhouses and then substitute male actors in the same roles during
provincial tours. Such a system of dual casting was, however,
precisely what Italian popular troupes did in order to play both in
the Papal States, where actresses were forbidden, and elsewhere in
Italy where they were allowed. English troupes could have used
their play-boys in the provinces and their actresses in London,
unless, as was suggested earlier, male actors clung to the time-tested
system of casting which had nourished many of their own careers.

If these hypotheses have any merit, then the economics of theatre
may help explain why casting men as women remained the standard
practice of the English theatre until 1642, and only changed after
theatre was revived in 1660 under a vastly altered set of conditions.
Framing the issue in such terms suggests an answer based on specific
conditions affecting the theatre before and after the Restoration: e.g.
gendered rivalries, concern over employment opportunities, methods
of recruitment, managerial assessment of practicality, availability of
potential actresses, and other factors which seem more distinctively
English than the cultural attitudes Orgel invokes. Formulating the
issue as Orgel does – 'Why were women more upsetting than boys to
the English?'[56] – invites an answer based on male fears of female
sexuality. The manifestations of that fear, at least those cited by Orgel,
seem fairly widespread throughout Europe and thus lack power to
explain what is said to be 'a distinctively English solution to the nearly
universal disapproval of actresses'. My attempts to explain the delay
in the appearance of actresses on the English stage are admittedly
speculative, as are those advanced by Orgel and other theatre
historians, but I propose a set of hypotheses derived from what we
know of the economic conditions of early modern English theatre,

rather than from attitudes towards women and female sexuality in European culture at large.

NOTES

1.   Reviews of the National Theatre productions are cited in Michael Shapiro, *Gender in Play on the Shakespearean Stage*, Ann Arbor: University of Michigan Press, 1994, 259 n2. For reviews of the Cheek by Jowl production, see Ben Brantley, 'How to Call a Play into Being by Smearing a Man with Mud', *New York Times*, 1994, C: 17; Vincent Canby, 'As You Like It', *New York Times*, 6 October 1994, 2:5; and Richard Corliss, 'Something to Sing About: A Very Traditional British Cast Finds Rapture in *As You Like*', *Time* 144 (12 December 1994): 84.

2.   Stephen Orgel, 'Nobody's Perfect', *South Atlantic Quarterly* 88 (1989): 7-8.

3.   Lesley Ferris, *Acting Women: Images of Women in the Theatre*, New York: New York University Press, 1989, 32-33.

4.   Elissa Weaver, 'Spiritual Fun: A Study of Sixteenth-Century Tuscan Convent Theater', in *Women in the Middle Ages and the Renaissance: Literary and Historical Perspectives*, Mary Beth Rose (ed.), Syracuse: Syracuse University Press, 1986, 173-205; Meg Twycross, '"Transvestism" in the Mystery Plays', *Medieval English Theatre* 5 (1983): 133; and James Stokes, 'The Wells Cordwainers Show: New Evidence Concerning Guild Entertainments in Somerset', *Comparative Drama* 19 (Winter 1985-86): 336.

5.   Kenneth Richards and Laura Richards, *The Commedia dell'Arte: A Documentary History*, London: Basil Blackwell for the Shakespeare Head Press, 1990, 39. See also Paul C. Castagno, *The Early 'Commedia dell'Arte' 1550-1621*, American University Studies, Series 26, Theatre Arts, Vol. 13, New York: Peter Lang, 1994, 53; Richard Andrews, *Scripts and Scenarios: The Performance of Comedy in Renaissance Italy*, Cambridge: Cambridge University Press, 1992, 224, 258 n65; Kathleen M. Lea, *Italian Popular Comedy*, 2 vols., Oxford: Clarendon Press, 1934, 1:113-14; and Kathleen McGill, 'Women and Performance: The Development of Improvisation by the Sixteenth-Century Commedia dell'Arte', *Theatre Journal* 43 (March 1991): 61.

6.   Glynne Wickham, *Early English Stages, 1300 to 1600*, 2 vols. in 3, London: Routledge and Kegan Paul, 1959-72, 2 (pt. 1): 10, describes this change as the substitution of image for emblem.

7.   Michael Anderson, 'Making Room: Commedia and the Privatisation of the Theatre', in *The Commedia dell'Arte From the Renaissance to Dario Fo*, Christopher Cairns (ed.) in *The Italian Origins of European Theatre*, VI, Papers of the Conference of the Society for Italian Studies, Nov. 1988, Lewiston: Edwin Mellen Press, 1989, 85; see also Richards, *The Commedia dell'Arte*, 88-90.

8.   Pierre Louis Duchartre, *The Italian Comedy*, Randolph T. Weaver (trans.), New York: Dover: 1966, 90, 93, 320; Richards, *The Commedia dell'Arte*, 268; Frances Barasch, 'Francesquina, the Transvestite Clown and Shakespeare's Maidservants', paper presented at the World Shakespeare Congress, Tokyo, 1991.

9.   According to Ireneo Sanesi, *La Commedia*, 2nd ed., Milan: Villardi, 1954, I, 508, the Cardinals granted a licence to the Desiosi so long as they agreed to perform 'without women' ('*senza donne*'). I wish to thank Janet Smarr for translating this passage. Carlo Goldoni (b. 1707), records first seeing actresses during a visit to Rimini, 'where women are admitted on the boards, and we do not see there, as at Rome, men without beards'. See *Memoires of Carlo Goldoni*, William A. Drake (ed.), John Black (trans.), New York: Knopf, 1926, 15. See also Richards, *The Commedia dell'Arte*, 67; Rosamond Gilder, *Enter the Actress: The First Women in the Theatre*, Boston: Houghton Mifflin, 1931, 64; John Roselli, 'The Castrati as a Professional Group and a Social Phenomenon', *Acta Musicologica* 60 (1988): Fasc. 2 (May-August), 143-79. Roselli sees the castration of vocally talented boys in a time of economic depression and Christian asceticism as a more extreme economic gamble than entering religious orders, where celibacy was enforced by vow rather than by the surgeon's knife.

10.   Melveena McKendrick, *Theatre in Spain, 1490-1700*, Cambridge: Cambridge University Press, 1989, 48-49; and N. D. Shergold, *A History of the Spanish Stage*, Oxford: Clarendon Press, 1967, 143ff. Ms Luz Vega-Vega informs me that Medieval and Renaissance Spanish records sometimes refer to female instrumentalists, singers, and dancers under such terms as *juglaresa*, but it is not clear whether they can be considered actresses. Ursula K. Heise, 'Transvestism and the Stage Controversy in Spain and England, 1580-1680', *Theatre Journal* 44 (October 1992): 357-74, argues that a *Pragmatica* of 1534, regulating performers' dress, refers to female as well as male *comediantes*, so that the Italian troupe was petitioning for a return to a previous practice. Such a request, however, would have been unnecessary had actresses still been employed in Spanish companies.

11.   Heise, 'Transvestism', 359-60, 366-68.

12.   W.L. Wiley, *The Early Public Theatre in France*, Cambridge MA: Harvard University Press, 1960, 20-25, 87-91; and Gilder, *Enter the Actress*, 82-99.

13.   E.K. Chambers, *The Elizabethan Stage*, 4 vols., Oxford: Clarendon Press, 1923, 1:246-47.

14.   Chambers, *The Elizabethan Stage*, 1:247-49.

15.   Richard Braithwait, *The English Gentleman*, London, 1630, quoted in Paul Whitfield White, *Theatre and Reformation: Protestantism, Patronage, and Playing in Tudor England*, Cambridge: Cambridge University Press, 1992, 234 n29.

16.   Henk Gras, 'All Is Semblative a Woman's Part?' (Ph.D. diss., University of Utrecht, 1991), 431. Leslie Hotson, *The Commonwealth and Restoration Stage*, Cambridge: Harvard University Press, 1928, 171, reports that an English actor-manager, George Jolly, who led a travelling troupe on the continent, was the first to bring actresses onstage in Frankfurt-am-Main in the 1650s.

17.   See J. W. Binns, 'Women or Transvestites on the Elizabethan Stage? An Oxford Controversy', *The Sixteenth Century Journal* 5 (Summer 1974): 95-120; *Gender in Play*, 38-39, 146-47.

18.   Edna Purdie, 'Jesuit Drama', in *Oxford Companion to the Theatre*, Phyllis Hartnoll (ed.), 3rd ed., Oxford: Oxford University Press, 1967, 508. In 1591, an official revision of the rules permitted only those female roles which were absolutely

necessary, while a dispensation of 1602 required such characters to be modest and serious and only rarely introduced (509).

19. Thomas Nashe, *Pierce Pennilesse His Supplication to the Divill*, in *Works*, R. B. McKerrow (ed.), 5 vols., London: Sidgwick and Jackson, 1958, 1:215.

20. Shapiro, *Gender in Play*, 15-28; Alan Nelson, 'Cross-dressing in English Renaissance Theatre: Business as Usual', paper presented at the Sixteenth Century Studie. Conference, St Louis, MO, 1993. As Nelson points out, their failure to encourage or at least allow plays with only male characters gives the game away.

21. John Rainoldes compares young male actors playing women to Sporus, Nero's homosexual favourite, while Prynne, citing Stubbes, refers to cases of men 'who have beene despaerately enamoured with Players Boyes thus clad in womans apparell, so farre as to solicite them by words, by Letters, even actually to abuse them' (quoted in Shapiro, *Gender in Play*, 38; see 37-41, 143 ff.). I am aware of current controversies in our attempts to understand homoeroticism in early modern England, but for purposes of my argument rely on Alan Bray's ground-breaking book, *Homosexuality in Renaissance England*, London: Gay Men's Press, 1982. As Bray has noted, except for antitheatrical tracts and a few satirical poems, it is rare in early modern England to find male homosexuality linked to cross-dressing. Indeed, outside of the theatre and folkloric rites (mostly rural rather than urban), it is rare to find any evidence at all of male cross-dressing in England. See also, Shapiro, *Gender in Play*, 37-4 1.

22. Heise, 'Transvestism', 371.

23. Doubling schemes are printed in David Bevington, *From 'Mankind' to Marlowe*, Cambridge: Harvard University Press, 1962, 265-73. See also Shapiro, *Gender in Play*, 32-34.

24. J.B. Streett, 'The Durability of Boy Actors', *Notes & Queries* 218 (1973): 46 1-65. My information about acting apprenticeship comes from Gerald Eades Bentley, *The Profession of Player in Shakespeare's Time, 1590-1642*, Princeton: Princeton University Press, 1984, 113-46; *The Jacobean and Caroline Stage*, 7 vols., Oxford: The Clarendon Press, 1941-68, 2:433-34; T. J. King, *Casting Shakespeare's Plays: London Actors and Their Roles*, Cambridge: Cambridge University Press, 1992, 48-49, 77.

25. Steve Rappaport, *Worlds Within Worlds: Structures of Life in Sixteenth-century London*, Cambridge: Cambridge University Press: 1989, 295 ff.; and Richard Rastall, 'Female Bodies in All-Male Casts', *Medieval English Theatre* 7 (1985): 28-35.

26. Ben Jonson, C. H. Herford and Percy Simpson (eds), Oxford: Clarendon Press, 1925-52, *Poetaster* (vol.4) 3.4.205-07, 3.4.273-76; and *Christmas, His Masque* (vol 7), II. 119, 132-37.

27. Bentley, *The Profession of Player*, 126-28.

28. G.E. Bentley, 'The Salisbury Court Theater and Its Boy Players', *Huntington Library Quarterly* 40 (February 1977), 137. Although masters of children's troupes held the power to impress or take up children, Henry Clifton's Star Chamber suit of 1601 identifies one of the Blackfriars actors, Alvery Trussel, as having been 'an apprentice to one Thomas Gyles', choirmaster of Paul's (quoted in Harold N. Hillebrand, *The Child Actors*, New York: Russell & Russell: 1964, 161. Hillebrand also reprints a contractual agreement dated 14 November 1606, in which Alice

Cooke agrees, in effect, to apprentice her son Abel for three years to Thomas Kendall, one of the managers of the Blackfriars troupe, 'to be practized and exercised in the. . . qualitye of playinge' (198).

29. Bentley, *The Profession of Player*, 144.

30. Sharers Papers of Cuthbert and Richard Burbage, as quoted in Bentley, *The Profession of Player*, 140.

31. Translated by Andrew Gurr, *The Shakespearean Stage, 1574- 1642*, 2nd ed., Cambridge: Cambridge University Press, 1980, 209, following Geoffrey Tillotson, '*Othello* and *The Alchemist* at Oxford in 1610', *Times Literary Supplement*, 20 July 1933, 494.

32. Colley Cibber, *An Apology for the Life of Mr. Colley Cibber*, 2 vols., London: John C. Nimmo, 1889, 2:90.

33. Stephen Orgel, in *Impersonations: The Performance of Gender in Shakespeare's England*, Cambridge: Cambridge University Press, 1996, 72 3, citing K.D.M. Snell's *Annals of the Labouring Poor: Social Change and Agrarian England, 1660-1900*, New York: Cambridge University Press, 1985, finds a surprising number of women admitted to the artisanal guilds in the sixteenth century, but notes a significant decline by the early seventeenth century. Comparison of theatre apprenticeships with those of craft guilds may be less relevant than Orgel believes: (1) As Rappaport (*Worlds Within Worlds*, 36-42), argues, as part of a general decline in the economic status of women, they were gradually being squeezed out of craft guilds, but it is incorrect to infer that they were also squeezed out of the acting profession because they were never a part of it; (2) Bentley, (*The Profession of Dramatist*, 125-26), finds that only three of the theatrical apprentices served actors who belonged to craft guilds, and although he suggests that Apprentice Books might yield more, I know of no examples which have come to light.

34. *The Dramatic Records of Sir Henry Herbert*, 95. I am not sure what is meant by 'habitts according to our sceanes'.

35. James Wright, *Historia Histrionica*, London, 1699, quoted in Bentley, *Profession*, 123.

36. Sandra Richards, *The Rise of the English Actress*, 8.

37. Thomas Jordan, *A Royal Arbour of Loyal Poesie*, quoted in John Harold Wilson, *All the King's Ladies: Actresses of the Restoration*, Chicago: University of Chicago Press, 1958, 6.

38. For information on Kynaston, Betterton, and Nokes, see Philip H. Highfill, Kalman A. Burnim, and Edward A. Langhans, *A Biographical Dictionary of Actors, Actresses, Musicians, Dancers. Managers, and Other Stage Personnel in London, 1660-1800*, 17 vols., Carbondale: Southern Illinois University Press, 1984, 9:79, 2:101-02, and 11:40-41. Even after the introduction of actresses, and contrary to Charles's revised patent, Nokes continued to play female roles, especially older women, such as the Nurse in *Romeo and Juliet* and in Henry Nevil Payne's *The Fatal Jealousy* (1672), for which he won the nickname of 'Nurse'. See also the entries for other known female impersonators in the years immediately following the Restoration: Edward Angel (1:83), Mr. Floyd (5:314), and John Mosely (10:329). Pepys's entry and Newport's letter are quoted in *The London Stage, 1660-1800*, William Van Lennep (ed.), 3 vols.,

Carbondale: Southern Illinois University Press, 1965, 1:12 and xxiv.

39. Quoted in Henry Wysham Lanier, *The First English Actresses*, New York: The Players, 1930, 42-43. To replace the systems of apprenticeship and covenant servants, under which training girls would have been difficult, one or two nursery companies developed in the years after the reopening of the theatres. See Hotson, *The Commonwealth and Restoration Stage*, 176-96.

40. Katherine Eisaman Maus, '"Playhouse Flesh and Blood" Sexual Ideology and the Restoration Actress,' *ELH* 46 (Winter 1979): 595-617. While Samuel Pepys's diary reflects his great delight with performances by Kynaston and by a number of actresses, John Evelyn's journal records his sense of the moral decline of the stage and his reluctance to attend plays, citing, among other reasons, the erotic power of actresses to arouse male spectators: 'Women now (& never 'til now) permitted to appeare & act, which inflaming severall young noblemen & gallants, became their whores, & to some their Wives.' See *The London Stage*, 1: 12, 96, 119.

41. Lea, *Italian Popular Comedy*, 2:352-58.

42. For evidence of French troupes in London, see *The Dramatic Records of Sir Henry Herbert*, ed. Joseph Quincy Adams, New Haven: Yale University Press, 1917, 59-62.

43. William Prynne, *Histrio-Mastix* (1632), quoted in Gras, 'All is Semblative', 528. Gras casts doubt on the evidence that French actresses were unpopular with London spectators is suspect. J.P. Collier, *History of English Dramatic Poetry and Annals of the Stage* (1832), as quoted by Gras, cited a letter from Thomas Brande to Archbishop Laud to the effect that a female troupe of 'vagrant French players . . . were hissed, hooted, and pippin-pelted from the stage'. Gras declares that this letter can no longer be found where Collier claimed to have seen it, suggesting that it is Collier's invention. Perhaps the French company, probably comprising men and women, was unsuccessful. Gras cites a letter (unknown to Collier) from John Mead to Martin Stuteville, dated 31 October 1629, which reports that 'certain French comedians, presuming to play before an English auditory in a playhouse, whereto belonged far better actors, were hissed off the stage', but there is no evidence of the French actresses being singled out for disapprobation. Sir Henry Herbert, *Dramatic Records*, 60, returned part of their licensing fees 'in respect of their ill luck', which suggests no lack of favour in the eyes of this court official.

44. Thomas Coryate, *Coryate's Crudities*, London, 1611, 247. For commentary on this passage and other English travellers' accounts of actresses on the continent, see Shapiro, *Gender in Play*, 247 n35.

45. Aurelian Townshend, *The Poems and Masques*, Cedric C. Brown (ed.), Reading: Whiteknights Press, 1983, 96, 98; Chambers, *Elizabethan Stage*, 1:371 n. 4. Bentley, *Jacobean and Caroline Stage*, 4:549-50, 917; and Suzanne Gossett, '"Man-maid, begone!" Women in Masques', 18 (Winter 1988): 96-113.

46. Quoted in Sandra Richards, *Rise of the First English Actresses*, New York: St. Martin's Press, 1993, 1 and 261 n4.

47. Wilson, *All the King's Ladies*, 10; for brief biographies of actresses, see Appendix A. See also Richards, *The Rise of the First English Actresses* 3-7; Kristina Straub, *Sexual Suspects: Eighteenth-Century Players and Sexual Ideology*, Princeton:

Princeton University Press, 1992, 90-91; and Elizabeth Howe, *The First English Actresses: Women and Drama, 1660-1700*, Cambridge: Cambridge University Press, 1993.

48. Andrews, *Scripts and Scenarios*, 190; Gilder, *Enter the Actress*, 67-81. Spanish authorities, as we have seen, tried to ensure that actresses did not practice prostitution. William O. Beeman, 'Mimesis and Travesty in Iranian Traditional Theatre', in *Gender in Performance: The Presentation of Difference in the Performing Arts*, Laurence Senelick (ed.), Hanover: University Press of New England, 1992, 22, describes how, in the rare instances when women enacted female roles in Iranian theatrical presentations, they took great pains to show that they were performers and not prostitutes: 'One was married and always had her husband close at hand. Another brought her aged mother and always sat with her when not on stage. A third had a baby that she would nurse conspicuously. All these devices were designed to prevent men in the audience from approaching the women'.

49. Andrew Gurr, *The Shakespearian Playing Companies*, Oxford: Clarendon Press, 1996, 36; Bentley, *Profession*, 177-205; Sally-Beth MacLean, 'Tour Routes: "Provincial Wanderings" or "Traditional Circuits?"' *Medieval and Renaissance Drama in England* 6 (1993), 1-14; Leeds Barroll, *Politics, Plague, and Shakespeare's Theater*, Ithaca: Cornell University Press, 1991, 106-11, 227-32; Virginia Gildersleeve, *Government Regulation of the Elizabethan Drama*, New York: Columbia University Press, 1908, 21-43.

50. See G.R. Quaife, *Wanton Wenches and Wayward Wives*, London: Croom Helm, 1979, 202-24; and Martin Ingram, *Church Courts, Sex, and Marriage in England, 1570-1640*, Cambridge: Cambridge University Press, 1987, 150 ff.

51. Paul Slack, *Poverty and Policy in Tudor and Stuart England*, London: Longman, 1988; A.L. Beier, *Masterless Men: The Vagrancy Problem in England, 1560-1640*, London: Methuen, 1985, 43. In a statement of rules and procedures, William Lambarde, *The Duties of Constables [,] Borsholders, Tithing Men*, London, 1583, which was often reprinted during the period, I can find no suggestion of this anxiety over the fear of women vagrants burdening local communities with newborn offspring. There are hints to be found in A.V. Judges, *Elizabethan Underworld*, London: George Routledge, 1930, xlvii; and Beier, *Masterless Men*, 53-54.

52. For discussion and examples of local concern with illegitimacy, see Susan Dwyer Amussen, *An Ordered Society: Gender and Class in Early Modern England*, New York: Columbia University Press, 1988, 111-17; see F. G. Emmison, *Elizabethan Life*, 5 vols., Chelmsford: Essex County Council, 1970-80, 2 (*Morals and the Church Courts*, 1973) on the same issue as well as on the related offence of 'Harbouring Unmarried Mothers', 25-31.

53. N. Bawcutt, 'New Revels Documents of Sir Geroge Buc and Sir Henry Herbert', *Review of English Studies* n.s. 35 (1984), 326-27.

54. *Records of Early English Drama: Norwich*, David Galloway (ed.), Toronto: University of Toronto Press, 1991, 142, 156-57.

55. *Records of Early English Drama: Lancashire*, David George (ed.), Toronto: University of Toronto Press, 1991, 68.

56. Orgel, 'Nobody's Perfect', p. 8.

5

FIGURES OF WORSHIP: RESPONSES TO ONNAGATA ON THE KABUKI STAGE IN SEVENTEENTH-CENTURY JAPANESE VERNACULAR PROSE

PAUL G. SCHALOW

THE ONNAGATA AS AMIDA NYORAI

In seventeenth-century vernacular prose texts (*kana-zōshi*), there is a persistent pattern of depicting onnagata (boy actors of female roles) on the kabuki stage as the salvific Buddha figure of Amida Nyorai. Like audiences everywhere, kabuki theatre-goers responded to actors on the stage in a variety of ways, many of which are recorded in prose accounts of what went on in the kabuki theatre. The audience's response took the form of organized clapping (by 'troupes of clappers', *teuchi renjū*); formal 'words of praise' (*home kotoba*); and spontaneous 'vocal outbursts' (*kake-goe*) expressing favour or criticism. Sometimes, members of the audience sent admiring notes backstage after the performance. All of these responses are fairly typical of the actor-audience dynamic in theatrical traditions world-wide. But the depiction in vernacular

prose of the audience treating an actor as a figure of worship is
something that may be unique to kabuki. Even operatic divas, who
evoke some of the same thrill in an audience that an onnagata
evokes, are not, to my knowledge, ever equated with religious icons;
and I wonder: when a boy made his appearance on the Elizabethan
stage, was his arrival ever greeted as 'the second coming of Christ'?
But that is exactly the sort of religious allusion routinely made in
seventeenth-century accounts of the kabuki onnagata when the
onnagata was equated with Amida Nyorai.

Two early examples of the equation of 'onnagata' with 'Amida'
occur in Asai Ryōi's *Ukiyo monogatari* (1661; Tales of the floating
world) and *Tōkaidō meishoki* (1661; Diary of a visit to famous places
along the Tōkaidō road). The hero of the first tale is a pleasure-
seeking samurai turned monk, Hyōtarō (Gourd-man), alias Ukiyo-
bō (Floating-world monk), whose exploits in gambling joints,
houses of prostitution and theatres are recounted in a series of
swift-moving episodes; the hero of the other work is Raku-amida-
butsu, or Raku-ami, whose name means something like 'Easy
Amidha Buddha', and the tale records his travels from the capital to
Edo and back. Since the images and decriptions of onnagata are
similar in each, I will quote only the example from *Tales of the floating
world*, the last episode (Episode 10) in Book 1, 'Ukiyobō's pilgrimage
to Kyoto' (Ukiyobō kyō uchi mairi no koto).

> [Hyōtarō] reached the dry riverbed [the theatre district at
> Shijō in Kyoto] where he could hear the noisy voices of
> doormen urging people into the theatres for puppet *jōruri*
> and onnagata kabuki. Among those displaying their skills
> were the acclaimed onnagata actor, Kichirōbei of the
> Ebisuya, along with Shōzaemon of Ozaka and Kanzae-
> mon of Edo. As Hyōtarō watched the youths dance
> across the stage, he was swept up in such excitement that
> all thought of his religious calling left him. He shouted
> uncontrollably: 'Yes! Yes! It is Amida, welcoming me to
> paradise. What sculptor could have carved such an image?
> Is it a moving, breathing Amida Nyorai? Yes! A living
> Buddha!'

There is a similarly graphic description in the first book of
Nakagawa Kiun's earlier *Kyō warabe* (1658; Citizens of the capital),

on which Ryōi is probably working a variation here. Despite the humour of the scene, Hyotarō's response to the actors is not entirely lacking in religious significance, for Hyōtarō positions himself *vis-à-vis* the onnagata actor on stage as a worshipper seated before a carved figure of Buddha, more specifically, the Buddha of the western paradise of the pure land, Amida (Amitābha), who in Jōdō (or Pure Land) Buddhist iconography is depicted descending to earth to welcome the dying to heaven.

The equation of onnagata with Amida is especially interesting because of the androgynous character of Amida in the visual arts. Amida is frequently depicted as a central figure flanked by the boddhistavas Kannon (Avalokitesvara) and Seishi (Mahāsthāmaprāpta), who is often conflated with the more popular boddhisatva, Jizō (Ksitigarbha). While buddhas and boddhisatvas are usually neither male nor female in their enlightened manifestations, Kannon is popularly regarded as a feminine deity in Japan, whereas Seishi, conflated with Jizō, is regarded as masculine. Amida, however, tends to stand somewhere in the middle of the male-female gender continuum, symbolized by the central position Amida occupies in religious paintings. If vernacular prose texts had recorded audience members shouting out 'It's Kannon!' or 'It's Jizō!' as the onnagata made his appearance on stage, it would have meant that the onnagata had a distinctly 'gendered' appeal to the audience, either feminine (Kannon), consistent with the actor's clothing and style, or masculine (Jizō), consistent with the actor's body under the clothes. The fact that onnagata were identified with Amida, who represented neither male nor female, but an intermediate blend of the two, indicates that the kabuki audience did not react to onnagata as an image of womanhood but, recognizing the man beneath the costume, saw a third and new creation produced by woman's clothing and style superimposed on a male body. The audience's response, then, was not to a woman or to a man in woman's clothing, but to an intermediate figure, which the audience equated with that most intermediate of Buddha figures, Amida.

In *Yodarekake* (The Bib), a work written in 1653 and first published in 1665, Books 5 and 6 recount a history of male love in Japan, beginning with the samurai tradition of love between man and youth, called Shūdō, and ending in the kabuki theatres of Kyoto where the practice of boy prostitution was institutionalized. There is a detailed description of the interior of the theatre and of the audience as it sits in anticipation of the appearance of the onnagata. The narrator expresses amazement at the sheer variety of theatre-going types: a wealthy and stylishly-dressed young woman; a poor man in a paper raincoat waterproofed with tree sap; a stylish man with a sedge hat on his head; an unwashed monk with a sunburned neck; an overweight farmer with soil under his fingernails: 'Old and young, highborn and lowborn all are thrown together, eyes wide open with excitement and filled with salty tears.' The passage culminates in the following description of the audience's reaction to the appearance of the onnagata on stage:

> A thrill sweeps the audience from one end of the theatre to the other. Slobber spills from their mouths as the words ring out, 'Yes! Yes! [S/He] must be the creation of Nan'ami [a famous sculptor]!' and 'It is a visitor from heaven!' Everyone looks to the stage in awe and expectation, and then Amida appears, dressed brilliantly in robes as bright as gold and silver and wearing a lustrous black wig with a cotton headband. The way [s/he] dances expresses [her/his] love for mankind, and [her/his] waving sleeves drive the audience mad with desire.

The electrifying effect of the onnagata on stage is captured here with Buddhist metaphors: the onnagata is equated with a carved image of Buddha covered with gold leaf, with Amida welcoming believers to paradise, and with a Buddha-like love for all mankind. The image of the onnagata is connected here with a convention of Amida iconography, the Raigō-zu, or paintings of Amida's descent from heaven, which usually depicted streams of light emanating from the hands of the approaching Amida. Believers, on their deathbeds, reach out to grasp the thread-like rays of light that will carry them to the pure land. The face of the dying one is filled with ecstatic joy as he grasps the light. Amida's face is the image of compassionate love.

Ihara Saikaku draws on the tradition of the Raigō-zu image in a story about the onnagata actor, Suzuki Heihachi, in *Nanshoku ōkagami* (1687; The Great Mirror of Male Love). The story is an elegy to the young actor, who died in the previous year, in 1686, at the tender age of twenty-three. Saikaku recounts:

> One spring day in this Jōkyō era, Heihachi starred in a
> wildly popular play called 'Tariki honganki' [Record of
> Amida's saving grace and the primal vow]. It attracted
> huge crowds of spectators who fell into the abyss of his
> love. They reached out to grasp the cords extending from
> his holy hands as if he were Amitabha come to welcome
> their eager souls to paradise. Even his lines echoed like
> the golden words of the Buddha in their ears.

Saikaku stresses the equally strong appeal this 'onnagata as Amida'
had for both men and women in the audience:

> It had been years since such huge crowds had gathered
> from villages outside the city, and it was all due to the
> infatuating beauty of this one actor, Suzuki Heihachi. They
> suffered and yearned for his love. No one knows how
> many broken-hearted men and women ultimately passed
> away like the evening dew.

The colour gold is central to the religious imagery equating Amida
and onnagata. *Tōkaidō meishoki*, the 1661 work by Asai Ryōi quoted
from earlier, has a passage where the boy's skin is compared to the
gold leaf on the surface of a sculpture of Amida in this very sensual
phrase: 'he touched the youth's golden skin; he brought Nyorai's
skin (*nyorai hada*) close to his . . . .' This is a clear eroticization of the
Amida image. Or, it might be more accurate to say that it is an
expression of the sensuality of Buddhist iconography, for the erotic
or sensual was never purged from religious icons as it was in the
Judeo-Christian religious tradition. For that reason, the equation of
onnagata and Amida, despite its humour, is not parody or slander,
but was the product of the audience's desire for an experience that
was serious and spiritual in nature. Thus, the audience positioned
itself as worshipper *vis-à-vis* the onnagata because that position
allowed the audience to experience the pleasure of the onnagata's
performance in ways the audience needed.

THE ONNAGATA AS TEXT OF BLISS

To understand how the audience experienced the pleasure of the onnagata, and to understand what the pleasure of the onnagata is, it is necessary to identify the onnagata as 'text', and the audience as engaged in a reading activity. In a performative process of interpolation, the onnagata, as the agent of ideological discourse, constitutes the members of the audience as subjects and draws them into a subject/text relationship. When members of the audience respond to the onnagata, then 'not only are they constructed as subject, but the text then becomes text, in the sense that the subject begins to construct meaning from the work and is constructed by the work' (Bobo 101). At the moment when the text and subject are constituted in their mutual encounter, men and women in the audience bring their personal and cultural histories to bear in the production of textual meaning. Meanings differ from person to person, depending on their gender, where they are situated within the social structure, and the competencies they bring to bear on the interdiscourse. Interestingly, the religious response described above is one that indicates the audience's desire to transcend gender, or at least to relieve the anxieties associated with maintaining rigidly-defined gender roles. The Buddha figure is a neutral, androgynous object, and it allows men and women alike to give up their male or female positions and prerogatives, to enjoy a pleasure not unlike the bliss of *jouissance*, based in the relief of gender anxieties. The interdiscursive subject constituted in the encounter with the onnagata experiences itself as genderless, and it is the experience of being relieved of gender that is the pleasure of the onnagata for the audience.

The audience experiences the pleasure of the onnagata by casting itself in a worshipful pose as it is hailed by the onnagata's subjectifying presence on stage. The audience is made a subject by its engagement with the onnagata text, and the audience's subjective gaze makes of the onnagata a Buddhist iconographic object. Yet, by positioning itself *vis-à-vis* the onnagata as Amida worshippers, the audience simultaneously relinquishes its subjectivity and becomes the *object* of the onnagata's salvific gaze. The onnagata is transformed from the *object* of the audience's worship into the benevolent, all-pitying, all-loving *subject*; the subjectivity of the audience is thereby displaced, and they instead become *objects* of the onnagata's symbolic heavenly grace. The audience, by being objectified in the interdiscourse between onnagata text and subject, suffers a pleasurable loss of position, and this loss complements and actuates the blissful gender reorientation, or at least temporary disorientation, which defines the pleasure of the onnagata.

How might we describe the pleasure an audience takes in the onnagata text? Roland Barthes, in *The Pleasure of the Text*, distinguishes between the 'text of pleasure' (*plaisir*) and the 'text of bliss' (*jouissance*). The text of pleasure is 'the text that contents, fills, grants euphoria; the text that comes from culture and does not break with it, is linked to a comfortable practice of reading'. Conversely, the text of bliss is 'the text that imposes a state of loss, the text that discomfits . . . , unsettles the reader's historical, cultural, psychological assumptions, the consistency of his tastes, values, memories, brings to a crisis his relation with language'. Barthes's framework, extended to the onnagata's performed text, shows the onnagata to be a 'text of bliss', for the audience loses its position as subject in the face of the onnagata figure of worship, and the audience's gender alignments are similarly unsettled. As in the case of the monk Ukiyo-bō quoted above, when all thoughts of his religious vocation were erased in the interdiscursive moment, all that remains of language in the moment of encounter between onnagata as text and audience as subject are words of Buddhist praise, and a resultant lingering sense of bliss. This is a fitting interdiscursive end point for the audience's encounter, in that Pure Land Buddhism teaches that the efficacy of calling on Amida's name alone is what brings believers to salvation. The pleasure of the onnagata is a bliss much like receiving religious grace. The crisis in the reader's relationship with language that Barthes associates with the text of bliss is symbolized in the audience's single-minded affirmation of Amida's name, equivalent to the recitation of the *nembutsu* (Namu Amida Butsu: 'I place my faith in Amida Buddha'). At the moment of its recitation, no other words have meaning. Moreover, the *nembutsu* has been described as being both 'the call of Amida Buddha to the authentic life, and the human response to that call, both of which are to be realized here and now' (Unno 52). The intermingling of subject and object positions, and the immediacy of the moment in the *nembutsu*, are elements which have exact parallels in the audience's experience of the pleasure of the onnagata on the kabuki stage.

THE ONNAGATA AS A SITE OF RESISTANCE

The equation of onnagata with Amida, and the onnagata's performance as a text of bliss, raises several questions about the nature of power in early-modern Japan. In North American critical discourse, we have grown used to the assumption that in patriarchal power structures, the human subject is male, and it thus seems natural to interpret the onnagata in kabuki as being structured around male pleasure. Thus, for North American critics of female spectatorship, the onnagata signifies yet another instance of what the critic Lea Melandri has called 'the two-fold concealment' of women's bodies (de Lauretis 177): women themselves are absent from the kabuki stage, and the image of 'woman' presented on stage in the form of the onnagata is constructed and presented by men. The presence of the onnagata thus signifies the absence of *onna* (woman). A feminist semiotics of theatre, film and television suggests that the representational context of entertainment media requires that 'female' has meaning only in its function as a primary, binary opponent to 'male', and that it is in the presence of the complementary but subsidiary 'female' that 'male' comes to life and achieves meaning. When 'female' serves this symbolic function in patriarchal ideology, the bodily presence of actual women is suppressed. The existence of the kabuki onnagata seems to prove that the female body-negating mechanism is as functional in the Japanese patriarchal system as it is in Europe and North America.

By extension, female subjectivity is as problematic for Japan as it is elsewhere. If the human subject is male, and if kabuki is structured around masculine pleasure, what can the onnagata mean to the female spectator? How can we explain the evident pleasure of the female spectator's response to the onnagata? Laura Mulvey has tried to explain the pleasure a female viewer derives from a typical Hollywood film in terms of 'trans-sex identification', in which the female spectator remembers the masculine, active stage of her psycho-social development and enjoys identifying with the masculine pleasures around which films are structured ('Afterthoughts on "Visual Pleasure and Narrative Cinema"'). Rejecting the Freudian model of female development, other critics have turned to Nancy Chodorow's model of female development based on object-relations theory (*The Reproduction of Mothering*) to describe how women find pleasure in male-centred film (Byars 112-15). But if the onnagata is a text of bliss, as I argue it is, then female identification with 'female-self' or 'male-other' or female empathy resulting from object relations is not at work in the female spectator's experience of the onnagata. Rather, her experience is parallel to the male spectator's experience, of identification with a neutral object which allows release from the very real anxieties of maintaining gender identification, by facilitating its temporary suspension.

But that is not to say that there are no repercussions for women related to the fact that the figure on stage is an onnagata – that is, it is a man's body dressed in woman's garb and carried in a feminine style. The neutral position of Amida Nyorai that the onnagata achieves would be a different neutral position from the one that could be achieved by a hypothetical *otokogata* – that is, a woman's body dressed in man's garb and carried in masculine style. And the way that men and women in the audience would respond to the hypothetical otokogata would not necessarily be identical to the response to the onnagata. For *jouissance* to occur, it seems important that the movement of cross-dressing be the condescending movement of man-dressed-as-woman, for in it the *powerful* embraces the *weak* in a compassionate, Buddha-like motion. The reverse movement would be entirely different in nature: woman-dressed-as-man is a *usurping* motion, an act of *insubordination* in a Confucian context where 'station' (*kurai*) was the central political fact of life. Looked at from this perspective, the onnagata who offers release of gender anxiety in the personal realm looks more like an opiate, in that the onnagata is by the nature of the ideological forces creating it unable to challenge or provide release from current configurations of power. In a sense, then, the reason the *otokogata* paradigm did not develop on the kabuki stage, and that the onnagata did develop, was that release from gender strictures and the anxiety they generated was allowed by the hegemonic powers only as long as the mechanism of release, the onnagata, maintained the hierarchy of power between superior (male) and inferior (female), such as was the case in the compassionate motion of Amida embracing the dying faithful. Release from gender anxiety through the act of insubordination of a woman-dressed-as-man would be an intolerable violation of the mechanisms of patriarchal power inherent in early modern Confucian ideology.

If the binary sex-gender system is an expression of the exercise of power dynamics, and the onnagata is a site of resistance to that power, then it is allowed because it resists only partially. While contributing to temporary personal release, the onnagata is not capable of facilitating permanent political release, and in fact could be viewed as contributing to the maintenance of current configurations of power. Only the hypothetical *otokogata*, by its violation of the hierarchy of power, could have posed a fuller threat to power configurations in early-modern Japan. I look at the kabuki stage as a theatre where a limited resistance in the form of temporary relief of gender anxiety was showcased in the figure of the onnagata, but the onnagata always exercised resistance in a manner that addressed the personal, not the political; and the self-interest of current power configurations saw to it that more powerful figures of resistance were suppressed.

Historically, kabuki moved through three phases before the role of onnagata was established. The legendary founder of kabuki, a shrine dancing girl from Izumo called Okuni, is said to have performed in skits and dances dressed as a youth, not unlike the hypothetical *otokogata* alluded to, opposite men in women's garb. Women continued to play roles as youths and women on the kabuki stage until 1629, when they were banned by government edict due to bloody rivalries among men for the affections of certain actresses. This ushered in a period of ascendance for youths' kabuki (*wakashū* kabuki), in which youths played male and female roles, though youths' kabuki existed well before the 1629 ban on women. Youths' kabuki lasted until 1652 when it, too, was finally banned for similar reasons. After that, young male actors were forced to wear the hairstyle of adult men on stage, to reduce their homoerotic appeal. Gradually, over a period of years, the onnagata role came into being and the pattern of equating the onnagata with Amida worship seems to have taken hold.

In each of kabuki's historical stages, we see a movement directed by the relentless pressure of goverment edict towards less threatening forms of release for gender anxiety. First, women and the female-in-male-garb are banned, consistent with the neccessity of preserving gender-based hierarchies of power. Next, the youth-in-female-garb is modified to a more symbolic level by forcing youths to wear their hair in the fashion of adult men. Finally, only the most symbolic form of woman is left: the man-in-female-garb. The longevity of the onnagata on the kabuki stage has a lot to do with the fact that, like good medicine, the onnagata provided the most relief with a minimum of 'undesirable' side-effects on Tokugawa political hegemony. As such, it proved to be as much a tool of maintaining current configurations of power as it was a site of resistance to that power.

REFERENCES

Asai Ryōi, 'Ukiyo-bō kyō uchi mairi no koto', in *Ukiyo monogatari. Kana zōshi shūsei*, vol. 6, Asakura Haruhiko (ed.), Tokyo: Tokyodo, 1985, 104-108.

Barthes, Roland, *The Pleasure of the Text*, Richard Miller (trans.), New York: Hill and Wang, 1975.

Bobo, Jacqueline, 'Black Women as Cultural Readers', in Pribram 90-109.

Byars, Jackie, 'Gazes/Voices/Power: Expanding Psychoanalysis for Feminist Film and Television Theory', in Pribram 110-31.

de Lauretis, Teresa, 'Aesthetic and Feminist Theory: Rethinking Women's Cinema', in Pribram 174-95.

Ihara Saikaku, 'A Terrible Shame He Never Performed in the Capital', *The Great Mirror of Male Love*, Paul Gordon Schalow (trans.), Stanford: Stanford University Press, 1990, 242-46.

Pribram, E. Deidre (ed.), *Female Spectators: Looking at Film and Television*, London: Verso, 1988.

Shively, Donald H., 'The Social Environment of Tokugawa Kabuki', *Studies in Kabuki: Its Acting Music and Historical Context*, James R. Brandon, William P. Malm, and Donald H. Shively, Honolulu: University of Hawaii Press, 1978, 1-61.

Unno, Taitetsu, 'Amida', *Kodansha Encyclopedia of Japan*, Tokyo: Kodansha, 1983, 52.

Yodarekake. Edo jidai bungei shiryō, vol. 4, Kokusho Kankōkai (ed.), Tokyo: Kokusho Kankōkai, 1916, 1-64.

6

FEMALE-ROLE SPECIALIZATION IN KABUKI: HOW REAL IS REAL?[1]

SAMUEL LEITER

K abuki's female-role specialists (onnagata), who originated in the seventeenth century, were only the latest in a long tradition of men playing women in Japan's performing arts. Unlike earlier examples, best represented by the *nō* and *kyōgen* theatres, however, what might be considered realistic – or representational – performances of feminine manners, movement, or vocalization were not highly developed until the appearance of kabuki. The beautiful boys who played so important a part in early kabuki, and who were often called upon to play female parts, were also same-sex prostitutes. They, therefore, learned to exploit the more overt aspects associated with femininity in their attempts to appear as sensually inviting as possible, but the images they projected were probably purely of a physical nature, rarely suggesting the complexity of women as three-dimensional human beings. Their performances were mainly limited to dancing, flirting, and acrobatics, not to fleshed-out characterizations. Only when the boys – like actresses before them – were banned did the emphasis turn from gay to *gei* (art). This was in the days of so-called *yarō* ('mature male') kabuki in the 1650s.

It was not long before the actors began to seriously explore the ramifications of feminine behaviour. According to a hint in

Matsudaira Yamato no Kami Nikki, the diary of a daimyo who regularly viewed kabuki from 1658 to 1695, and in which the first use of the word onnagata appears, we may surmise that characters other than beautiful young women were beginning to appear by 1658 (Leiter 1997, 499). Danced women seem gradually to have been replaced by dramatized women for whom physical beauty was not their first prerequisite. The actors responsible were those who originally had starred in boys' or *wakashū* kabuki and were now maturing not only in age but also in artistic perception and dimensionality. Various stars of the day were described in contemporary critiques for qualities that went beyond their physical or vocal beauty, demonstrating that audiences were finding other qualities to praise in onnagata than had previously been the case. The greatest leap, however, occurred in the last decade of the seventeenth century, during the Genroku period (1688-1704), a time of spectacular artistic growth, when a number of outstanding onnagata appeared, none more so than the brilliant onnagata Yoshizawa Ayame I (1673-1729).

Ayame was the first to articulate the importance of psychological distinctions in the art of acting women. For example, he observed that a samurai's wife, who might find herself in various circumstances in which she would be forced to draw her sword and fight, should do so differently depending on the nature of the situation. If she is attacked by a group of armed men and must battle to defend both her life and that of her lord's daughter, she must – because of the intensity of her samurai loyalty – display martial skills even better than those of a man. If, however, the circumstances pit her against an enemy in a drawing room, her manner must be calmer than in the other situation. This kind of advice – coming at a time when kabuki acting was still in a relatively simple state and when actors tended to display the same bellicosity regardless of the conflict – was considered a breakthrough in making kabuki more believable (see Dunn and Torigoe 1969, 50).[2]

Ayame's comments on this and other matters were posthumously published in the *Ayamegusa*, known in English as 'The Words of Ayame' and for many years revered as the onnagata's bible. His greatest contribution lay in his belief that the key to becoming a convincing onnagata artist was to live one's life as a woman, both offstage and on. He says, for example, that if the onnagata loses his femininity when fighting, or seems consciously to be making his acting elegant, the result will be inferior:

> For these reasons, if he does not live his normal life as if he
> was a woman, it will not be possible for him to be called a
> skilful onnagata. The more an actor is persuaded that it is
> the time when he appears on the stage that is the most
> important in his career as an onnagata, the more masculine
> he will be. It is better for him to consider his everyday life
> as the most important. (Dunn and Torigoe, 53)

The practice of living as a woman, even if married and even if a father (as Ayame was), became *de rigeur* for all important onnagata until modern times and the influence of Westernization. Iwai Hanshirō VIII (1829-82) and Onoe Kikujirō III (1882-1919) were among the last onnagata stars to have followed this procedure, at least in their public lives. Such actors believed that only by a process of complete self-deception could they acquire the requisite artistry that would enable them to convey artistic sex appeal (*iroke*).

Ayame felt that if one were to live as a woman offstage, it would have to be not just as any woman but as a virtuous woman, the kind of gentle, gracious, modest woman revered in traditional Japanese culture. Moreover, it was only such women that should appear in plays, he averred, and an onnagata artist should refuse to play women whose virtue was questionable. This has nothing to do with *keisei* (courtesan) roles, as kabuki courtesans are typically women who have not chosen their profession but have been sold into it because of financial need; they are just as virtuous – in the broad sense – as women in ordinary life. In fact, they are often more virtuous because of the dramatic interest thus established between their characters and the general perception of the world they inhabit. In other words, kabuki prostitutes, like those in so much Western drama, typically have hearts of gold. Nevertheless, despite Ayame's advice to onnagata to refuse the roles of immodest women, kabuki would never have progressed dramatically if only the kind of women he admired were put on its stage. Here is one area where the reality that Ayame sought was very selective; clearly, any truthful representation of Japanese society would have necessitated the depiction of all kinds of women, which is exactly what post-Ayame kabuki went on to do.[3]

Also extremely important to the onnagata – and closely related to *iroke* – is the concept of *tashinami* ('etiquette'), originally referring to the linguistic and behavioural choices made by the onnagata in his daily life as a woman. A famous, but possibly apocryphal, anecdote illustrating *tashinami* concerns Sawamura Kodenji I (1665?-1705?), a contemporary of Ayame's, who, after being bounced around all day in a palanquin while on a religious pilgrimage, referred to his physical unease by saying he was having his period (*chi no michi*). His companions laughed at his woman's locution but the great Genroku novelist, Ihara Saikaku (1642-1693), whose story was reported years later in the encyclopaedic *Kokon Yakusha Taizen* (1750), found it touching, given that Kodenji had been raised since childhood to play female roles, and Saikaku insisted that onnagata should use only female language from the time they began their training (quoted in Hirose 1978, 78).

Another example comes from Ayame himself, where he notes that he refused to eat a certain sweet potato concoction (*tororo jiru*) when dining with the male-role actor Arashi San'emon II (1661-1701), who was impressed by Ayame's single-minded devotion to female etiquette. According to later commentators, it seems that the food was objectionable to a proper lady either because eating it required an objectionable sucking noise or because it was somehow used in male lovemaking (Dunn and Torigoe, 51).

A much later example, recorded in his memoirs by Onoe Kikugorō VI (1885-1949) and often referred to by Japanese commentators, occurred when Kikujirō III (1882-1919) played the prostitute Michitose against Kikugorō's romantic hero Naozamurai, in the play popularly known by the latter character's name. The scene required Michitose to greet Naozamurai when he came to visit her during midwinter as he fled from the police. Having overheard Kikugorō say that 'When one meets a woman with cold hands, one will want to warm up those hands,' Kikujirō prepared for the scene offstage by dipping his hands in ice water so as to stimulate his character's own desire to have her hands warmed and his theatrical partner's desire to warm them. (Onoe 1947, 119-20).

The business, which suggested the urgency with which Michitose wanted to greet her lover and gave Naozamurai something real to respond to, may be an example of the appropriate etiquette for an onnagata *vis-à-vis* his regular onstage partner, but it also conveys to us the realism with which actors in this highly conventionalized theatre often approach their roles.

Not a few modern critics believe that the quality of onnagata acting has declined with the abandonment of the custom of living offstage as women. But there are also those who argue that a kabuki woman is a theatrical construction, an idealization, a stylization, and not reality, and that it is a mistake to think you must live like a woman to effectively inhabit this construction. Another reason for what is perceived as a weakening of the onnagata's art is the practice of onnagata occasionally playing male roles, which – following the epochal success of Iwai Hanshirō V (1776-1847) in playing multiple role-types – gained popularity in the nineteenth century when versatility took precedence over specialization. Ayame himself attempted to switch from female to male roles, but his failure in this line only confirmed his own oft-stated belief that those onnagata who attempt such boundary crossing could not do so successfully. Fukuoka Yagoshirō, the amanuensis through whom Ayame's words were handed down, noted: 'I have come to the conclusion that this is because essentially there can be no person who can be both a man and a woman' (Dunn and Torigoe, 54-55). And Ayame is quoted as saying that 'A real woman must accept the fact that she cannot become a man. Can you imagine a real woman being able to turn into a man because she is unable to endure her present state?' (Dunn and Torigoe, 55). Whatever Ayame's reactions to modern surgical miracles might have been, when he says these things he seems to conflate the idea of a 'real woman' with the true onnagata, the player of female roles who takes so seriously his psychological transformation from man to woman that he is, to all intents and purposes, just that, a woman. He conveniently overlooks the contradiction that the onnagata he idealizes is a 'real man' who has become a woman, because what concerns him is the need to emphasize the technique required to make the onnagata – an artist who has trained in this line since childhood –

achieve as high a level of conviction in it as possible. If you are an onnagata, he is saying, do not imagine that you can also play men and still preserve the quality of your art.

Until the mid-nineteenth century, the onnagata took a backseat in the kabuki hierarchy to the actors of male roles, just as women did with men in the non-theatrical world. Now, with their appropriation of male roles, the onnagata began to claim increasing power within their troupes, even having female versions of the great male roles written for them. Also, the nineteenth-century development of a line of female characters – the *akuba* or 'evil women' – known for their rough-edged qualities, led some onnagata who played such roles to assume crude characteristics in their offstage lives, like the mid-nineteenth-century actor Matsumoto Kosaburō (fl. 1834-60): 'There's a story that when he went flower-viewing at Mukōjima dressed as a maiden in a long-sleeved kimono, a country samurai thought him a real girl and snuggled up to him. He thereupon raised himself a bit from his seat, lifted his hem, took a leak, and went off just like that . . . ' (quoted in Tobe 1971, 146). Of course, an onnagata from earlier years would never have been so uncouth as to deflect a man's unwanted attentions by choosing to urinate.

Today, only a few onnagata devote themselves to complete (or nearly complete) specialization, although most of their roles are female. Ayame admits that he made a big mistake at one point in his career when he attempted to switch to male roles; he cautions others not to try the same thing, but his advice eventually went unheeded. The devotion of an old-time onnagata to playing only females is represented by a story dating from around 1805 when Segawa Kikunojō III (1751-1810) was asked to play a male page in a new play:

> He faced the playwright and said, 'I'm an onnagata. I should play female roles. A page is definitely a male. I therefore can't play it and am turning it down.' The writer replied, 'I wrote this as a rare opportunity for you to play a youth and if you don't play it my efforts are in vain.' 'Well, well,' [responded the actor], 'if you revise the play so that the boy really is the female character – Lady Yamabushi – who, because of her fear of the Genji clan, has disguised

herself as a boy, I'll play the part; I'll play it if she's really a woman.' (quoted in Hirose, 79)

One of Kikunojō III's disciples, Segawa Kikujirō (dates unknown), declared, 'If you pay attention to the Chinese characters in the word "onnagata", you'll be a very bad actor. My advice is never to look at the "gata" ['person' in this example] part of onnagata' (quoted in Hirose, 79). In other words, the actor should concentrate only on the part of the word using *onna*, or woman.

Even an actor's name, said Ayame, should not suggest too much strength; an actor named Karyū spelled it with the characters for 'perfumed dragon', but Ayame argued that 'dragon' was too strong a character for an onnagata's name and the actor subsequently changed the characters to those for 'song stream', which can be pronounced Karyū (Dunn and Torigoe, 50).

Further weakening the position of pure onnagata acting has been the practice of great male-role actors now and then choosing to play female roles, which became increasingly popular from the time of the late-nineteenth-century stars Ichikawa Danjūrō IX (1838-1903) and Onoe Kikugorō V (1844-1903). This is not unlike our seeing Dustin Hoffman playing Tootsie-like characters as a regular practice. What this has done, it seems, is to replace the emphasis on lifestyle with one in which pure skill is demonstrated, so that onnagata acting becomes a technical achievement instead of the natural by-product of training and personal behaviour totally dedicated to the embodiment, both externally and internally, of a feminine ideal. Because of the traditional nature of kabuki acting in which an actor hands his art on to his son, the handing on of onnagata performances by a nonspecialist father, like Kikugorō VI, to a specialist son, like the late Onoe Baikō VII, whose private life was conventionally masculine, leads, some believe, to a diminution of the art.

We should recall that the original intention of Ayame and his peers was not to *act* as women but to be women, at whatever cost, in the interests of art. They were not necessarily thinking of themselves as men playing women but sought to be as true as they could to women as they understood them. This was not a conscious process of observation but a lived experience. Ayame told his followers such things as to hide the fact that they were married, to blush if their wives or children were mentioned, to observe female rules of decorum when eating in their dressing rooms, to treat their stage lovers with the proper respect, and so forth. Here is a famous example from the *Ayamegusa*:

> The onnagata should continue to have the feelings of an onnagata even when in the dressing room. When taking refreshment, too, he should turn away so that people cannot see him. To be alongside a *tachiyaku* [actor of male roles] playing the lover's part, and chew away at one's food without charm and then go straight out on the stage and play a love scene with the same man, will lead to failure on both sides, for the *tachiyaku*'s heart will not in reality be ready to fall in love. (Dunn and Torigoe, 61)

This comment suggests that not only is the onnagata's art affected by his offstage behaviour, but so is that of his onstage partner. If the *tachiyaku* can't believe in the total femininity of his partner, he will be unable to give a truly believable performance. Thus stage reality will suffer in general if the onnagata is anything less than completely faithful – at least while in the presence of other actors – to the ideal of femininity he represents. In fact, there are stories like that of Sakata Tōjūrō I, the great Genroku-period actor, who fell in love with his 'leading lady', Kirinami Senju I (1679-?), whom he found overwhelmingly believable as a woman.

Ayame's comments are contained in a literary form known as a *geidan*, which essentially means a 'commentary about art', in this case, the art of acting. Many later *geidan* also focus on the problems and techniques of the onnagata, but the one that most modern scholars use to contrast with Ayame's is that of Segawa Kikunojō I, a younger contemporary of Ayame's who achieved greatness in his field. This actor's *geidan*, called *Onnagata Hiden*, reveals how discussions of onnagata acting evolved from Ayame's preoccupation with the authenticity of female experience and how this could be translated into effective performance. Kikunojō, of course, also lived like a woman offstage, but by his time this was a given, so his principal concerns were with the specific technical details of performance rather than with (like Ayame) the personal experiences that had led to various insights. This ultimately became the foundation upon which subsequent onnagata *geidan* were and still are written. These writings tell you how to look beautiful, how to hold your lover when sincere and when insincere, how to do your make-up, how to hold and manoeuvre your fingers, how to differentiate between character types, how to manipulate the kimono's hems and sleeves (which, by the way, are among the most crucial aspects of onnagata acting in conveying the essence of different character types), how to hold a pipe, and how to play specific roles. They may even be concerned with the way an actor crafted his career in terms of fan interest. For example, Kikunojō's *Onnagata Hiden* has this statement:

> It's bad for an onnagata to have female fans. It would be inconvenient if one wanted to marry him. He should have many male fans who wish there were a woman like him. If he is going to receive female support, he should work to get them to admire the kinds of hair ornaments, combs, headdresses, and so forth, that he likes and that palace maids, prostitutes, and city girls will emulate. He should be setting his sights on making fans of those women who see in him a woman like themselves. (Suwa 1979, 36)

The increasing tendency, especially after the end of the Edo era, to formalize the male actor's technical observations of feminine behaviour reveals a need that was not as necessary in a time when the onnagata's behaviour flowed naturally out of his female life-style. What Kikunojō set in motion, apparently, was a concern with form that led to a gradual ossification of stage behaviour in set patterns (*kata*) rather than a naturalness that grew out of a fundamentally realistic approach to spirit and character (*shōne*). The modern actor, therefore, strives to be an onnagata rather than to be a woman. Because it is no longer possible to observe the type of female behaviour available during the Edo period, today's actors have no opportunity to do anything but repeat the patterns they have learned. But it was not unusual during the Edo period for serious actors to make special attempts to observe women with whom they might not ordinarily come in contact. For example, Hanshirō IV, preparing to play a cheap whore, went with his playwright collaborator to a real lower-class brothel to study the women and to copy their coarse speech mannerisms. This was part of a nineteenth-century trend away from the idealized female characters who had come to dominate kabuki and to expand the repertoire in the direction of more naturalistic effects. It also serves to remind us once again of how even the most formalistic acting traditions must be based on truth derived from observation. The Moscow Art Theatre's famous visit to a doss-house to prepare for *The Lower Depths* is actually a late example of the kinds of things great actors have always done, in Japan as well as elsewhere.

The practice of male actors living as women suggests that, for all the stylization associated with kabuki acting, these early actors – unlike the dancing women and boys who had pioneered kabuki in the first half of the seventeenth century – believed that realism was at the core of their art. Ayame refers, for example, to *jigei* (literally, 'ground art'), which was an early term for realistic acting as opposed to dance (*shosagoto*). His comments continually underline the need for complete believability in acting. If the actor is to achieve femininity beyond femininity, he must first be completely feminine, as much like a woman as possible. Ayame and his peers felt that anything they did to betray their masculinity was a weakness in their acting. Unless they believed themselves to be women they could not express the feminine truth of their characters. Thus, to compensate for their innate maleness, the women they created had to be even more overtly feminine than real women, although the latter were in turn influenced by the stage performances and borrowed many items of behaviour and appearance from the actors. The importance of being completely believable as a woman may even have superseded the quality of one's acting. We are told of one Kyoto actor, Yamamoto Kamon (1682-?), contemporary with Ayame, whose acting, dancing, and looks were not especially impressive but whose popularity was tremendous. According to the *Kokon Yakusha Taizen*, he was beloved because 'He was like a real woman and had absolutely nothing rough about him. The first thing for an onnagata, said [the great Genroku actor] Sakata Tōjūrō I, is to be a woman, the second is his acting' (quoted in Hirose, 77).

As several of the stories I've presented reveal, kabuki actors have a long history of attempting to make their characters as realistic as possible within the conventions of the form. They often examined each motivation of their characters for its psychological truth. When appropriate, they made an effort to observe real people whose behaviour could be appropriated for authenticity in performance. And, despite their frequent use of obviously artificial conventions, the onnagata's female characters were no more artificial than the similarly stylized men of every description who appeared on stage with them. I thus find it hard to accept Peter Hyland's remark that 'A man who plays a woman on the stage is always playing "a kind of woman", not a realistic woman' (1987, 6-7). There is little to suggest that, if women had created these roles, they, too, would not have been playing 'a kind of woman'. As Mette Laderierre wrote, 'The actor must not symbolize a woman, but must create the illusion that he is a woman on stage' (1989, 31).

NOTES

1.   This essay was first published in Samuel Leiter, *Frozen Moments: Writings on Kabuki 1966-2001*, Ithaca: Cornell East Asia Series, 2002.
2.   Kawatake (1972), offering a brief comparative survey of the history of theatrical female impersonation, East and West, claims that the acting (not the writing) of women's roles in the West, from the Greeks to the Italian castrati of the eighteenth century, was more conventionalized and less psychologically dimensional than that of the onnagata. He suggests that the Western actors' primary function was to express the values of poetic drama, whereas Japanese actors of female roles – once such acting began to be taken seriously in the light of Ayame's breakthroughs – were more concerned with the depth and quality of their acting as art. He notes, for example, the absence of any known 'artistic path' (*geidō*) associated with classical acting of women's roles in the West. Kawatake also provides a concise examination of the history and development of female-role playing in Japan, and its relationship to the tradition of male-male sexual relations (*shudō*).
3.   For an overview of onnagata roles (apart from those of old women) and their relationship to Edo-period women, see Leiter (2001).

REFERENCES

Dunn, Charles J., and Bunzō Torigoe (eds and trans.), *The Actors' Analects*, Tokyo: University of Tokyo Press, 1969.
Hirose Chisako, 'Onnagata no Geidan', *Engekikai* 36 (June), 1978.
Hyland, Peter, '"A Kind of Woman": The Elizabethan Boy-Actor and the *Kabuki Onnagata*', *Theatre Research International* (Spring), 1987.
Kawatake Toshio, 'Onnagata no Kiseki', *Kabuki* 19, 1972.

Laderierre, Mette, 'The Early Years of Female Impersonation in *Kabuki*', *Maske und Kothurne* 35, 1989.

Leiter, Samuel L., *New* Kabuki *Encyclopedia: A Revised Adaptation of* Kabuki Jiten, Westport, Ct.: Greenwood Press, 1997.

_____, 'From Gay to *Gei*: The *Onnagata* and the Creation of *Kabuki*'s Female Characters'. Originally published in *Comparative Drama* (Winter/Spring 2000). Reprinted in *A* Kabuki *Reader: History and Performance*, Samuel L. Leiter (ed.), Armonk, NY: M.E. Sharpe, 2001.

Onoe Kikugorō VI, *Gei*, Tokyo: Kaizōsha, 1947.

Suwa Haruo, *Kabuki no Denshō*, Tokyo: Senninsha, 1979.

Tobe Ginsaku, 'Onnagata no Gihō to Seishin', *Kabuki* 12, 1971.

THE STAGING OF A KABUKI VERSION OF HAMLET

ORITA KŌJI

TRANSLATOR'S INTRODUCTION
by Scott Johnson, Kansai University, Osaka

The 1991 Japan Festival introduced audiences in London, Dublin and Newcastle to a neglected adaptation of *Hamlet* by the versatile Japanese writer and critic Kanagaki Robun (1829-94). The working script for the production had been put together by Orita Kōji, now the artistic director of the National Theatre, Tokyo. In August 1995, Orita gave an informal talk about the Japan Festival performances, and how the production originated, from the choice of the 1886 playtext, and its background, to the selection of the cast and performance details. The occasion was an international symposium called 'Traditions of Cross-dressing and Cross-gender Casting', sponsored by The Shakespeare Society of Japan, The Kabuki Academic Society of Japan, The Japanese Society for Theatre Research and Osaka University. The original format of his slide-show talk has been preserved, although dates have been added for writers and performers mentioned, since they are not so well known outside Japan.

Orita comments on the 1886 adaptation of *Hamlet*: 'By the last instalment the author, Kanagaki Robun, had triumphed with a powerful work of absolutely crystalline clarity. . . . The momentousness of this script cannot be over-estimated.' The intensity, and obvious sincerity, of Orita's praise offers readers a fresh assessment of a writer who has been much maligned when not totally neglected.

Donald Keene's *Dawn to the West* (1984), a survey of post-1868 Japanese literature, devotes a good many pages to Robun as a writer of popular literature from the 1850s into the early 1870s. While recognizing Robun's productivity, he finds little to praise. He refers to early works as 'frivolous' and quite baldly states: 'Robun's only concern was with selling books.'[1] But with the impending collapse of the Tokugawa government, the comparatively bloodless establishment of Emperor Meiji as titular head of state, and the corresponding departure of one group of career bureaucrats, and the entry into Tokyo of a new stable of bureaucrats, the book-buying public was pretty much baffled as to Japan's future. With this in mind, success in 'selling books' was no mean achievement. But Robun was aided in his commercial ventures by a wide acquaintance with *ukiyo-e* artists, who were also eager to succeed commercially in changing times. He was especially close to two of Utagawa Kuniyoshi's students – Utagawa Yoshiiku (1833-1904) and Kawanabe Kyōsai (1831-89), and both artists shared Robun's 'wait-and-see' attitude towards trendy attempts to become Westernized.

Almost grudgingly, Keene reports that the humour in his longest popular work *Seiyō Dōchū Hizakurige* (By Shank's Mare through the West) (1870-76), 'is still intermittently effective'. (p.18)

Keene notes that Robun publicly announced his withdrawal from comic writing in the early 1870s, but he gives no hint that the writer's later work improved in subtlety and sophistication, or included kabuki scripts. So, one happy surprise offered to us in Orita's talk is a dramatic re-assessment of Robun as a writer. (In fact, with rising interest in popular culture, Robun's entire output is due for a re-assessment.)

But Robun himself offers a surprise that was unknown to Orita and the other planners of the 1991 Japan Festival performances. Those performances were to climax in London, but it turns out that

Robun had once dreamt of putting London on the stage in Tokyo. *By Shank's Mare through the West* (to use Keene's translation of the title) was mostly illustrated by Utagawa Yoshiiku, the same artist who illustrated the 1886 serialized publication of Robun's *Hamlet* adaptation. One of the more surprising book illustrations is in the form of a poster announcing a kabuki version of the novel, with the two main characters, Yaji and Kita, brandishing an umbrella, with London in the background. The script adaptor was named Nakamura Utanosuke, as was one of the principal performers, Ichikawa Danjurō IX, later to be Robun's dream actor for the role of Hamuramaru (Hamlet).

A kabuki adaptation of *Shank's Mare* was never performed, but the timing of Robun's imagined play, partly set in London, intersects with his growing interest in both kabuki and Shakespeare's play. The final volume of *Shank's Mare* appeared in 1876, but the last volumes were finished by another writer. Robun bowed out of his role as storyteller in 1874, introducing readers to his successor. And as Orita informs us, he began to write an early draft of a *Hamlet* play in 1875, serialized in a short-lived newspaper.

In other words, he abandoned his most ambitious comic fiction, and shortly began publishing his first attempt at *Hamlet*. The timing may be coincidental, but it does appear that the kabuki stage and London were very much on Robun's mind in the mid-1870s.

In the ten years or so between his first and final adaptations of *Hamlet*, Robun wrote extensively. In fact, although he had publicly vowed to give up comic writing, he cheated somewhat. His name pops up on title pages of books well into the 1880s, as a 'reviser' of comic fiction by various followers, and in other cases a book is advertised as 'based on a story by Robun'.

But he also wrote as a drama critic for various newspapers, and this may be where he honed his craft and sharpened his awareness of what might work on the stage. He knew everyone in the kabuki world, and was quick to report on fads and trends. Kabuki was thriving. Keene is enthusiastic about the playwright Kawatake Mokuami (1816-93): 'it might be argued that Mokuami was the finest dramatist active anywhere in the world in the late 1850s'. (p. 13) As you will see, Orita confirms that Mokuami's brilliance continued well into the 1870s and '80s.

But widespread awareness of Robun's mature writing of a kabuki
scenario had to wait some hundred years for Orita Kōji's efforts to
get it staged. How it came to be is a good story, and he tells it well,
with the aid of Robun's illustrator Utagawa Yoshiiku, as well as the
colour pictures of the Japan Festival production.

Yoshiiku's promotional illustration for a kabuki production of Robun's *Shank's
Mare*, from Vol. 19 (of 30).

A Yoshiiku illustration from Robun's *Hamuretto Yamato Nishiki-e* featuring portraits of the characters representing Claudius, Polonius and Ophelia.

As Orita's translator the only major change I have made is to simplify character names for English readers familiar with Shakespeare's *Hamlet*. Robun gave the characters in his play long and complex names, rich in allusion. But he also gave most of them familiar names, nicknames, as it were, which are similar to character names in *Hamlet*.

The ghost, for example, is named in the play Shiba Shūri-dayū

Minamoto no Kaneyori, but also known as 'Hamuretto'. For the sake of simplicity, I have generally used these 'nicknames' in reference to the characters.

Photo credits:

The Yoshiiku picture from *Shank's Mare* is used with the permission of Dr M.F.M. Forrer, Royal Museum of Ethnology, Leiden.

All the Yoshiiku illustrations for Robun's *Hamuretto Yamato Nishiki-e*, as well as colour pictures of its 1991 Japan Festival production, are courtesy of Orita Kōji, and used with his permission.

NOTES

1.   Keene, Donald, *Dawn to the West*, New York: Holt, Rinehart and Winston, 1984, p. 16.
2.   Robun's published books are duly noted in Yamaguchi Takemi's *Meiji Zenki: Gesaku-bon Shomoku* (A Catalogue of Popular Fiction of the Early Meiji Period), Tokyo: Seishōdō, 1980.

A TALK BY ORITA KŌJI
Artistic Director, National Theatre, Tokyo

In 1991, the Japan Festival brought a variety of events and performances to venues in England, Ireland and Northern Ireland, culminating in London. Prominently featured in this attempt to introduce many aspects of Japan to an English-speaking audience was a production of Shakespeare's *Hamlet* in the manner of a Kabuki production. I was the person asked to prepare a script and appropriate stage action for this production.

On the face of it, *Hamlet* and kabuki may seem an exotic coupling whose child could only see light in such a festival atmosphere. In fact, Shakespeare and Japan have shared a long history. From the mid-nineteenth-century 'opening' of Japan to the West, there has been a documented history of Japan's fascination with the best of Western culture, and obviously Shakespeare is important in such a history.

To the extent that Shakespeare is important, *Hamlet* must be seen as a vital link in Japan's understanding of Shakespeare's undying popularity. *Hamlet*'s connection with kabuki is the subject of *Hamlet in Japan* (Nansōsha, 1972), by the noted scholar Kawatake Toshio (1924–). My report to you at this 1995 international conference on Shakespeare and kabuki is one aspect of this larger subject of Shakespeare in Japan, but I want to narrow my focus to an unashamedly impassioned look at the staging of one play, *Hamuretto Yamato Nishiki-e* (A Japanese Colour-print Hamlet). This is not really a scholarly report or even a proper lecture, but anyway, I do hope you will listen to what I have to say. For an analysis of the play, quotes and other scholarly points, I will draw on Kawatake's *Hamlet in Japan*.

I. CONCEPTUAL UNDERPINNING OF THE STAGE ACTION

In February 1990, at the coldest time of winter, Tamura Seiya of the Panasonic Globe Theatre in Tokyo said he wanted to discuss something with me. Amid the various preparations for the autumn 1991 Japan Festival he wanted to involve me in assembling various types of speakers for a symposium entitled 'A History of the

Acceptance of Shakespeare in Japan'. Using the 1903 Shakespeare performances by Kawakami Otojirō (1864-1911) and his company as a model, a planning group was assembled. This group included Ishizawa Yūji (1930-), who had directed *Othello*, Ninagawa Yukio (1930-), who had directed *King Lear*, Takahashi Yasunari (1932-2002), who had created a script for a Kyogen-style *Falstaff* and Yamada Shōichi (1925-), who had created a script in the style of a Bunraku puppet play called *Tempesto: Arashi nochi Hare* (The Tempest: After the Storm, a Calm), all of which had kabuki inspiration. Tamura, Kawatake and I had only one meeting. An 1886 newspaper item referred to the creation of a version of *Hamlet* by the satirist Kanagaki Robun (1829-94), and this caught our attention, but we did not spend much time discussing it.

So now, just what is this 'Japanese Colour-print Hamlet' that I promised to tell you about?

II. THE HISTORICAL POSITION OF 'A JAPANESE COLOUR-PRINT HAMLET'

The earliest reference to *Hamlet* in Japan is in the Nakamura Masanao (1832-91) translation of Samuel Smiles' *Self-Help*, published in 1871, predictably Polonius's 'neither a borrower nor a lender be' advice to Laertes. The next reference is in an 1874 issue of the Yokohama newspaper *The Japan Punch* in which Hamlet's 'To be, or not to be' soliloquy is burlesqued into a sort of pidgin Japanese by the editor, Charles Wirgman (1832-91), who in more serious moments wrote articles on Japan for the *Illustrated London News*. The *Japan Punch* soliloquy is accompanied by an illustration of Hamlet in tights and doublet, and it is possible that some sort of sketch was performed at Yokohama's Goethe Theatre.

Then, in 1875, Kanagaki Robun began editing an illustrated newspaper he called *Hiragana E-iri Shimbun*, and in it Robun included an intriguingly-titled article, 'Seiyō Kabuki Hamuretto' (Hamlet: a Western Kabuki). Due to lack of popularity, the newspaper folded after only three issues, but it was the first Japanese publication to introduce the story of *Hamlet*.

Six years later, Toyama Shōichi (1848-1900) published his 'Reigen Ōji no Adauchi' (A Virtuous Prince's Revenge, 1881), which makes no pretense at being a complete translation of *Hamlet*. The following year, an anthology of poems edited by Toyama, called *Shintai Shishō*, included a translation of the 'To be, or not to be' soliloquy by Toyama (or possibly Yatabe Ryōkichi (1851-99)). In 1885 Tsubouchi Shōyō (1859-1935) published his 'Denmaru Ōji Hamuretto no Katari' (The Dialogue of Hamlet, the Prince of Denmark) in the ninth issue of the literary journal *Chūō Gakujutsu Zasshi*. In spite of the title, only parts of the play are translated, but he introduces a *'jōruri'* (puppet theatre recitation) style in his translation of Act I, Scene One. There are several episodes, but it finishes incompletely, so it cannot really be considered a script.

Now, it must be pointed out that the versatile and prolific kabuki playwright Kawatake Mokuami (1816-93) made a rather accurate outline of all of *Hamlet*, apparently beginning as early as 1878. In 1879, Mokuami adapted Bullwer-Lytton's *Money* as one of his attempts to create a new style of kabuki. Mokuami was sixty-four at this time. What courage, what a young mind! Either Mokuami or the Shintomi Theatre producer Morita Kanya considered using the story of *Hamlet* for a theatre piece, and encouraged its dramatization by Fukuchi Ōchi (1841-1906), according to a recollection by Mokuami's son, Kawatake Shigetoshi (1889-1967), called 'Sheikusupia to Mokuami' (Shakespeare and Mokuami) published in the 125th volume of the literary journal *Waseda Bungaku* in 1916. Succeeding waves of Western-influenced dramatic reforms following Mokuami's lead struck the kabuki world, challenging its leaders to make fundamental changes. Unfortunately, however, after Mokuami no playwright with such ability and vision followed. One cause of this reversal of momentum was the arrival in 1879 of British and French performers who appeared in a play-within-a-play in Mokuami's ambitious melodrama called *Hyōryūkidan Seiyōshibai* (Adventure Adrift: a Western Play) which failed to appeal. The cool response by the public was probably a reaction against the over-heated interest in things Western at the time. Then, as now, producers of popular entertainment talked about reforms and ideals, but did not do much of anything. But regardless of this, one kabuki playwright of that time, whose popularity was coupled with real ability, set his sights on bringing Mokuami's outline of *Hamlet* to reality.

We are now approaching the birth of 'A Japanese Colour-print

Hamlet'. From September to November of 1886 it appeared in twenty-two instalments in the *Tokyo E-iri Shimbun* (Tokyo Illustrated Newspaper). By the last instalment the author, Kanagaki Robun, had triumphed with a powerful work of absolutely crystalline clarity. Happily, the time was ripe for just such a complete version of *Hamlet*. The momentousness of this script cannot be over-estimated. To bring it to the kabuki stage, an acting scenario was prepared in 1889 by Kawatake Shinshichi III (1842-1901), under the title *Hamuretto Takumi no Engeki* (Hamlet's 'Mousetrap' Play), but unfortunately it never was actually staged, and at the present time even the whereabouts of Shinshichi's scenario is unknown.

In June 1891, the *Yomiuri Shimbun*, one of Japan's national newspapers, announced Fukuchi Ōchi's 'Toshima no Arashi' (The Storm at Toshima), which was purportedly based on *Hamlet*, but in fact was such a free adaptation that no part of Shakespeare's play was actually discernible. *Hamlet* had again been forsaken.

The first actual performance of *Hamlet* on a Japanese stage finally came to be in 1903 when the Kawakami Otojirō troupe performed a series of Shakespeare plays at the Tokyo Hongo Theatre using adaptations by Yamagishi Kayō (1876-1945). Kawakami staged *Hamlet*, *Othello* and *The Merchant of Venice*, and following close upon the death of kabuki luminaries Ichikawa Danjuro IX (1838-1903) and Onoe Kikugoro V (1844-1903), his company breathed much-needed fresh life into the theatre world. First calling this new style 'Seigeki' (True Drama), a later epithet, 'Shimpa-geki' (New Style Drama) caught the public's imagination. The firm establishment of the Shimpa movement is inextricably linked with the flourishing of performances of Shakespeare in Japan. Later, in October 1907, Kawagishi's version of *Hamlet* for the Ichikawa Sadanji II (1880-1940) troupe, was staged at the Meiji Theatre. This script called for narration by a traditional reciter, which began the actual stage history of kabuki versions of *Hamlet*. This production was staged at Osaka's Naka Theatre the following March by another innovative kabuki actor, Nakamura Ganjirō (1860-1935), firmly establishing a link between the kabuki world and *Hamlet*. However, it is hard to say whether this *Hamlet* was a real success.

'A Japanese Colour-print Hamlet', 'Hamlet's "Mousetrap" Play' and 'The Storm at Toshima ', with their puppet play and kabuki scenarios were soon forgotten. But in November 1907 a new version of *Hamlet* was performed by the Bungei Kyōkai (Literary Society) troupe, translated for them by Tsubouchi Shōyō (1859-1935), which initiated a new era of genuine translations of Shakespeare to the Japanese stage.

III. THE SIGNIFICANCE AND OVERALL CONSTRUCTION OF ROBUN'S 'A JAPANESE COLOUR-PRINT HAMLET'

In 1886, at the age of fifty-seven, Kanagaki Robun showed how Shakespeare could flourish if linked to the old performance technique of recitation, not only of narration but of a character's innermost thoughts. This style rightfully took its place within the new developments in Japanese literature as well as the theatre and kabuki worlds. But the reform movement for drama, including works by Mokuami, was somewhat countered by Robun, who was almost anti-reformist. His *Hamuretto* has a 'classic' tone, and clearly Robun revelled in being out of fashion, even though this kept his *Hamuretto* from actual production at the time. With the advantage of hindsight, we can see that both the reformist and Robun's anti-reformist ideas had their merits. But let us look more closely at this 1886 version of *Hamlet*, its special pleasures and strengths.

Robun's *Hamuretto* is divided into five acts and nineteen scenes; the play is divided into character dialogue and kabuki recitation. Written on traditional lined sheets of 400 characters, the entire script takes up 120 pages. If performed in its entirety, the play would take about seven hours. This was and is clearly impossible. But by judiciously cutting the play to eleven scenes, a script could be prepared preserving the core of Robun's *Hamuretto*. For some unknown reason Hamlet's 'Get thee to a nunnery' scene was not part of Robun's plot. And there is no equivalent of Fortinbras at the end of the play. By interpolating these parts of the play from Tsubouchi Shōyō's translation, a complete Japanese *Hamlet* could be created.

This edited script, in three acts and eleven scenes, is eminently stageable, so let us take a closer look at the nature and strengths of the storyline.

IV. THE STORY

The play is set within Japan's only period of disputed reign, when two Imperial courts were set up, a time embracing the years 1353 to 1370. The time of the play is set in the reign of Go-Kōgen, the 99th Emperor, and the place is Yamagata in the far north, in the feudal palace of the Shiba family, just after the sudden death of Feudal Lord Shiba Shūri-dayū Minamoto no Kaneyori, also known as Hamuretto. The main characters and the parts divisions are:

- The late Lord Hamuretto's son and heir: HAMURA-MARU (Hamlet) [principal performer]
- Koroshasu, the current Feudal Lord, the late king's brother and now stepfather to young Hamura-maru; known formally as SHIBA DANJŌ TADAKANE (Claudius) [principal performer]
- Chief Minister Horoniusu, formally known as MIYAUCHI SHŪZEN MUNEHARU (Polonius) [supporting performer]
- A military commander, formally known as IWAMURO CHIKARA TORANAGA (Horatio) [principal performer]
- The daughter of the Chief Minister, Princess Aperia, formally known as MIKARIA HIME (Ophelia) [performer of young women's roles]
- Serutoru Utonomae, Lady to the late Lord and still Lady as wife to his successor, formally known as SERITONOMAE (Gertrude) [performer of women's roles]
- Ghost of the late Lord Hamuretto, SHIBA SHURI-DAYŪ MINAMOTO NO KANEYORI (the Ghost) [doubled by a principal performer]

These are the roles and parts divisions as Robun envisioned them, but now let us look at the actors he is known to have wanted to use in his Hamlet.

HAMURA-MARU (Hamlet): Ichikawa Danjuro IX (1838-1903)
KOROSHASU (Claudius): Ichikawa Sadanji (the First) (1842-1904)
APERIA (Ophelia): Fukusuke (later Nakamura Utaemon V) (1844-1903)

Now it is time to examine the act divisions of Robun's 'Japanese Colour-print Hamlet', but let us begin with the first picture by

Yoshiiku, in the form of a theatrical billboard featuring the title of the play, and portraits of Toranaga (Horatio) on the right, Hamuramaru (young Hamlet), centre, and Aperia (Ophelia), left.

1

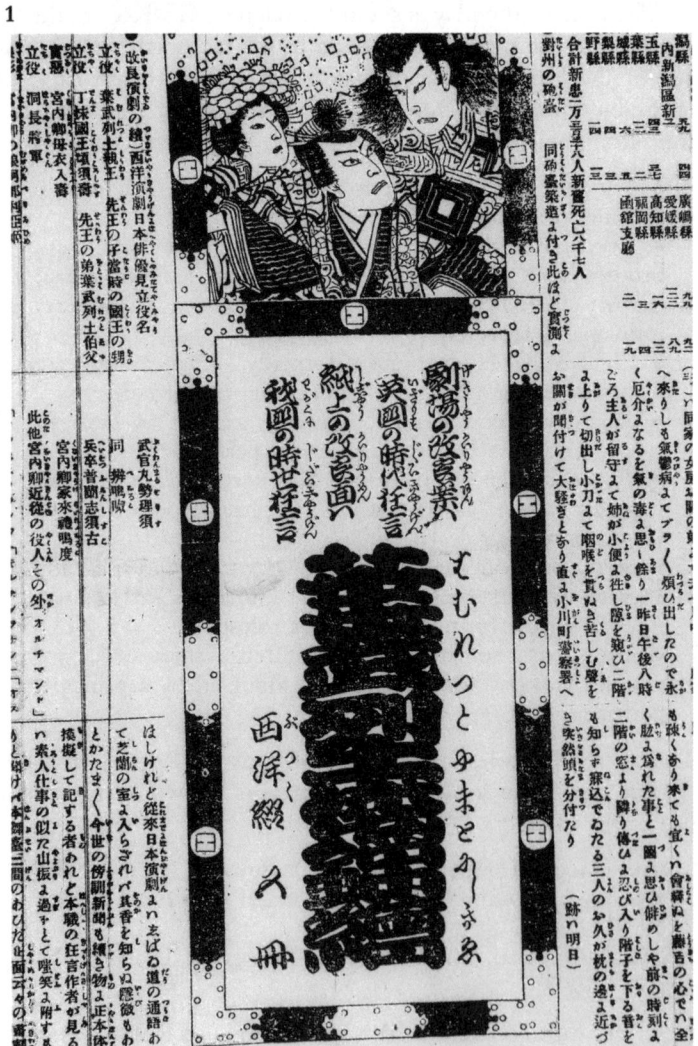

A Japanese Colour-print Hamlet

ACT ONE

Scene One: The Eastern Wing of Shiba Castle

Minister Horoniusu's son Reinojō (Laertes) is about to depart for schooling in distant Kyoto, and the minister gives him advice, as his sister Aperia (Ophelia) listens.

2

Koroshasu (Claudius), the new Lord, assures Hamura-maru (young Hamlet) that in due time the rights of lordship will be his and Lady Seritonomae (Gertrude) also comforts her son Hamura-maru, as Reinojō listens.

3

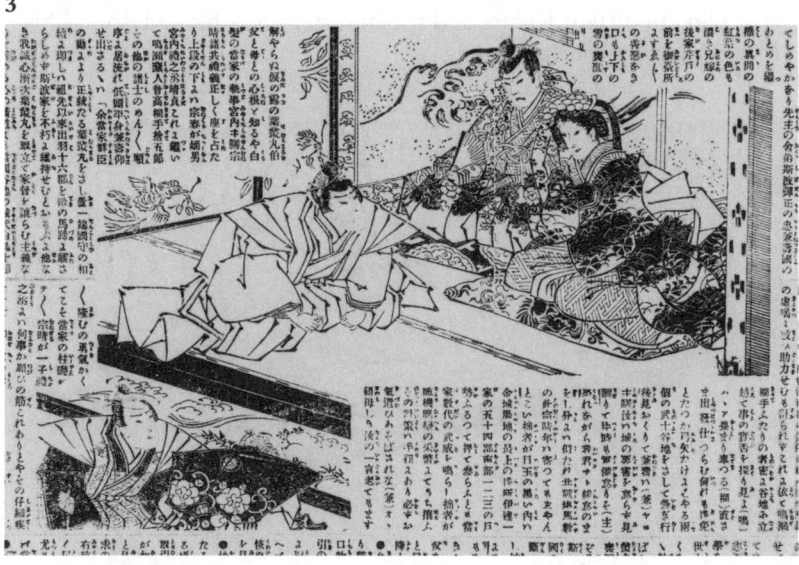

Toranaga (Horatio) tells Hamura-maru that he has seen the ghost of the late Lord Hamuretto.

4

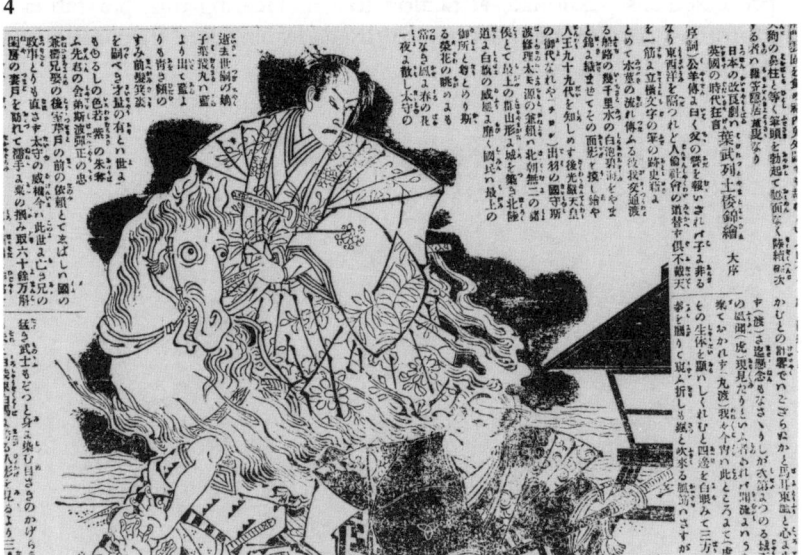

Scene Two: The Residence of Chief Minister Horoniusu

Aperia tells her brother Reinojō that Hamura-maru had once professed his passionate attraction to her. Hearing this, her father Horoniusu orders her severely to dissuade him, and in confusion Aperia is reduced to tears.

5

Scene Three: *A Tall Cherry Tree by a Canal*

Toranaga (Horatio) and a companion follow Hamura-maru's orders and take him to the place where they saw the dead Lord's ghost. The ghost reappears.

6

The ghost then tells Hamura-maru that he had been poisoned and his place taken by the murderer as both Lord and husband.

7

Learning of the new couple's wickedness, Hamura-maru and Toranaga make plans for revenge.

8

ACT TWO

Scene One: Koroshasu's Quarters; Hamura-maru Gone Mad

Koroshasu and his Lady hear of Hamura-maru's mad talk, but Minister Horoniusu wishes to test whether or not this is true madness. Horoniusu engages Hamura-maru in conversation to test his sanity.

(In Kabuki, madness was indicated traditionally by tying a cloth around the head, knotted on the left, as here with Hamura-maru.)

9

Later Hamura-maru orders that a troupe of actors from Kyoto prepare a performance in which he intends to trap the royal couple into revealing their guilt.

Scene Two: A Special Room: the Play within the Play

The puppet players from Kyoto perform a play which follows the Ghost's description of his own murder.

10

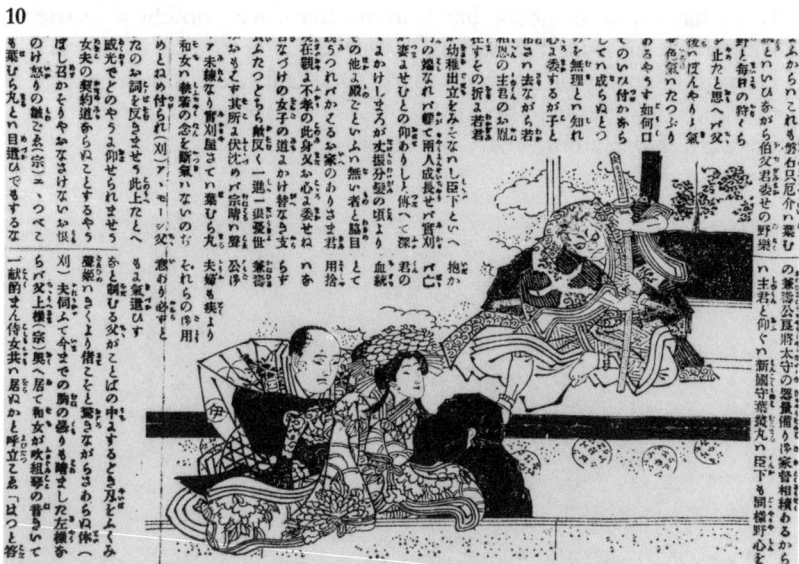

Seritonomae becomes agitated and Lord Koroshasu orders that the play be stopped. Hamura-maru now knows the truth of the Ghost's accusations and intensifies his plans for revenge.

ACT THREE

Scene One: An Inner Room in Koroshasu's Quarters

Koroshasu now suspects that Hamura-maru has somehow learned something of old Hamuretto's murder, and in his fear, asks Horoniusu to spy on Hamura-maru. One night Koroshasu prays to the ghost, confessing his disloyalty and begging for forgiveness, unaware that Hamura-maru is listening.

11

Scene Two: A Bedroom in Koroshasu's Quarters

Hamura-maru and his mother speak. Hamura-maru kills the concealed Horoniusu.

12

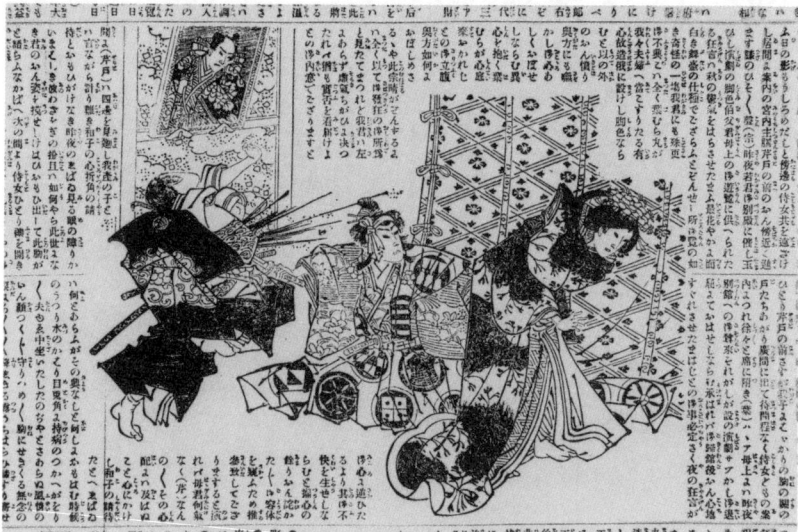

Hamura-maru then boldly leaves the room as if nothing has happened, but watched by his mother and attendants.

13

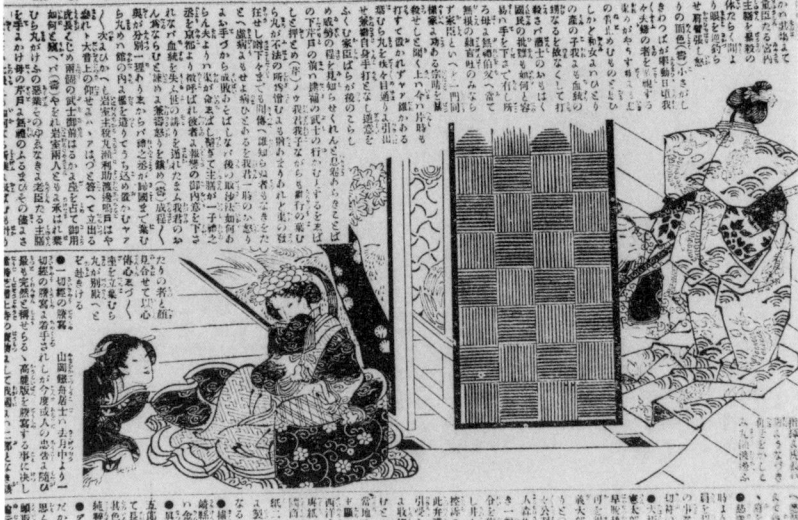

Scene Three: The Same

Toranaga tells Lord Koroshasu and Lady Seritonomae that Hamura-maru has been locked in a secure room. Aperia (Ophelia) comes, mad with grief. Reinojō (Laertes), hearing of his father's death, returns from Kyoto.

14

Scene Four: An Inner Room in Another Part of the Castle

Reinojō goes to the room where Hamura-maru is confined to rebuke him for Horoniusu's death and challenges him to a duel. Hamura-maru accepts the challenge. At this point it is reported that Aperia has plunged herself into a stream and drowned.

15

Scene Five: The Shiba Family Cemetery

Two gravediggers are digging a grave. Hamura-maru talks with the gravediggers and holds a skull in his hands which they have dug up. Hamura-maru recalls the face of Aperia and grieves at her imminent burial, as the ghost of her father Horoniusu glowers.

16

Scene Six: *A Large Room*

The day set for the duel has arrived. Reinojō and his retainers prepare for the duel and its possible consequences.

17

Lord Koroshasu has arranged for poisoned wine. However, Lady Seritonomae drinks the poisoned wine in suicide, and on the verge of death confesses her part in the crimes and begs forgiveness. Seeing this, Koroshasu gets furious as his plans for Hamura-maru's poisoning backfire and then he is killed.

18

Hamura-maru, having killed Lord Koroshasu, commits *seppuku*, formal suicide, and Reinojō follows with his own death by *seppuku*. At this point the late Lord Hamuretto's younger sister returns to the realm and mourns the death of Hamura-maru.

And amid the spectacle of all these corpses the play comes to an end.

Stripped of all its subtlety, that is the story of Robun's play, but now let us look at the points of difference between Robun's and Shakespeare's *Hamlet*s and those aspects of Robun's script which make it seem so successful as a Japanese play.

V. THE JAPANESE ELEMENTS IN ROBUN'S *HAMURETTO*

But when one speaks of a Japanese-style 'kabuki adaptation', what was meant in Robun's time? Even for Japanese people, ideas about kabuki were undergoing change. Plays by Kawatake Mokuami (1816-93) were at the forefront of kabuki reforms which have had lasting effects, such as the still-performed *Mekura Nagaya Ume ga Kagatobi* (1886) or *Sakanaya Sōgorō* (1883) or *Shisen Ryō* (1885), all of which Robun, in his journalistic criticism at the time, labelled 'Western Kabuki'.

For readers, or before that, for a theatre audience, what was appealing in those times? How important to audiences were familiar themes and techniques? How important were human concerns? The scope of Robun's theatrical common sense, then, was challenged. How does he measure up?

1) The apparition of a dead person traditionally appeared in white garments in an antiquated style, astride a white horse. On the stage, Robun's actor was expected to wear a broad silver split-skirt *hakama* over a costume appropriate for a ghost in a Noh play, with a gaunt man's mask; in short, a very Japanese ghost. Yoshiiku's illustrations to the play #4 and #6 show the ghost linked with horse images.

2) The ghost's story begins before the poisoning, and only as the story unfolds does it become clear that the character is dead. This technique is quite typical in Kabuki.

3) Even in his student days at Wittenburg, Shakespeare's 'Hamlet' had been different from his classmates, but he is quite lucid at the beginning of Shakespeare's play. In contrast, the character Hamura-maru from the beginning plays the fool. This is not so different from the feigned madness strategy of Lord Ōkura Ichijō in the play *Kiichi Hōgen (Sanryaku no Maki)*[1] (1731).

4) In Robun's play several spies appear. Near the end of a number of scenes spies are cut down, somersaulting splendidly while sticks are clacked for emphasis, lending importance to minor roles, as in the following picture.

19

5) In the grave-digging scene, Hamura-maru holds a skull which seems to foreshadow his own death. This underscoring of the catastrophe awaiting Hamura-maru can be seen as fundamentally Japanese-style. This point will be taken up shortly.

The appearance of the ghost, the play within a play, Hamura-maru confronting his mother, Aperia's drowning, the comic tone of the grave-digging scene and other plot devices of Robun's text are full of life, but in addition, all these theatrical elements have been thoroughly Japanized.

The scholar Kawatake Toshio has written: 'Shakespeare's anti-classical Baroque approach to playwrighting has unexpected affinities with similarly "Baroque" Kabuki playwrights which facilitates adaptation.'

VI. FUNDAMENTAL DIFFERENCES BETWEEN ROBUN'S TEXT AND SHAKESPEARE'S

Let us examine the nature of the characters in the play and their function within the plays.

Hamura-maru feigns madness, and in fact until well into the play he seems a quintessential dotty royal. He does this strategically to help him deal with a double plot to overthrow the royal house. This aspect of the play is quite different from Shakespeare's. Koroshasu (Claudius) kills his older brother, who had been the feudal lord and forcefully weds his widow, effectively becoming the local feudal lord. But at the same time, the old lord's retainer, Chief Minister Horoniusu (Polonius), also aims at usurping the throne. There are then two treasonous plots.

Shakespeare's Polonius is basically a good person, not a villain. He is fainthearted to the point of being a comic character. He is manipulated by Claudius, who is a distillation of evil, and ridiculed by Hamlet, who then kills the unfortunate old man, mistaking him for Claudius.

Robun's Horoniusu, however, is a 'real villain'. He flatters Koroshasu, and tries to get Hamura-maru killed to set up his son Reinojō (Laertes) as the prince's successor. At one and the same time he tries to steal the throne while overseeing the government. If anything, Horoniusu is more villainous than Koroshasu. As a result the relations between Horoniusu and his children are complex. The relationships between Polonius, Laertes and Ophelia seem utterly typical of father-child relations. This is in stark contrast to Robun's play in which father and child relations, hinging on bloodline and obligations, are filled with conflicting emotions, all of which are fundamental Edo-period themes. Unlike their father, Reinojō and Aperia are true-hearted, exemplifying the virtues of devotion and filial piety. This is where Robun's double tragedy has its birth.

Hamura-maru acts on behalf of his late father. Avenging an enemy was a rule of Edo society. But Reinojō (Laertes) is aware of his own father's villainy and therefore suffers. He deeply sympathizes with Hamura-maru and understands him. After he witnesses Hamura-maru's suicide, Reinojō himself quickly seeks release in the same way. In contrast, Hamlet and Laertes are fundamentally different. The same contradictions that afflicted Reinojō, drive Aperia (Ophelia) to madness. At the command of the late feudal lord, Hamuretto, Aperia had become engaged to Hamura-maru, a pure case of feudal authority. As it happens, Horoniusu is opposed and cuts off this relationship. Aperia suffers

Scenes from the 1991 Japan Festival (London) performance of Robun's *Hamuretto Yamato Nishiki-e*

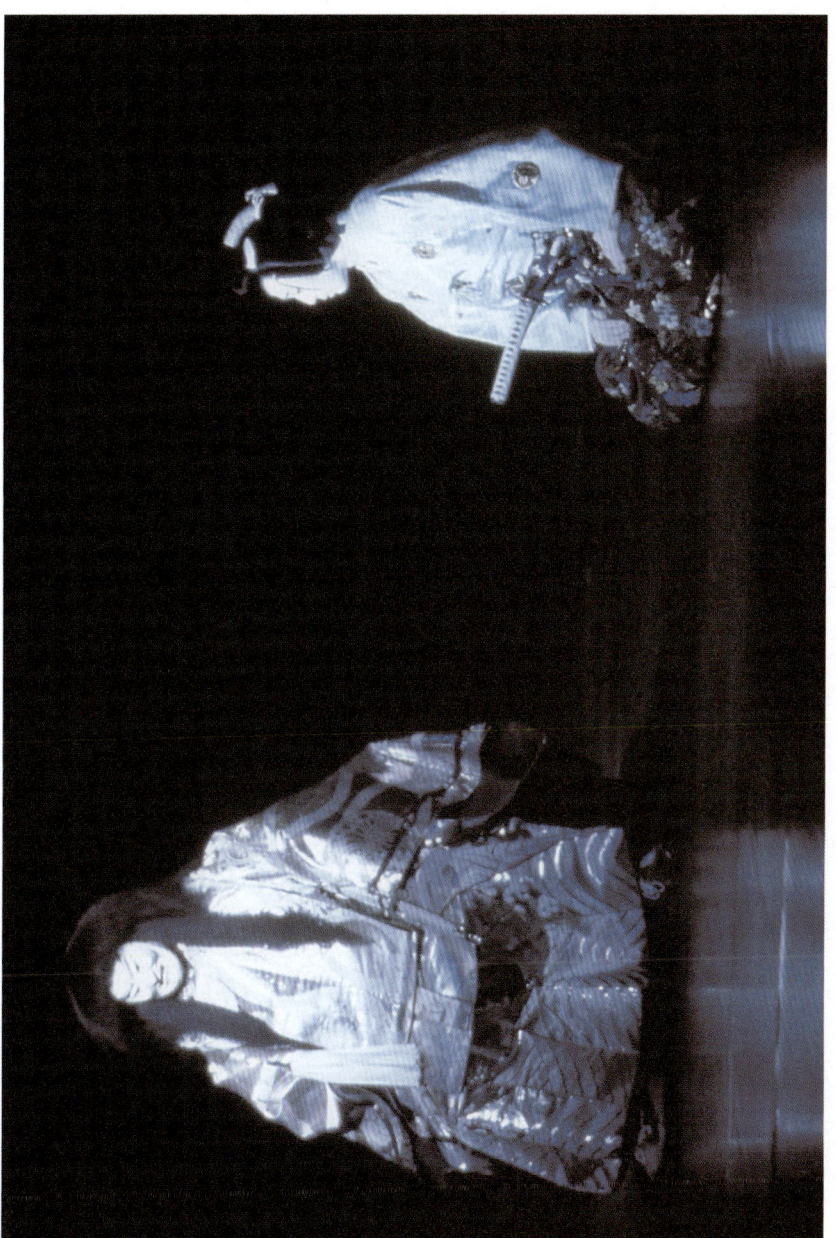

The (masked) ghost of Lord Hamuretto, revealing details of his death to his son, Hamura-maru. [This picture corresponds to the 1886 Yoshiiku illustration No. 7: see Orita, page 100]

Hamura-maru, determined for revenge
[This picture corresponds to Yoshiiku illustration No. 8: See Orita, page 101]

Ichikawa Somegorō (then 17), as Hamura-maru, appearing to be mad, threatens a retainer
[Corresponds to Yoshiiku's illustration No. 9: Orita, page 102]

The 'mousetrap play', as the Queen pours poison into the ear of her unsuspecting husband. [Corresponds to illustration No. 10: Orita, page 103]

Hamura-maru mistakenly kills Minister Horoniusu in front of his mother, Lady Seritonomae
[Corresponds to illustration No. 12: Orita, page 105]

Somegorō, as Aperia, on the verge of suicide
[Corresponds to illustration No. 15, Orita, page 108]

Hamura-maru by the grave, open for Aperia's burial
[Corresponds to illustration No. 16, Orita, page 109]

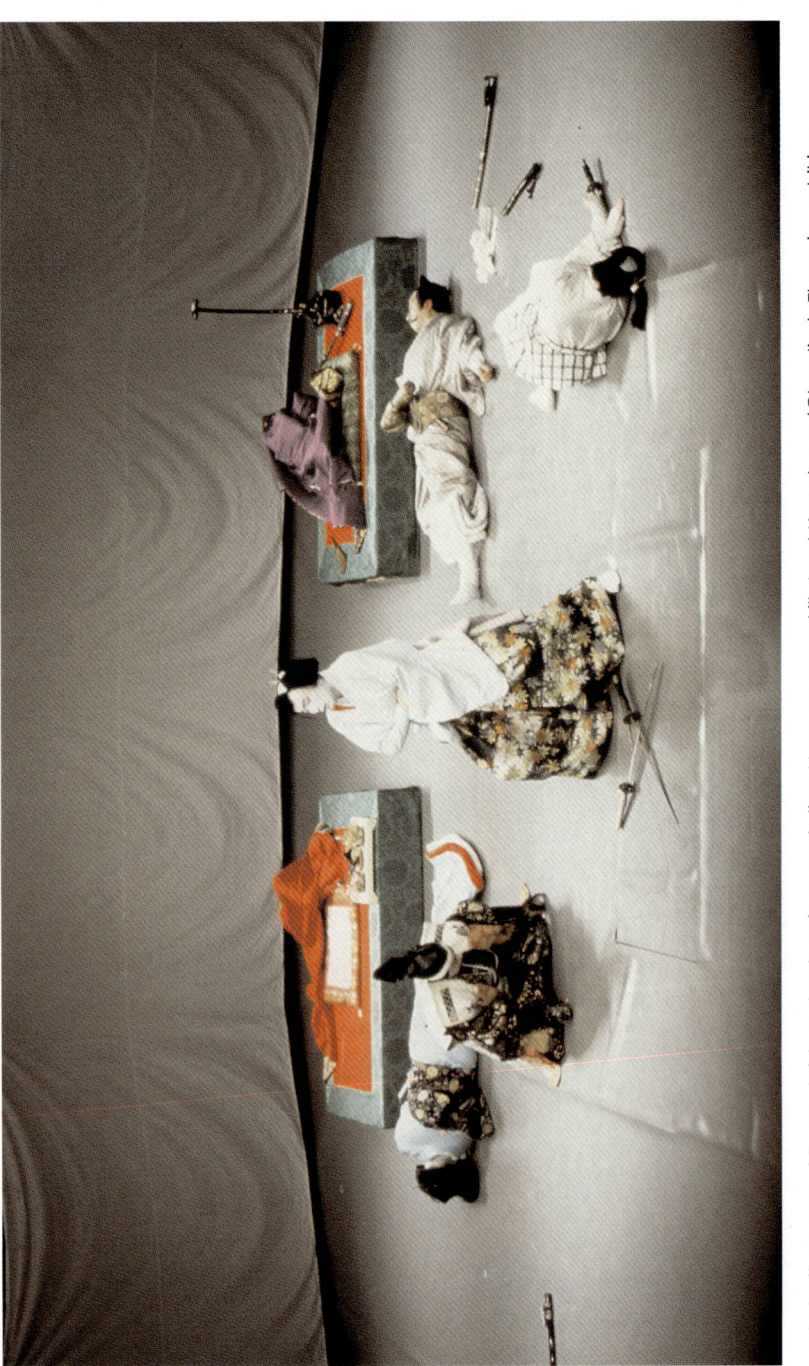

Lady Seritonomae (Gertrude) has drunk poison and dies; Hamura-maru kills Lord Koroshasu (Claudius). Then, in a striking departure from Shakespeare's *Hamlet*, Hamura-maru prepares to commit *seppuku* (formal suicide); Reinojō (Laertes) bows to acknowledge the propriety of this suicide, and will then kill himself to atone for the evil of his father, Minister Horoniusu. [Corresponds to illustration No. 18, Orita, page 111]

Four scenes from the Maurice Béjart's dance
King Lear: La mort de Cordlia
[See Yumiko Yamada's essay (Ch. 10): 'Shakespeare and Kabuki in Maurice Béjart: his *King Lear: La Mort de Cordelia'*]

The opening of the Béjart dance *La mort de Cordelia*. Lear (Maurice Béjart) kisses the hand of the dead Cordelia (Bandō Tamsaburō) as attendants lift her body from a cart. See Yamada, 'Shakespeare and Kabuki in Maurice Béjart: His King Lear: *La mort de Cordelia'*

Lear fruitlessly attempts to revive Cordelia.

In a flashback, Lear removes his crown and robes, seated next to Cordelia.

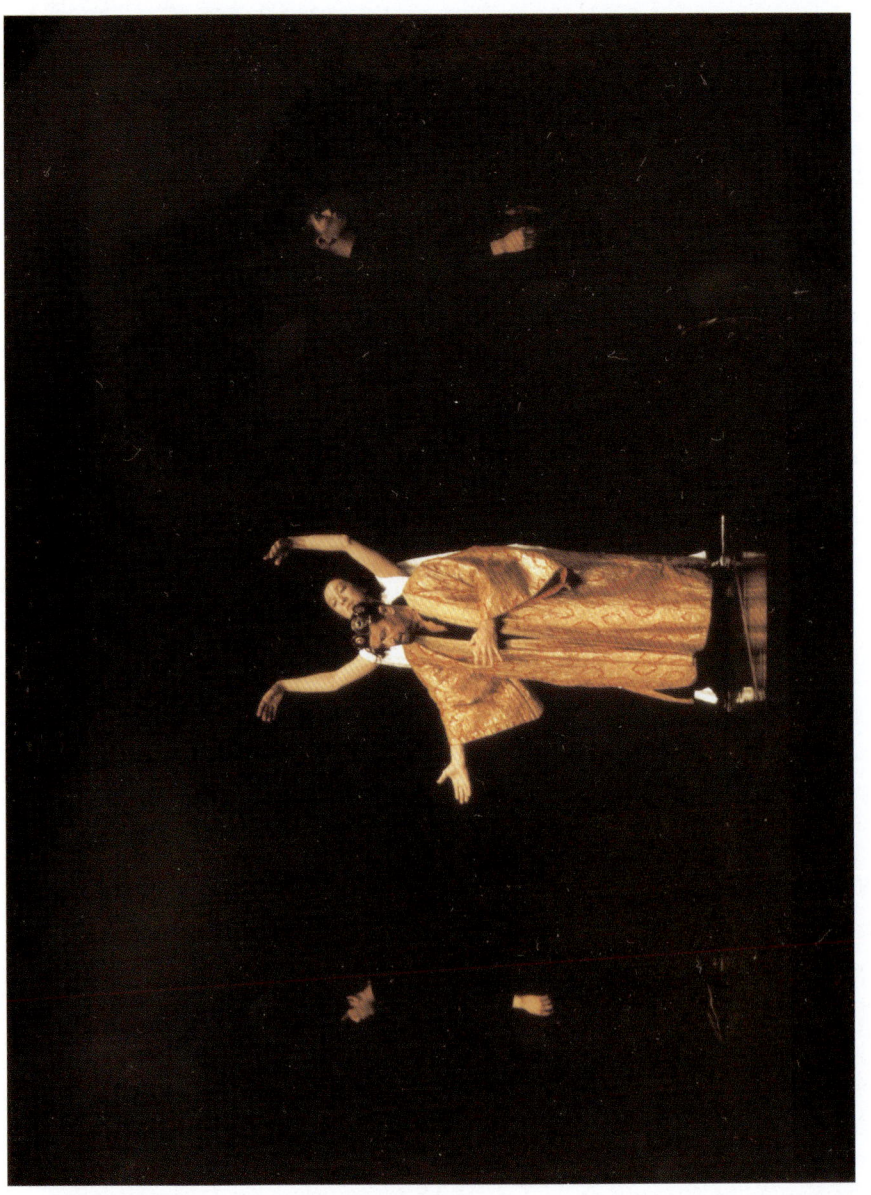

Later in the flashback, Lear and Cordelia dance.

from the dilemma of her duties of devotion and filial piety. In contrast, Ophelia's madness is triggered by the sudden death of her father.

Let us now examine the Queen character. Shakespeare's Gertrude is a strong character, not unlike Lady Macbeth, which means the 'wicked woman' type. In Robun's play, when the ghost of the late Lord Hamuretto speaks of Seritonomae's role in his murder, a scene illuminated by a flickering alcohol lamp, it is a revelation of parental torment, but Lady Seritonomae never reveals her feelings to Hamura-maru. However, in the climactic dialogue, when the poisoned cup is prepared, she, not Hamura-maru drinks the poison. Such an unexpected reversal is called *modori* in kabuki, meaning that a character who has seemed to be totally evil, in an extreme situation reveals its true, virtuous nature, in this case through suicide.

In this climactic scene, up to the point when the Queen character's complicity is revealed, *Hamlet* and *Hamuretto* are quite similar. But after that the action of the two plays is strikingly different. Although they share a desire to overcome their fathers' enemies, the fates of Reinojō and Hamura-maru are different. The monologue during the gravediggers' scene is critical; more pointedly, there is Aperia's suicide. Reinojō understands this action. Only people steeped in the feudal Japanese ethic could fully appreciate such a suicide. It certainly is not acceptable in the context of Christian morality, but such thoughts and actions cannot be separated from a traditional Japanese sense of duty.

The conclusion of the play, on the other hand, is far from a traditional Japanese felicitous ending. All the main characters of the play are dead. There is no exact equivalent of Fortinbras in Robun's play. We seem to see the destruction of an entire family line. When performed, Robun's character Shiratoritarō was given a title equivalent to that of Fortinbras. A pure white curtain was drawn to represent burial, and behind it were set up three torches, the central torch for the late Koroshasu, the left and right for Hamura-maru and Seritonomae, the three lights in turn becoming a single central light as an image of the ascension of souls, or even a Japanese style image of salvation.

This singular conclusion is not exclusively 'Japanese', but as a final curtain for a tragic play, it has a certain newness. And as this ending is based on Shakespeare's *Hamlet*, and in part rounds it out as a kabuki play, it is this illumination that justifies the 'Japanese Colour-print' of Robun's subtitle.

What is a human being? There seem no questions or significant observations about human existence that Robun left out. Which means a term like '*Kindai*', the usual term for post-Edo art and literature as it struggled to find new significance in a wider world, is limp and useless here.

But this is with the advantage of hindsight. Kanagaki Robun's challenge was to sell his version of Shakespeare's *Hamlet* as a kabuki model when there were no other real translations available for comparison. And with this in mind, his ability to challenge the accepted masterpieces of kabuki with something new was exceptional and brilliantly done.

VII. PERFORMANCE NOTES

A. Casting and Performance in 1991

It was perfectly natural to consider the entire spectrum of kabuki performers for the Japan Festival performance of Robun's adaptation of *Hamlet*. Ichikawa Somegorō VII (1979-) was cast on the basis of the playtext and the image of the character Hamlet. Somegorō was sixteen at the time he was cast, seventeen when performing at the Japan Festival. He simply rose above all others considered in the three-hundred-seat theatre used for the auditions. In addition, he had access to the insights of his father, then Matsumoto Kōshirō IX (1942-), with his wide theatrical experience, and indeed his experience performing Hamlet.

Ultimately, it was a question of Somegorō's face-to-face meeting with the director (myself) and our conversation. Sawamura Tanosuke VI (1932-) as Seritonomae (Gertrude) and Ichikawa Shōsuke (1933-) as Koroshasu (Claudius) were expected castings, and their performances were splendid. In kabuki there are families of performers, and the master-disciple relationship creates other 'families', notably Kōshirō's disciples Matsumoto Kingo (1956-) as Toranaga (Horatio) and Ichikawa Komazō (1957-) as Reinojō

(Laertes). There are also 'families' of actors who have performed the same roles, such as Kōshirō and his son Somegorō who now have both performed Hamlet. In all there were fifteen performers. This necessitated some doubling, and Somegorō was also cast as Aperia (Ophelia) as well as the late Lord Hamuretto's younger sister who comes on at the end of the play.

Let me explain a little more about Somegorō's performance as both Hamlet and Ophelia. It must seem impossible, if not absurd, for the two lovers to be played by the same actor. However, in kabuki, there is no special problem. I mentioned earlier that Robun had left out the 'Get thee to a nunnery' scene, and that we had used Tsubuouchi Shōyō's translation in our production. Here, of course, Hamlet and Ophelia are both onstage at the same time. In this scene Somegorō played Hamura-maru, and had all the spoken lines. Another actor, more or less the same height and build as Somegorō, wore Aperia's costume and wig. The character's grief made it perfectly appropriate for that actor to weep, concealing his face. In other scenes, the two characters are not onstage at the same time, and Somegorō used kabuki's 'quick change' tradition to change costumes in order to play both parts.

The script served as the determinant of parts divisions, and made it possible to calculate the smallest number of performers possible. All in all, there were fifteen performers.

From the beginning, it was a fundamental premise that this play should be presented in the performance style of kabuki, including old techniques. It seemed especially important to attempt to embody traditions that would have been current in 1886 when the play was written. It was hoped that such an approach would bring back the spirit as well as the text of this play after a century of neglect. For the London performances everything had to be re-thought. Theatre size and problems of staging, not to mention money considerations, compelled new solutions, all of which were difficult, but in the end a solidly kabuki performance style was created. Rather than a 'kabuki version' of *Hamlet*, it became a performance of the kabuki play *Hamuretto Yamato Nishiki-e*. It would be a falsehood to say that we stopped thinking about Shakespeare's *Hamlet*, but I do believe that in the end we created a new kabuki work.

Hamlet's suicide onstage was 'improper' according to some comments, especially after the first performances in Japan. In addition to regular audience members, Japan Festival organizers and even Foreign Ministry staff members voiced their concerns. I got exhausted having to make the same explanations over and over, to the point where I joked that if Hamura-maru's *harakiri* were cut I would have to resign and commit *harakiri* myself. This is a play written in 1886, within vivid memory of Edo-period custom. If this *harakiri* were considered improper, what kind of future could we expect for plays full of *harakiri*, such as *Chushingura*[3] or *Terakoya*[4]?

In London, when I told a member of the Shakespeare Society about all this Japanese concern for propriety, he said: 'There have been as many stage interpretations of *Hamlet* as there are London telephone directories. Yours is just one of them.' Throughout the performances in Britain, there was no problem with the suicide or any other aspect of the production.

B. The Music

To create *gidayū kabuki* music, you need someone from the Takemoto gidayū tradition. For this work, Nozawa Matsusaburō (1912-) was asked to be the composer. Everything was performed live, from the *geza ongaku* music ensembles to the clacking of the *tsuke* sticks. Nothing was recorded.

Gidayū kabuki originally referred to music used in plays based on the puppet theatre tradition, but there are also 'grand opening' prologues, the most famous now being the opening of special performances of *Chushingura*. In addition, the Takemoto tradition includes adaptations of such music. A *gidayū* reciter embodies many classical techniques, and with them can create new music.

For this play, the cast comes onto a dimly-lit stage in two groups of three and two groups of five; they put on their costumes onstage and assemble according to their status. The sticks are clacked and music begins as the lights come up and the Takemoto chanter takes his place. As he identifies them one by one, each character moves into position, ready for the action to begin.

C. The Stage

This was the biggest worry. The seemingly impossible challenge was to come up with a design for the eleven scenes which would look like traditional kabuki scenery, but be adaptable to the Panasonic Globe stage in Tokyo, the Oriental Theatre in Kobe and the various venues in the British Isles. Then came the idea of folding screens. A memory of a folding screen with day and night images on opposite faces offered us a solution. An opened screen presents six faces, but can be folded to reveal three, two or even one, as needed. For use onstage, a monumental folding screen was needed; ultimately, each face was 3.6 metres in height, 1.2 metres in width. The architect Isozaki Arata (1931-), our art director, painted two six-panel screens, as is traditional, but on a colossal scale, and by turning them around daytime images could be replaced by moonlit images, and various combinations gave us scenery for each of the eleven scenes.

To divide the upper and lower stage areas, again the screen idea was useful, making grey enclosures, each with a grey gauze curtain behind which a musician could be concealed. The stage floor was grey linoleum. Although the folding screens carried the burden of scenery, a white carry-on curtain could also be set up near the front of the stage, as for the climactic duel.

A pair of folding screens gave us the scenery for every scene, which was also a wonderfully economical solution to our design problem. During the time of our London performances the Japanese Gallery in the British Museum displayed a sun and moon folding screen, which seemed delightfully serendipitous.

Costumes, props, wigs and so on were all standard kabuki fare.

An Episode

In London, no, not just London but all over Europe, the fire regulations were extremely strict. All scenery had to be fireproof. For the grave-digger's scene we had brought a brushwood fence, but since this was flammable, we could not use it. We could not think what to do, but Simon Ashe, the technical director, showed up with a bundle of leafy bamboo. It was just what we needed, and the fire chief said we could use it since it would not catch fire. We were relieved but baffled as to where he could have found live bamboo in

London. He explained that, to help the London Zoo feed their pandas, bamboo from China was grown at the zoo. So, we were rescued by pandas.

D. Conclusion

Performances in Japan were given in June of 1991 at the Panasonic Globe in Tokyo and the New Oriental Theatre in Kobe. Japan Festival performances were: 19-28 September at the Mermaid Theatre in London; 2-4 October at the Tivoli Theatre in Dublin and 9-11 October at the Playhouse Theatre in Newcastle. In London and Newcastle there were also lecture-demonstrations.

Perhaps I am biased, but I think everything went extremely well. Critical comments were also very good, which was an additional relief.

Listening to the comments of audiences at various venues in Japan and the UK, I was pleased to hear much the same comment from audience members: 'I had always felt that kabuki techniques belonged only in kabuki theatres, but now I have realized for the first time how effectively this wealth of traditional technique can enliven a new work.'

And that is how it was. We had taken it for granted, but now we had proof, that people who had never seen classic kabuki could be astonished at its freshness.

I see that the time is up, so I'll finish my talk here.

Translated by Scott Johnson, Kansai University, Osaka

NOTES

1.   The play is set during the time of rivalry between the Heike and Genji clans. Ōkura, who is accepted as a feeble-minded Heike loyalist, pretends to be mad in order to conceal his Genji sympathies.

2.   Toshio Kawatake, *Nihon no Hamuretto* (Hamlet in Japan) (Nansōsha, Tokyo, 1972), p. 173.

3.   The play *Kanadehon Chushingura* (1748) is a revenge play based on a historical incident in which forty-seven loyal retainers kill the man responsible for their clan leader's forced suicide. There are prominent suicides during the play, but from the

beginning the loyalists know beforehand that the price of their revenge will be for each of them to commit *seppuku*, formal suicide.

4. *Terakoya* is a scene from the play *Sugawara Denju Tenarai Kagami* (1746) which features, in addition to *seppuku*, the display of the severed head of a boy.

SUKEROKU YUKARI NO EDO ZAKURA — ITS TEXT AND PERFORMANCE

IZUMI KADONO

The texts of plays seem to have been one of the literary art forms most vulnerable to alteration in order to suit individual performances and preferences of actors. Various elaborate productions demonstrate the almost infinite variety of text interpretations. When we compare and contrast Shakespeare and kabuki in the way that texts have been treated, one of the big differences seems to be attitudes towards the text. In kabuki, we find a curious contradiction between the high esteem for mimesis or representation by means of traditional acting and the low regard for play texts. They have suffered considerably from free alteration and abbreviation, whereas the texts of Shakespeare used for productions of the last 150 years have been carefully edited to align them with the most reliable early printed versions and except for cutting to save time have remained fairly stable during that time.

However, it is important to consider that many kabuki texts were too long to perform. It is almost inevitable that abridged texts were used for performance, so that texts tend to be regarded as changeable rather than inviolable. Even when a text is of acceptable length, the use of a shortened script is taken for granted. *Sukeroku Yukari no Edo Zakura* (*Sukeroku and the Cherry Blossoms of Edo*), one of the most popular plays as well as being a famous Edo kabuki, appears to be a good example of this. First, we will survey the process of the establishment of the standard text. We will then examine why an abbreviated text is used, which parts have been deleted and how the abridged script affects the play.

To clarify this point, we shall survey the process of the establishment of the cult of Shakespeare's language, and then focus on *Sukeroku*.

Today the plays of Shakespeare are recognized as first-rate literary art. No one would consider that his language needs to be refined, or the contents of his plays improved upon since the dramatist's texts are regarded as sacred and inviolable. However, in the early stage of Elizabethan drama as well as in the Edo Kabuki, a script was not generally accepted as a literary work. In 1616, Ben Jonson took the initiative in claiming literary credit for his plays, giving a collection of them the title *The Works of Benjamin Jonson*. Jonson must have been keenly aware of the need to stabilize his plays, having already seen them suffer from free alteration. Shakespeare's colleagues were not inclined to use the word 'work' in the title of a collection of his plays, but the publication of the First Folio (1623) suggested that they had been recognized as literature, and this publication helped to establish a form of authorized text, although several kinds of quartos had already been published.

Although the First Folio had placed stress on the author's language, the cult of Shakespearean texts was established only after many twists and turns, and the evaluation of his texts varied for more than two hundred years. After the reopening of the theatres in 1660, the taste of the audience had changed dramatically. In spite of certain flaws, the Restoration dramatists valued what Shakespearean plays represented. They believed that the playwright's genius lay not in his language but in representation. As his texts had not been canonized, they felt free to change his plots and to polish the language in order to improve the coarse, old-fashioned style. Radical adaptations such as John Dryden's *All for Love* (1676) and Nahum Tate's *History of King Lear* (1681) were much preferred to the original plays.

It was Nicholas Rowe's critical edition of *The Works of Mr William Shakespeare* (1709) that heralded the high esteem of the original texts.

The critical editions such as those of Lewis Theobald and Edmund Malone indicate that the plays had gradually become recognized as objects of scholarship.

Although theatrical entrepreneurs of the eighteenth century, like David Garrick and others, continued to produce foreshortened and adulterated adaptations as if these were truly the work of Shakespeare, beginning in the 1830s and 1840s, William Charles Macready led a movement to restore fuller and more accurate texts to the British stage.

In contrast to the long period of adaptation, Shakespeare's texts are now highly respected in current productions. Almost all directors adhere to Shakespeare's language, and stage the plays with only minor cuts and alterations, if any, mainly in view of performance time. Strictly speaking, it is very difficult to define what a Shakespearean text is. Yet it is taken for granted that the dramatist's original work, whichever edition it may be, and not later adaptations, should be staged.

Compared with the established evaluation of Shakespeare's words, kabuki texts have generally been vulnerable to undue alteration. As far as texts are concerned, kabuki is in a situation similar to that of Shakespeare during the Restoration period. Besides the special treatment of texts already mentioned, the innate emphasis on physicality affects the concept of unstable texts. Kabuki is often said to be an actor's drama, since major actors have attracted much attention. There is no denying that drama greatly depends on the actors' charisma and appeal as well as the conventions of stylized acting and gorgeous staging. While interest in the actor's art of performance and theatricality is growing, the lack of regard for texts is striking. Play texts are recognized as changeable scripts rather than established literary works, so that there is little hesitation in meddling with words and plots. Such a low estimation of play texts originated in the Edo period. The outstanding playwrights such as Chikamatsu Monzaemon, Tsuruya Nanboku and Kawatake Mokuami made great contributions to the development of kabuki, but even their plays could not escape from many alterations. This suggests that the authority of texts was not established.

The modern audience may consider kabuki to be static because it is a classic drama with many traditional rules, a highly stylized acting technique and a lot of stage conventions. In the Edo period, however, kabuki was expected to show novelty of direction, new staging devices and music fit for each season, just as in today's Shakespeare productions. Though considered classic drama today, kabuki originally involved flexibility as an acute reflection of public sensibility and contemporary society.

A marked combination of novelty and tradition created particular theatrical conventions. One of these was that the New Year productions in Edo had to use *Soga Monogatari (The Tale of the Soga Brothers)* as a framework for the dramatic world. Each company had to present a new version of the Soga drama with novel devices every year. This 'rule' was observed for more than 300 years, indicating that the public taste for Soga plays was insatiable. Within the framework of the same story, writers came up with various ingenious ideas to make the play interesting as well as new. They renewed not only the script but also the music and libretto every year. The script was regarded as something expendable, and therefore the concept of a sacred text did not exist.

Presumably, the play *Sukeroku* originated in Osaka, but the first production of it was said to have been at the Yamamuraza in Edo in 1713.[1] It formed part of the play *Hanayakata Aigo no Sakura*, and Daidoji Tabatanosuke was Sukeroku's real name. Ichikawa Danjuro II played the role. Although inheriting the *aragoto* (bombastic) style of acting, he seemed to play the part as a gallant rather than a masculine hero of fiery temperament and to represent an aspect of the lover's tenderness.[2] The play then advanced to a *sewamono* (a realistic play depicting contemporaries). Compared with the present stylish Sukeroku, the Ur-Sukeroku character must have been much closer to the *aragoto* hero with a violent disposition.[3] Yet Danjuro II's performance was a new attempt to infuse a refined touch into an *aragoto* play.

Danjuro II played the part for a second time in 1716, when *Sukeroku* was drastically revised. Strictly speaking, it was a new and different drama. The first innovation was a change in the dramatic world to which the play had been attached. It was separated from *Hanayakata Aigo no Sakura* and transferred to *Soga Monogatari.*

Sukeroku was presented as a part of *Shikirei Yawaragi Soga*. In accordance with the change in the drama from which the new *Sukeroku* was excerpted, the true identity of the title role was changed from Daidoji Tabatanosuke to Soga no Gōrō, one of the Soga brothers. Thereafter, Sukeroku was provided with the conventional attributes of Soga no Gōrō, one of the Soga brothers. His true identity was implied in Sukeroku's *mukimi-guma* makeup and a headband, both of which symbolically represented Gōrō's youthfulness and vitality. The first innovation contributed to forming the fundamental character of the role of Sukeroku.

The second innovation of *Shikirei Yawaragi Soga* was that, as the title suggested, the art of *wagoto* (the gentler, realistic style of acting) which had been derived from a variety of the courtesan plays popular in Osaka and Kyoto, was introduced into a Soga play, a typical Edo kabuki. Danjuro II acted Sukeroku in the *wagoto* style. Adopting its conventional plot of a love affair between a dandy and a courtesan into a Soga play, the playwright contrived to mingle a valiant *aragoto* hero and a gentle, refined *wagoto* lover to create a new type of hero. The coarse, masculine soldier in the first *Sukeroku* was transformed in the second production into a smart high-spirited gallant with a touch of gentleness. The flute and the *kamiko* (paper kimono) indicated his dual character of an *aragoto* hero and a *wagoto* protagonist: the former was a kind of tool for fighting and the latter a symbolic costume of *wagoto* used to prohibit him from fighting. His new charm appealed to the taste of many theatre-goers. Despite having the same title, the two plays were very different both in plot and performance.

In 1749, the 62-year-old Danjuro II acted the role for a third time. As the *jojuri* style title, *Sukeroku Kuruwa no Ie Zakura*, implies, the scene was set in Yoshiwara (the licensed quarters) and the stage was decorated with cherry blossoms. The actor's stylish costume became very similar to the present-day one: a black silk kimono bearing the five family crests of Danjuro and a bluish-purple silk headband. It was about this time that *Sukeroku* came to be independent from Soga plays and became considered a one-act play. The form of *Sukeroku* was thus nearly complete, and the music of *Edo Bushi* (a kind of music style) or *Katō Bushi* was used. Hereafter it also became a convention to stage the play in March.

Thus the text, the style of performance and the music were gradually refined and polished through various kinds of *Sukeroku* productions over many years. It had been a rule to renew the music and words in every production until the tenth *Sukeroku* production of *Edomurasaki Kongen Soga* (1761). The first production of *Sukeroku Yukari no Edo Zakura* in the *Katō Bushi* style was the fore-runner of the current *Sukeroku Yukari no Edo Zakura*.[4] Thereafter, it was made a practice to use *Katō Bushi* in the *Sukeroku* plays, although the Onoe lines were and are accustomed to using *Sukeroku Kuruwa no Momoyogusa* in *Kiyomoto* (a more lyrical music style). The music and words of this *Katō Bushi* version have been handed down to the present day.

The script of *Sukeroku Yukari no Edo Zakura* (1811) at the Ichimuraza in Edo was the model of the present-day *Sukeroku*, and is recognized as a standard text. It had taken about one hundred years for the play to establish its mode of direction, acting style, costumes and music. Unlike Shakespeare's plays, it is difficult to specify the author. The play was a result of the amalgamated effort of several playwrights, actors and musicians over the course of several decades to attain the most refinement. The changing of the text over the course of a century demonstrates the play's essential dramatic vitality, but the changes also show that the text was accepted as a work-in-progress rather than an inviolable literary work.

Moreover, the playwrights bear some responsibility for prejudice against set texts. After *Sukeroku* had established a standard form of script, music and style of performance, the actors in several roles were expected to throw in some jokes that had not been written in the script. The audience was pleased with the *ad libs* and topical allusions in every performance. In order to give some savour to the drama, the playwright entrusted a particular player with certain lines and acting, deliberately writing 'Yoroshiku' (I'll leave the dialogue up to the actors) in the script. Shakespeare gave Hamlet the famous lines, 'let those that play your clown speak no more than is set down for them' (III.ii.39).[5] He desired players to stick to the text. The lines must be an echo of Shakespeare's intention. Kabuki playwrights, on the other hand, understanding that a lively performance was favoured, submitted to actors' preferences and were sufficiently tolerant not to demand the strictest adherence to lines written in the script. This malleability of the text might well have been promoted by the familiar actor-playwright relationship, which was also an intrinsic quality of kabuki.

Besides the innate nature of kabuki, the current production system is greatly responsible for the use of abridged or adapted texts. They are usually used to meet the requirements of the current performance system of 'midori' (performance of several plays, in each of which only part of a whole play is extracted for performance). The programme usually consists of three or four plays, and the performance time is approximately four or five hours, including several intermissions. Plays are therefore of necessity cut short, and only one or two scenes from the whole play can be presented. The highlighted scenes of the popular plays are arranged in the programme, and yet there is no connection between them. Because of the present performance system, an abbreviated script is much preferred to the lengthy original play.

The present script of *Sukeroku Yukari no Edo Zakura* is an abridged version based on the script of the 1915 production at the Kabukiza theatre in Tokyo. The performance time of the unabridged version is approximately three hours, whereas the current stage version is little more than one hour. The reduction in the performance time to less than half suggests a radical abbreviation. After touching on the two major deletions, we shall examine what results from the cuts.

The first cut covers the story from the entrance of Soga no Mankō, Sukeroku's mother, to the exit of Shimbei, Sukeroku's elder brother. Anxious about Sukeroku, both of them hide their real identity and respectively come to look for him. The introductory scene involves a riddle. The disguised Mankō, dressed in *kamiko*, visits Yoshiwara to see Agemaki, a high-ranking courtesan. Mankō comes across Shiratama (Agemaki's colleague) and other employees and guests of Miuraya, a famous brothel. While their humorous conversation ingeniously recreates the merry atmosphere of Yoshiwara on stage, Mankō learns from the chatter about Agemaki's personality, her devotion to Sukeroku and her popularity. After Mankō's exit, Shimbei, who has disguised himself as a vendor of white saké, enters the stage to see Sukeroku. Shimbei entertains the guests and employees by promoting the saké, which is one of the most attractive moments. The lively scene in front of Miuraya provides the audience with a pseudo-experience of Yoshiwara. While Sukeroku and Agemaki take the major roles in the shortened version, the unabridged text of the play also paints a colourful picture of Edo commoners placed within the Soga family story.

The other deleted part is the lovers' quarrel and subsequent love scene in which Sukeroku suddenly transforms himself from a dapper gallant to a sweet lover. The revenge of the Soga brothers is skilfully interwoven with the play. Sukeroku is a disguised revenger searching for a lost sword named Tomokirimaru. Once the *kamiko* is introduced in the play, however, it makes a momentary digression from a revenge theme to a love plot. The kaleidoscopic change in performance style has much to with dressing in *kamiko*, a symbol of *wagoto*. From the modern realistic view, his abrupt change may appear illogical and contradictory. Free from modern realism, however, it is one of the specific characteristics of kabuki that the two different styles of *aragoto* and *wagoto* fuse into Sukeroku. He is required to express different aspects with the changes of his costume. The *kamiko* functions as a significant catalyst to transform his acting style and personality, since his dalliance with Agemaki is closely connected with the convention of *wagoto*. Wearing the *kamiko*, Sukeroku demonstrates the art of *wagoto* while he remains an Edoite with a frank and open disposition. His delicate transformation and more subtle acting must have been part of the attractiveness favoured by audiences. Therefore the deletion of the lovers' quarrel and love scene violates the convention of kabuki as well as marring the intrinsic quality and charm of *Sukeroku*.

Although it is possible to follow the main plot in the abridged production, there is no denying that these major cuts distort the compound structure, the duality and the leisurely tone which the original play created.

CONCLUSION

Masakatsu Gunji states in *The Kabuki Guide*: 'A product of the popular culture of Edo at its zenith, *Sukeroku* still delights contemporary audiences with a vibrant beauty that literature has failed to capture.[6] No-one would deny his praise, since a dazzling stage production is fascinating. With a concern for vindicating the unabridged text of the play, however, an uncut performance could delight audiences not only with external beauty but also make a much deeper impression. Adherence to a shortened script may make it difficult to see the play in its proper perspective, and undermine the rich attraction of kabuki.

Sukeroku Yukari no Edo Zakura is an especially important play in the sense that it is one of the *Kabuki Juhachiban* (a collection of eighteen plays in the repertoire of the Ichikawa Danjuro line of actors), and, furthermore, it is the only *sewamono* among them. A revival of the unabridged play could be a significant attempt to represent on the contemporary stage the essence of Edo kabuki, which we are in danger of losing track of. The play confirms that kabuki depicts the profound depth and variety of human nature, as well as providing the pleasure of visual beauty and kinetic acting.

A brief study of *Sukeroku* encourages us to emphasize that it is not only the appeal of superb acting but also the elaborate texts that have contributed to the popularity and charm of kabuki. The quintessence of kabuki has been created by the ultimate combination of the refined physical appeal of the actors and the kinetic dramaturgy of the play texts. My conclusion is that it is time to appreciate the significance of the play scripts of kabuki, as well as the physical tradition of acting. The fruitful results of the revival of the original texts have already been proved in Shakespeare.

NOTES

This article is based on my earlier essay, '*Sukeroku Yukari no Edo Zakura* – Its logos and mimesis–', *Eibeibunka*, 22 March 2002.

1. See Kokuritu Gekijo Geinoshiryoshitsu (ed.), *Joen Shiryoshu*, 134 (1977), 1. I have consulted the dates of performances of *Sukeroku* in this book.

2. With regard to kabuki terms, I have consulted, and owe much, to the following books: Ronald Cavaye, *Kabuki: A Pocket Guide*, Rutland & Tokyo: Charles E. Tuttle, 1993. Masakatu Gunji, *The Kabuki Guide*, trans. Christoper Holmes, Tokyo: Kodansha International, 1987.

3. Cf. Masakatu Gunji, 'Sukeroku', *Joen Shiryoshu*, 134: 30.

4. Haruo Suwa, commentary, *Sukeroku Yukarino Edo Zakura Kotobuki Soga no*

Taimen, by Kanai Sansho, Hakusuisha: Tokyo, 1985, 154. Cf. Seitaro Atsumi, *Joen Shiryoshu,* 134: 47.
5.   Harold Jenkins (ed.), *Hamlet,* London and New York: Methuen, 1982.
6.   Gunji, *Kabuki,* 130.

9

Onnagata in Kabuki and the London Globe Theatre

Minoru Fujita

A distinctive feature of kabuki in Japan has been and still is the female impersonation, namely, the use of actors whose acting involves dressing and performing as women on stage; those players skilled in impersonating female roles are called onnagata. Etymologically, *onna* means woman and *kata* (here as '*gata*') figure or form. Similarly, the word kabuki, when transcribed in three Chinese characters, signifies the combination of three types of performance, namely, music or singing (*ka*), dancing (*bu*) and acting (*ki*), although 'kabuki' is a word originally deriving from the older Japanese verb *kabuku*, connoting the idea of decadence or self-indulgence mirroring the general moral and cultural decline after a peak or culmination of achievement. This general decline took place when kabuki was at the time of its genesis and even in earlier stages of theatrical development in the Japanese feudal ages.

Another significant feature of kabuki, noticeable especially with respect to its rise and development, is the remarkable parallelism that is observable between the Elizabethan theatre and kabuki. The time of the rise of the theatre and the high time of the two Globes more or less corresponds with that of the earlier stages of kabuki's growth and development. The earliest theatre form of kabuki can be located in an outdoor open stage near the riverside in Kyoto, which reminds us of the form of an open amphitheatre found close to the riverbank of the Thames, and significantly enough, the time during the day when an Elizabethan drama was performed coincides with the time of the day when kabuki was enacted onstage. A more remarkable paralleling fact can be found in the two theatre traditions belonging to these two island countries situated off the east and the west coasts of the vast Eurasian Continent, and that is that female roles were performed exclusively by male actors. It must, at the same time, be remembered that kabuki as a theatre form was first initiated by a female dancer, Okuni, earlier in the seventeenth century.

I do not know whether women dressing as men came to be regarded as threatening to the feudal society of the time or not, but, when, as I shall later refer to it, kabuki became men's exclusive business under the strict control of the absolutist feudal government, it started to have its own particular development. Onnagata is, therefore, something unnatural by birth, and, taking advantage of its unnatural origin, it has achieved its own accomplishment as an art of theatrical performance. Between the two theatre traditions, one British, the other Japanese, there is a difference equally remarkable; in England, the theatre custom of female impersonation ceased to exist coincidentally with the close of the London theatres at the time of the Puritan revolution in the 1640s; when the theatres reopened in the Restoration, actresses appeared. Whereas, in Japan, female roles have continued to be performed solely by male actors in kabuki, and onnagata (female impersonation) has developed into one of the most representative features characterizing and upholding the kabuki tradition.

There have been a certain number of men of the theatre in England who are conscious of the parallelism, and there have been a few who are exceptionally aware of or sensitive to the difference referred to above. Certainly among the latter group of people is found Mark Rylance, the art director of the Globe in London today (2005). In the 1990s he visited Japan several times and became acquainted with the onnagata actor Nakamura Ganjiro III. What Rylance personally has learned from that distinguished actor is beyond our knowledge, but the extent of Rylance's interest in onnagata is known from the fact that Nakamura Ganjiro was invited to perform on the stage of the London Globe in 2002.

Ganjiro chose to give a performance of the dance drama entitled '*Fuji-musumé* (The Wisteria Girl) on the characteristic open platform stage of the London amphitheatre that August. This piece of dance drama is one of those preferred by the highest-ranking onnagata actor in a troupe to exhibit the quintessence of the skill with which genuine sophisticated qualities of traditional onnagata dance performance can successfully display the extremity of feminine grace and spirit in the Kabuki stage space. The story of the dance drama is almost plotless; a lovely girl, whose love has been unrequited, laments her failure to receive an answer to her letter, and in her lamentation the actor impersonating her, in a kimono embroidered with wisteria flowers and bearing a wisteria twig on her shoulder, performs a graceful dance on the stage covered with wisteria flowers. The traditional manner of Japanese dance features a circular or rotational style of movement, a movement with a sliding step, and at the same time with elements of physical expression associated with acting. As a whole this particular dance drama is meant for the full display of the traditional skill of female impersonation by a skilled male actor, and also designed to show off the beauty of the movements of femininity and to evoke an unlimited admiration of the beauty of the spectacle of botanical efflorescence itself. Very carefully direct reference or pertinence to daily actuality is minimized in this aesthetic performance, and movements are abstracted from reality as much as possible.

This episode of the appearance of an onnagata on the stage of the Globe may possibly serve to suggest an aspect of the potential of the Shakespearean stage space newly restored in London. As an onnagata actor Nakamura Ganjiro is a living national treasure of Japan, ranking among the few top kabuki artists. Ganjiro III, who performed as Fuji-musume on the Globe stage, was born as early as 1931. Concerning this particular performance, no theatre critic in London seems to have written any reviews, although critics were very enthusiastic about praising the marvels of Ganjiro's kabuki productions of Chikamatsu's drama put on the stage in London and Birmingham. I do not believe that this attempt of the introduction of kabuki elements or onnagata traditions will immediately bring any meaningful addition that will encourage the exploitation of a new scope of Shakespearean performance on the Globe stage or even remotely provide any significant inspiration to those performers in the Globe stage space who will further try to expand new dimensions in their female impersonation in their future Shakespearean productions. What little I can say with confidence is that the newly-built Globe amphitheatre should not, as I shall later discuss, be taken simply as a replica of a celebrated old building serving further to inspire the worship of Shakespeare. It certainly is an authentic playhouse where players can revive the true energy of Shakespeare's drama which the Elizabethan Renaissance gave birth to, but which, since the loss of the Globe stage tradition at the time of the Puritan revolution, has been lost sight of. In modern Western theatres Shakespearean productions have been mostly confined in the framework of their proscenium arch stages, and evidently Shakespeare's plays have lost their initial Renaissance magnificence and vigour; this has caused a theatre critic to remark that Shakespeare's drama has exceedingly been 'dwarfed' in modern theatres.

Any sophisticated director of any Shakespearean play is expected to produce a novelty of interpretation and presentation which necessitates extraordinariness in respect to the manner of performance. Presumably, the Epiphany of 1602 saw the performance of *Twelfth Night* given in the Middle Temple, and this seems to be the first direct reference to the date of its earliest production available today. In 2002, Mark Rylance and his troupe produced the play in the Middle Temple to commemorate the 400th anniversary of the play's production there. In 2004, Mark Rylance and his men gave Shakesperean productions at Hampton Court. The particular reason why the latter venue was chosen is unknown, but as to the former, it is clear that the revival of the (almost) original production of the play was not meant as a curiosity but part of Rylance's endeavour to examine the way *Twelfth Night* was originally performed in a traditional milieu full of signs and symbols of the Medieval and Renaissance times and teeming with architectural features of Elizabethan antiquity. Presumably, all the architectural features, such as the hammer-beam roofs that spanned the great hall built by Henry VIII, square-headed mullioned windows, stained-glass windows, sharp-pointed lancet windows, red-bricked flattened arches, hall screens – all of them – would have reminded the Shakespearean performers of the traditional cultural milieu of the Tudors. Shakespeare's drama did not subsist alone; it was created in close relativity with his own theatre space, which, so far as the Globe is concerned, was a space full of historical, architectural and artistic features contemporary with and preceding the English Renaissance. Similarly, the theatrical idea of female impersonation in Shakespeare's time did not exist by itself. Like onnagata in Japanese kabuki, it was born as a historical and artistic necessity, and because of its sheer and unavoidable necessity, it came to be an entity with a profound depth of theatrical meaning and also with a considerably high level of perfection and artistic refinement.

When Mark Rylance encountered kabuki and the distinguished onnagata actor Ganjiro, he must have sensed how deeply the tradition of kabuki art, and the onnagata artifice, were rooted in the cultural circumstances in which they had had their birth. The reconstruction of the Globe has, at least so far as female impersonation is concerned, supplied an important and promising clue to the true idea of female impersonation still lying hidden in the core of the Elizabethan drama, and actors performing on the Globe's stage have received a fresh impetus to bring the idea somehow into practice. Mark Rylance was planning to bring his troupe to Japan to give a Shakespearean production in an old country kabuki theatre, named Kanamaru-za, which is designated as an important national cultural property, in Shikoku Island of Japan, and we expected to welcome them. However, only a few months before it was to be brought into effect, it was decided that the plan would not, financially, work out very well. Because of this sudden unlucky interruption of the plan, Rylance and his men changed their schedule and made a tour of the United States, and, owing to their ill-luck in Japan, they proved to be lucky enough to succeed in drawing great crowds in Chicago, Los Angeles and several other cities. Even though this plan of placing Shakespearean drama on a traditional kabuki stage did not materialize, their interest in the Japanese theatre tradition will surely survive and bear fruit in the future.

Bando Tamasaburo V, another distinguished kabuki onnagata actor, once played the part of Lady Macbeth. Scholars and theatre critics were astounded to see how he performed in the scene where the heroine looks at her hands and tries to cleanse the blood stain from her hands in vain, saying: 'What, will these hands ne'er be clean? No more o' that, my lord, no more o' that; you mar all with this starting. . . . Here's the smell of the blood still. All the perfumes of Arabia will not sweeten this little hand. O, O, O!' (5.2.43-5, 50-2) Professor Hapgood, who formerly taught Shakespeare at the University of New Hampshire, once told me that no people in the West had ever seen Lady Macbeth scrape her hands together, even to the tips of her fingers, so elaborately, ceremoniously and so full of energy and grace. We know that Tamasaburo's performance was by no means the nearest approach to what is real and truest to nature; presumably it was one quite opposite from the way actresses in the West rub their hands together desperately onstage. In this respect Professor Pronko is perceptive enough to know the difference between the East and the West:

> The play, *Who's Afraid of Virginia Woolf?*, may be violent, even inhuman, but violence and inhumanity are represented in a recognizable, believable human way, with gestures, voices, and facial expressions that could be used in everyday life as we live it. The Oriental actor, given such a play, might feel free within the traditions of Chinese opera, kabuki, or Balinese dance play to develop moods, emotions, and character in a dozen different ways forbidden us. He has another freedom denied us: the freedom of the perfectly disciplined artist who is working within clearly defined traditions and who, within those limits, may develop his individuality. (*Theatre East and West*, 189)

I wonder if the Shakespearean actor Mark Rylance himself has directly seen how Tamasaburo played the part of Lady Macbeth, or even known by hearsay how ingeniously the femininity was enacted by this distinguished female impersonator. Moving quickly and energetically, to the point of springing up into the air, which is so usual and essential in Western ballet, is an element most irrelevant to Japanese dance found in kabuki and *Noh*. 'Dance' in the Japanese sense does not signify any movement, such as hopping, skipping or jumping, that is quick and light. It is always serene and sedate, and yet grave and obeying the influence of the force of gravity. The gravest movement of the limbs expresses or emphasizes the idea or sentiment of the deepest wish, and, in the case of playing Lady Macbeth, the cleansing of her hands is nothing less than the physical posture and gesture in which a kabuki or *Noh* dancer does his best to give expression to any of the human passions. Ganjiro III, Tamasaburo V and other great masters of dance in kabuki and Noh are certainly those initiated into the essential principles of performance. Mark Rylance became acquainted with Ganjiro III and started to learn something from kabuki, and he began respectfully to call the distinguished kabuki actor his '*Shisho*' (master). This, however, does not necessarily mean that Rylance started to learn how to copy after the fashion of kabuki or onnagata. I understand that he was, first and foremost, impressed, like Professor Hapgood, by Ganjiro's exquisite onnagata performance and showed his deepest respect to Ganjiro as an actor and paid his homage to the tradition of the theatre arts of kabuki, which has enabled generations of kabuki actors to be masters of the still-living tradition of onnagata performance.

The main interest in this long kabuki tradition does not lie in its persistence, but in the fact that the time-honoured tradition has handed down treasures of theory and wisdom achieved by generations of celebrated actors and their skilled art and practice of performance. Shakespeare must have inherited from the medieval and Elizabethan Renaissance tradition of the theatre, and absorbed a great deal from it while he developed his career as a playwright writing for his own theatre. The presumably rich theatrical tradition, as I have suggested earlier, became at risk of not being transmitted to any later generations when the Globe and other public theatres were closed and destroyed by Puritans in the 1640s. It must have seemed that, together with the loss of the Elizabethan theatre with its characteristic stage space, all the principles and practices essentially native to Shakespeare's own theatre space were destined to be deracinated and irretrievably lost forever, except the texts of the dramatists. Mark Rylance and some other Shakespearean actors today must have thought that 'the cease' of the theatre 'dies not alone'.

The counterpart of the onnagata in kabuki is, needless to say, the so-called boy actors in the Elizabethan and Jacobean times. From the comparative study of the development of female impersonation in Japanese kabuki, it can easily be supposed that those boy actors must have developed and further elaborated their own particular art and artifice of female impersonation, and even from Hamlet's own remark about such boy actors, we may also assume that their popularity must sometimes have reached the level of that of the adult theatre groups or gone beyond them. Onnagata is one of the most time-tested resourceful means of theatrical presentation developed in the earlier stages of kabuki history in the seventeenth century, and one of the most remarkable features enjoyed by today's kabuki audience still is the female role enacted by the male onnagata actor.

This onnagata tradition started as early as 1652. The Tokugawa feudal government issued an order which prohibited the employment of women for the enactment of female roles, presumably because kabuki had more or less become implicated in the matter of prostitution. The remarkable phenomenon that followed in the wake of this prohibition is that not only young actors but also older ones gradually proved to be superbly talented at representing, in their skilled and experienced stage performance, the deepest soul of femininity. Traditions of onnagata expertise then began to form themselves through the accumulation of superior experiences by master actors. Basically understood, female impersonation is a theatrical fiction, but, because of this fictional basis, generations of female impersonators could freely and limitlessly elaborate the artistic stylization of performance. This successful development of the art of impersonation, in due course, made itself authorized as an indispensable orthodox feature of kabuki. The feudal shogunate government, taking advantage of this specialization of onnagata actors, exercised rigid control over kabuki theatres. Severe regulations and prohibitions were enforced on kabuki by the shogunate government, because there was, in kabuki, an innate tendency towards moral depravity and decadence. The patronage the French absolutist kings gave to French classical drama may exhibit a striking contrast with the severe persecution of kabuki theatres often meted out by the absolutist Edo government. However, both the French drama protected in Versailles and Japanese kabuki subjected to shogunate pressure came to achieve the highest qualities as theatre arts and equally rank highest in the history of world theatre.

In the wake of Japanese modernization, in its effort to survive, kabuki tried to reform itself and groups of actors called 'New School', 'New Drama' and 'New National Drama' were formed; all of them decided to adopt the principle of employing actresses. In the hundred years or so following Japan's modernizing revolution, all of these 'new' reform groups became extinct, but kabuki, with its onnagata tradition still succeeds in maintaining its life. It has survived, and the National Theatre in Tokyo has, together with the Kabuki-za (Kabuki Theatre) also in Tokyo, become the stronghold of the classical kabuki drama in today's Japan.

Modern Japanese drama developed under the strong influence of modern drama in the West, ranging from Ibsen to Ionesco, and naturally this category of Japanese contemporary drama has necessitated the use of actresses, but this rise of the female performer has never in any way undermined the time-honoured use of the traditional onnagata performers in kabuki. On the contrary, we have seen a new theatre company formed by the young generation, with the specific purpose of giving performances resembling and reinterpreting classical kabuki drama, and that with onnagata actors.

As mentioned above, Mark Rylance calls Ganjiro III '*Shisho*' and this certainly shows his deep respect for him as a kabuki onnagata performer, but this does not mean that Rylance immediately began to perform after the manner of Japanese onnagata. It was certainly a daring and audacious attempt, even a theatrical sensation, for him to play the role of Cleopatra. So far as I observed the performance of *Antony and Cleopatra* at the London Globe in the 2000 season, no conscious attempt was made on the part of Rylance to imitate an onnagata performance. It seemed to me that Rylance acted very freely and not a speck of the flavour of the style of the traditional Japanese female impersonation could be detected in what Cleopatra showed on the Globe stage. In 2003, Rylance again made an attempt at the male impersonation of a feminine character, this time, in *Twelfth Night*. He played the part of Olivia, and his performance received favourable criticism. However, so far as I understood, what Rylance attempted to do was to employ a manner of walking or stepping with short feminine steps, which was amusing enough and enlightening enough to bring the idiosyncratic character of Olivia effectively into relief. The tiny short steps the white-faced and queenly-attired Mark Rylance was seen to take was certainly an onnagata-like method of walking, which could be described as superbly feminine mincing. Indeed, when presented on the Globe stage, it was stylized to the extreme and, so to speak, was so well theatricalized that the actor became almost totally immersed in a performance approaching a solemnized form of dancing. The important question about this form of the presentation of feminine behaviour is, on the one hand, whether this *pas d'action* can become a performative element to be so refined and polished as to form a supreme piece of artistic acting style; and, on the other, whether this *pas d'action* was so effective as to induce later actors playing the role of Olivia to follow this particular skilled combination of steps exemplified on the Globe stage of 2003.

My approach to the problem of female impersonation in Shakespeare is from the angle of the nature of the Globe stage and what the dramatist wrote for this stage space in his play texts. I do not think that what we call female impersonation can be discussed as a subject in sociology or folklore lying outside, or independent of, any sort of theatre study or text reading. Female impersonation can only, in my mind, subsist as a core or a central nucleus of a larger category of the study of drama or theatre. I particularly mention 'the Globe Theatre' in the title of this chapter, since the Globe Theatre rebuilt in the Southwark area in London is, in a way, more trustworthy and authentic as a Shakespearean theatre meant for reproducing Shakespeare's plays as they were originally produced on the Renaissance stage. As one of the representatives of the Shakespeare Globe Centre of Japan, I participated in the 2001 conference where fundamental issues concerning the reconstruction of the Globe were discussed. The purpose of the reconstruction of the Globe is more than to provide a near-perfect reproduction of the Elizabethan Globe. There has been a hot controversy as to whether the reconstructed Globe is an *authentic* Shakespearean theatre, and, so far as I have understood, there certainly are a number of Shakespearean scholars who are of the opinion that the new theatre on the Thames cannot monopolize authenticity. With respect to its architecture, Andrew Gurr, John Orrel and other scholars engaging in this field of study have collaborated in order to make the closest approach to the idea of the original Elizabethan Globe. And archaeological investigations of the former sites of the Rose, and only very limitedly of the Globe, made by the archaeological section of the London Museum, yielded an enormous amount of material proof concerning the wooden architecture, limestone foundations and all the details of the amphitheatre, with the open platform stage extending forward into the circular yard and having on each side of the stage two pillars supporting the stage heaven, the roof, that covers the stage proper. For the purpose of constructing the new Globe, numbers of scholars co-operated to gather information so as to produce an idea of the theatre supported by all the possible architectural proof and evidence available since the conscious effort of the research on the Globe playhouse was started by J.C. Adams and other scholars in this field of Shakespearean study earlier in the nineteenth century. It must be admitted, however, that the proof and evidence are, however extensive, essentially partial and limited in quantity and conjectural in quality, and therefore far from being satisfactory or exhaustive. Any attempt at the restoration of the original Globe is destined to be more or less short of being ideal and complete.

From the architectural point of view, therefore, the Globe Theatre is not authentic, although not at all a far cry from fully conforming to the known facts of Elizabethan amphitheatre construction. We may, nonetheless, accept the reconstructed Globe Theatre as acceptable and trustworthy in the sense that Shakespeare himself wrote his masterpieces such as *Hamlet, King Lear, Macbeth* and *Othello*, and other works for the open platform stage with two classical pillars supporting the stage heaven. Here I may justifiably remember what Mark Rylance himself once said to me some years ago. His remark was that he was fortunate enough to be able to do now what none of those celebrated Shakespearean actors in England could have dreamed of doing. According to what he has said, no distinguished actors such as Kemble or Kean or Olivier could dream of playing the roles of Shakespearean heroes on the stage of the *Globe*, and he is now able to do what none of those merited actors could do. For Mark Rylance the space of the open platform is almost exactly that in which Richard Burbage stood about 400 years ago. The stage façade is what Burbage had behind him when he faced the groundlings standing in the yard and the audience seated in the three-tiered galleries. The stage heaven and the blue sky which Richard Burbage could see above the gallery roof, and the afternoon sunshine that Shakespeare himself saw, and the air of London that Elizabethan actors smelt, namely, everything that they saw and felt through their own senses within the Elizabethan roofless amphitheatre is what Mark Rylance can enjoy seeing and sensing today on the platform of today's Globe, which is similar in size and nearly identical in form with that of Richard Burbage's original Elizabethan public theatre. Because of these theatrical circumstances which Mark Rylance is proud of enjoying today, actors/actresses who can perform on today's Globe stage are able to share very similar, or almost identical kinds of experiences that any one actor belonging to Shakespeare's own company enjoyed four centuries ago. Is there any other theatre in London or elsewhere where actors are similarly able to enjoy such a blessed and thrilling experience? That is why I dare to say that the Globe theatre in London today is 'more authentic' than any other kindred theatre in the world. What Mark Rylance consciously does when performing on the Globe stage is to expose himself, and to urge his colleagues to expose themselves, to the totality of the influence of the theatre itself, including its open platform stage, the symbolism of the architectural stage façade, the three-storeyed circular galleries, the nut-cracking groundlings in the yard, and everything that is contained within the theatre.

It is almost unnecessary for him consciously to imitate the manner of Japanese onnagata performances. He has only to wait for the moment when the very stage space of the Globe, in which boy actors once performed, silently begins to work on his imagination to develop his own intuitive idea of female impersonation. In this respect it is worth our while to consider what Professor Pronko has to say from the viewpoint of the parallelism between the Elizabethan drama and kabuki, and that is: 'The kabuki actor, using every facet of body and voice to portray character and emotion, presents himself quite frankly as a theatrical creation on a stage before an audience.' Professor Pronko further argues that the Elizabethan actor tended to play not so much *in* a setting as *against* it, and the kabuki actor 'enjoys a stage structure and type of decor that thrust him toward the audience'. (Pronko, 163-4) There is, in the heavily symbolic and emblematic stage space of the Globe, a strong sense of relativity pervading, and an actor's performance has to be one which is exactly controlled, choreographed and after all stylized in accordance with the closely standardized visual plan of the scene settings such as the pair of imposing classical stage columns. In the case of kabuki, the *hanamichi* ('Flower way'), which is an elevated walkway, serves as an extension of the main stage area, running from the rear of the auditorium through the audience to the front of stage right, and often performs a similarly crucial feature of its formal stage setting. To me, the pair of classical columns symmetrically arranged at the front part of the stage is an equally important crux as a structural feature of the Elizabethan stage.

In the development of the onnagata tradition in Japanese kabuki, the stylized architectural scenic scheme of the stage space, whether in *jidai* (historical plays) or *sewa* ('dramas of contemporary life'), was first and foremost the factor that determines the very nature of actors' performances unfolding on the stage. Nakamura Utaemon VI is the most distinguished and oldest ranking onnagata actor I have ever seen on the kabuki stage. He was born in 1917, and when I saw him play the part of a high courtesan of nonpareil beauty at an elderly age, I immediately believed that his performance was undoubtedly an acme of the art of presenting the most brilliant stateliness or glamour of femininity realizable on kabuki's stage. I remember him performing as the high courtesan and, at the very beginning of the play, making a procession-like entry onto the main stage through the *hanamichi*. (I was reminded of the processional entry which takes place at the very outset of Act I, Scene I of *Antony and Cleopatra*. 'Egypt's queen', accompanied by Antony, enters the stage in a pageant-like royal procession, to be met by Demetrius and Philo, who look at the 'strumpet' and her 'fool' with a most critical eye.) Not only the performance by Utaemon with his costume and makeup, the traditional architectural features of a kabuki theatre, including the *hanamichi*, a time-honoured traditional stage setting and lighting, but also the aural aspects of theatre such as the actor's voice, stage effects and music performed by instrumentalists on and off stage, various narrative recitals of chanters with *shamisen* accompaniment, are, all of them, delicately and exquisitely combined, and they acted as superb foils to the splendour and magnificence of the processional entry of the distinguished courtesan heroine. The whole theatre focuses its attention on the spectacle of dazzling gorgeousness of the courtesan in her flowery ornate attire slowly advancing along the flower way, to be met by a wealthy but ugly and boorish farmer. He is instantly captivated by the coquettish courtesan's sidelong glance and instantly and fatally becomes enamoured with her.

Another time I saw Nakamura Utaemon VI appear in *Meiboku Sendaihagi* performing as the '*tate oyama*' ('chief female impersonator') and playing the part of the heroine Masaoka, who is the paragon of feminine stoicism, impersonating infinite patience and severest suffering when she has to endure seeing her own young son cruelly killed and sacrificed in her presence in order to save the life of her lord's son. When the distinguished actor played this difficult, medieval, feminine role equalled by none in the kabuki repertoire, I witnessed in the heroine a superb image of a woman with her infinite spiritual dignity and solemnity developing in the total scheme of a stage tableau.

All the scenic settings found in kabuki are standardized, and in this drama the scenic arrangement of the inside of a spacious solemn palace, with its grand stairway and gravely painted sliding screens, and a solemnizing perspective, created the dramatic tableau of tragic agony and womanly perseverance after she has unavoidably had her young son sacrificed. The palatial scenic setting serves as a background to support the full-scale manifestation of the tragic onnagata's art of performance unfolded on the stage. The audience may participate in the thrill of witnessing the spectacle of tragically graceful femininity or the symbolic vision of enhanced womanly virtues, when, in terms of these spectacles and stage visions, a highly moving female impersonation takes place on the stage. In connection with these spectacles and visions, we may rightly assume that there is a strong parallelism between the Globe theatre and the kabuki playhouse, which is that a very strongly formulated architectural pattern governs the scenic design of the stages of an Elizabethan public amphitheatre and of a Japanese kabuki playhouse. In the case of the latter, as I have previously noted, the *hanamichi*, a raised walkway, leads straight from the rear of the theatre through the auditorium to the main acting stage, and this walkway joins the stage at a right angle. The important fact about this is that all theatres prepared to present kabuki plays are, without exception, provided with this platform. For kabuki historical plays ('*jidaimono*') standardized scenery is provided, and among the scenic elements that are included are plllars, banisters, railings, front stairs, stately sliding doors, background screens, the front of the solemn palace building, etc. While, in a citizens' play (*sewamono*), a residence of a townsman is often chosen for the setting, and a house with a wooden gate, curtained entrance, and a *tatami* room is standard scenery. There seem to be two patterns of this category of scenic setting; one for the inside of an ordinary citizen's household and the other for the inside of shops, both having in common a *tatami*-matted spacious room meant as a drawing-room, with an exit in the rear and a home temple (*butsudan*) and an alcove (*tokonoma*) fit on the back of the stage. On the stage left there is a sliding door (*fusuma*) leading to the next room.

In an Elizabethan public theatre, as we know from De Witt's so-called Swan Sketch, there is a rectangular open platform stage extending precisely to the middle of the circular yard. The stage-façade has a two-storeyed architectural structure with three doors on the stage level, and this architecturally designed façade, in Kernodle's idea, combining several medieval symbols of throne, tomb, altar, castle wall, city-gate, etc., serves as the background or scenic device for the scene of any comedy, tragedy or historical play enacted on the stage. In addition to this, on either side of the front of the rectangular stage stand two posts supporting the roof or canopy covering the stage. These two posts seem to be classical columns, presumably, of the Corinthian order. This standardized scenic background with the classical pillars and the two-storeyed stage-façade, all symmetrically arranged, must have invariably been found in the Globe and other Elizabethan public theatres. With respect to the way the scenery is rigidly formalized and also with respect to the manner in which scenic elements are uniformly set according to a fixed pattern suitable for traditional ways of performance, the Japanese kabuki stage is doubtlessly an almost exact counterpart of the standardized formal Elizabethan stage.

The ranking onnagata is, and was, the quintessential symbol of kabuki theatre art. Mark Rylance himself must have understood this fundamental priority of onnagata in kabuki, and therefore as an actor he seems to have limited the extent of female impersonation to the role of Olivia when he became the 'master' of the play *Twelfth Night*. Since the important thing about this comedy is to concentrate the audience's attention more on the Cesario-Viola impersonation, it was necessary for Rylance to limit the theatrical effect of female impersonation to the idiosyncrasy and peculiarity of behaviour and character of the aristocratic Olivia.

The reason why the Globe is at least more authentic as a 'Shakespearean playhouse' than any other theatre is that Shakespeare began to write plays mainly for the stage space of the Globe after his company started to use the playhouse in 1599. For the purpose of understanding a certain deeper meaning of the sort of female impersonation that presumably took place in the characteristic stage space of the Elizabethan Globe, let us focus our attention on the significance of the two stage posts, which even today are, from time to time, liable to be regarded or treated as a nuisance to performers and/or spectators in the gallery. The two stage pillars were evidently classical pillars as we know from the so-called Swan Sketch and as we conjecture from the statement of The Fortune Contract made in 1600. The latter, in particular, includes a statement that refers to the two stage posts with some classical association and to be made after the manner of the stage columns of the Globe that had been built the year before. In Western architectural history the most distinguished use of classical pillars can, of course, be found in Greece. Needless to say, the Parthenon still remaining on top of the Athenian Acropolis shows how unequalled a Greek temple is in splendour and magnificence with its series of simple but stately marble columns of classical Doric order as its main architectural elements. The magnificence of the Roman Empire could not have achieved such a satisfactory expression without a full exploitation of the architectural resources of classical pillars, as is so clearly manifest from a glimpse of the Foro Romano that still remains in the centre of today's Rome. As part of the revival of classical literature and artistic styles, Renaissance architecture could not have found full expression without the revival of the Vitruvian architectural theory, in which the meaning and function of the 'column' is of crucial and supreme importance. Not only architecture itself but also Renaissance art was under the great influence of the idea of Classical columns.

Fra Angelico produced a series of works having the theme of the 'Annunciation'. One of them painted *c.* 1430-45, and today found in the Prado Museum, Madrid, illustrates the biblical theme; the angel Gabriel is positioned on the left-hand side in the tableau and Maria on the right, and under the arched structure the angel and Maria are seen facing each other, and several rather slender columns are seen to support the arches. Another work dealing with the theme of the 'Annunciation' painted by the same artist in *c.* 1435 remains in Cortona; in the picture we find the angel and Maria, both positioned similarly in this tableau, surrounded likewise by a series of classical columns, which look less thin than those found in Madrid. The artist's most famous *Annunciation*, a fresco of the late 1430s for the convent of San Marco, Florence, features a composition very similar to the preceding two tableaus on the same theme, but far more artistically finished and technically accomplished. The columns composing the colonnade especially are more imposing and looking more like those actually employed by Palladio in his Renaissance *rotonda* architecture. 'Annunciation' means the words by which the angel Gabriel foretold the incarnation to the Virgin Mary, and the incarnation in this context refers to the embodiment of God in human form as Jesus, the union of the divinity and humanity, which signifies an extraordinary miracle and at the same time a reality in Christianity. In order to give full expression to this transcendental miraculous theme of incarnation, a theme which essentially refuses to be rendered in terms of practical human experience or reason, it was necessary for a painter of the Annunciation theme to adopt an artistic means or plan whereby he could convincingly represent this solemn and transcendental theme through visual artistic means. For the Renaissance artist Fra Angelico, classical columns must have meant the only inestimably effective method available to him for solemnizing the composition of the divine theme in an artistic tableau.

As for other Renaissance artists dealing with the same religious theme, Donatello for one made an admirable stone relief (*c.* 1430) now found in Santa Croce, Florence, and it is not a tapering cylindrical column but a square stone pillar that he placed on either side of the sculptured scene of the Annunciation. The two stone pillars, though not round but rectangular in shape, serve nonetheless as a means in terms of which the theme of transcendence is truly successfully and artistically framed and solemnized. Earlier in 1333, the *Annunciation* was painted in tempera, by Simone Martini and Lippo Memmi, as part of the altarpiece in the Siena Cathedral, and the remarkable thing about this painting is that Maria looks very surprised by the sudden appearance of the angel Gabriel and 'shrinks away in a movement of awe and humility, while looking back at the messenger from Heaven' (Gombridge, *The Story of Art*, 212). Human elements on the part of Maria are certainly given emphasis in her painted gestures, but in order to support the total sacred significance of this biblical episode, the two figures in this painting are placed under a solemn structure with lancet arches symmetrically arranged and supported by slender spiral-shaped pillars. In the Bible, with reference to the Annunciation, Gabriel says to Maria: 'The Holy Spirit will come upon you, and the power of the Highest will overshadow you; therefore, also that Holy one who is to be born will be called the Son of God.' (Luke: 1.35) Essentially, the Holy One and The Holy Spirit belong to divinity and conceptually they are infinitely separated from human beings. No two entities are more totally different and dissociated from each other than the divine and the human. According to the Bible, however, a messenger and servant of God visits a maid living in a town in the Middle East.

This is a happening that is totally incredible and beyond human imagination, and moreover it cannot be explained by any law of nature. In order to help people suspend their disbelief, artists like Fra Angelico had to create a framework within which they could convincingly represent a biblical episode, and those two young people in the tableau are made to seem spritually solemnized and aggrandized. Since the time of the Greeks and Romans, columns have been an effective architectural means in terms of which the holy and divine might possibly be given simultaneous habitation on the earth, as the Greek temple in the Athenian Acropolis unmistakably exemplifies. Anything that transcends everyday life could, in an artist's mind, be solemnized in some sanctifying framework of imagination. Without the Renaissance fashion of employing columns of the five orders of classical architecture, namely, Tuscan, Doric, Ionic, Corinthian and Composite, Fra Angelico could not have composed a scene essentially transcending human experience and imagination.

As a corollary we may notice the fact that, a few centuries later, a Plutarchian theme was painted in a neoclassical picture named *The Oath of Horatii* in 1784, by the French artist Jacques Louis David. In this painting, the decided spiritual stance of the three brothers is found positioned on the left-hand side of the tableau and an equally resolute posture of their father confronting them is placed on the right-hand side. Here, David gives an eloquent illustration of the spirit of honour and bravery among ancient Romans. However, if it were not for the two stately classical columns that stand in the background of this heroic tableau, this marvellous masterpiece illustrating the solemn scene of the patriotic oath would surely have lost much of its solemn and intense spirit as an expression of Roman stoic morality. Obviously, the two classical pillars are of the Doric order with its round shaft and plain capital. They are columns signifying the spirit of ancient simplicity, sincerity and moral strength. David, as a master artist of French neoclassicism, was well aware of the importance of the meaning of classical columns, and succeeded in rendering the heroism of Roman youth in a solemnized and aggrandized scale, supplying the heroic tableau with the forceful visual effect of classical columns. As a reaction against the decorous excesses of Baroque and Rococo in the field of the visual arts, neoclassicism started in Italy and spread throughout West Europe, and undoubtedly reached its peak in the works of David, particularly in his *The Oath of the Horatii*. The visual effect of the Doric columns in this work is unmistakable, and the tableau as a whole inspires those who see it with an upsurge of highly moralistic sentiment as well as an enhancement of rarest aesthetic pleasure, and the people in this masterpiece of fine art are made to look more aggrandized and enhanced in moral or spiritual stature than ordinary soldiers or citizens.

Ben Jonson's Folio edition of his *Works* was published in 1618, and the title page of the volume is quite memorable in that the design was based upon the illustration of a triumphal arch which is supported by classical columns. Ben Jonson, the great classical writer of Shakespeare's time, was undoubtedly well versed in the classical architectural significance of those columns, and the design as we see it on the page at the front of the Folio edition of his *Works* looks impressive and dignified, and successful in paying tribute to the author's literary achievements. The aim of this publication was to glorify an Elizabethan playwright as ranking among the great English men of letters and to immortalize the value of Jonson's literary fame. The classicist Ben Jonson himself must have known the architectural and aesthetic value of the classical columns, since his contemporary Elizabethan public theatres, including the Swan, the Globe and the Fortune, were supplied with classical columns on both sides of their stages, and the Roman architect Vitruvius himself was of the opinion that: 'Tragic scenes are delineated with columns, pediments, statues and other objects suited to Kings.' (Chambers, *Elizabethan Stage*, IV, Frontispiece).

Needless to say, De Witt's drawing of the Swan allows us to suppose that certainly there were two classical pillars supporting the stage heaven. They were not real stone pillars but 'wooden columns, painted in such excellent imitation of marble that it might deceive even the most prying' (quoted as translated by Hodges, *The Globe Restored*, 95.) According to The Fortune Contract, made between Phillip Henslowe and Edward Allen, and the carpenter Peter Street in 1600, 'all the pryncipall and maineposts of the saidde fframe and Stadg forwarde shall be square and wrought plasterwise, with carved proporcions called Satiers to be placed & sett on the top of every of the same postes' (Chambers, II. 439). From this statement of the contract we know that there certainly were posts which were not circular like those found in the Globe but square, and had on top of them some capital-like portions carved with satyrs. All of this evidence, together with the amassed facts known from the comparatively recent archaeological excavation of the Rose, collectively show that there certainly were stage posts or pillars, which more or less looked like classical columns. According to the theatre historian George Kernodle: 'Most of the new buildings erected in England in the latter half of the sixteenth century were of the newer Renaissance architecture, with its classic orders of columns and arches and its marble and gold.' (*From Art to Theatre*, 134)

In *Othello*, Act II, Scene I, when Desdemona arrives in Cypress, Cassio, waiting for her, remarks:

> Tempests themselves, high seas, and howling winds,
> The guttered rocks and congregated sands,
> Traitors ensteeped to clog the guiltless keel,
> As having sense of beauty do omit
> Their mortal nature, letting go safely by
> The divine Desdemona.
>   (2.1.68-73)

Previous to these lines, Cassio, in all sincerity and seriousness, praises the unparalleled beauty of Desdemona, which 'paragons description and wild fame' and 'excels the quirks of blazoning pens', and in her native beauty Desdemona defeats all attempt of the inventive poet to praise her adequately. Desdemona, now Othello's wife, 'our great captain's captain', is:

> One that excels the quirks of the blazoning pens
> And in th' essential vesture of creation
> Does tire the ingener.
>   (2.1.63-5)

It is interesting to find that E.A.J. Honigman, in his edition of *Othello*, explains the quoted lines in a gloss: 'exhaust the (powers of the) divine inventor (God); i.e. she is God's masterpiece'. Because of her natural beauty, therefore, all the obstacles and difficulties that might prevent Desdemona's voyage to Cypress seem to have avoided blocking her safe passage as if they held beautiful Desdemona in awe and reverence and refrained from giving free rein to their murderous wild instincts. In order to bless 'the divine Desdemona' with safe passage, what Cassio means to express here is his own high praise and respect for her feminine grace and virtue, and, through his own eulogy, to impress the audience with the high-bred dignity in her character and personality. Like Utaemon's Masaoka, Desdemona looks equalled by none on stage, and the true beauty and the nobleness of character in Desdemona as stated in Shakespeare's text, somehow, induce people to have the belief that Desdemona does somehow partake of the nature of God, or 'God's masterpiece', but Shakespeare, by bringing out the contrast between divinity and 'mortal nature', caused the loftiness of her personality to stand in bold relief.

As a dramatist specially writing plays for the Globe stage, Shakespeare must have known all the specific characteristics and distinctive qualities of the stage space, such as the multi-levelled stage and three stage doors fixed in the stage-façade, the stage heaven and the stage hell, and the pair of imposing stage posts supporting the stage heaven; for the dramatist, these must have had special significance when he wrote tragedies, comedies and historical plays. In view of the classical columns provided on the Globe stage, Shakespeare must have been encouraged to write *Julius Caesar* – presumably as one of his first plays to be presented at the Globe after the theatre opened in 1599.

Drama is intended to portray human life or character, or to tell a human story by actions and, usually, dialogue tending towards some result based upon them. The paradox about drama is that the portrayal of human life or character can become more dynamic and intense when there is an intrusion of more than human life or character. Desdemona can most humanly be portrayed when something more than natural and human becomes involved. In this context, kabuki onnagata seems to take on special meaning. Because of the severest tempest that has thrown Othello and Desdemona into despair, what they have felt and known goes by far beyond their everyday experience and seems to reach the extremity of height and the infinity of depth:

> It gives me wonder great as my content
> To see you here before me. O, my soul's joy,
> If after every tempest come such calms,
> May the winds blow till they have waked death,
> And let the labouring bark climb hills of seas,
> Olympus-high, and duck again as below
> As hell's from heaven. If it were now to die,
> 'Twere now to be happy; for I fear
> My soul hath her content so absolute
> That not another comfort like to this
> Succeeds in unknown fate.

> (2.1.175-85)

To surpass the ordinary dimension of humanity often characterizes Shakespeare's imagination; to counter this transcendence on the part of the hero and heroine, Iago's evil gradually grows to be that of a devil in its extreme severity and subtlety. Iago himself in the course of the drama, gradually goes through the process of aggrandizement, in proportion as his malignity grows more and more inhuman, merciless and motiveless. *Othello* is a domestic tragedy, since, unlike *Hamlet* or *King Lear*, its hero is neither royal nor aristocratic by birth or origin. Nevertheless, Othello is a tragic hero because his tragic suffering is as great and as magnificent, and Desdemona herself gradually comes to acquire magnificence as a tragic heroine beyond the range proper to domestic life. The extent of Othello's love and devotion and his attachment to Desdemona grows more and more absolute and unswerving, although, through the wiles of Iago, jealousy inexorably goes on to corrode Othello's mind. The stage of the Globe must have shown its audience as well as Othello himself how noble and dignified the heroine looked to Othello the moment she enters the stage and he meets her:

> Excellent wretch! Perdition catch my soul
> But I do love thee; and when I love thee not,
> Chaos is come again.
> (3.3.90-92)

The exclamation mark suggests how serious and intense the impact which the noble figure of Desdemona has made on Othello's mind is, and the audience, having witnessed the perfected image of feminine dignity on the stage, must have rightly assessed the enormity of the shock the hero has experienced at this moment. Similarly, when, in the same scene, Desdemona again enters to be met by Othello, he again makes a shuddered remark at the solemn sight of the unspoiled and dignified purity embodied in his wife: 'Look where she comes./ If she be false, O then heaven mocks itself,/ I'll not believe it.' (3.3.280-1) Shakespeare is daring enough to let Othello be extremely astounded or rather horrified at the sight of the matchless beauty of Desdemona with her nonpareil purity and chastity, and, through the remark of shocked horror, to make him, paradoxically, an encomium of the magnificent dignity of her womanhood. It would be interesting to know how the Elizabethan dramatist was enabled to feel it justified to portray Desdemona, quite so imaginatively, in such magnificent proportions in the limited dimensions of the Globe stage space. Similarly, it is worth our while to ask why Shakespeare, in the finale of *Antony and Cleopatra*, was not made to feel it unreasonable to induce Cleopatra to determine to leave her everyday life and kill herself ('Now no more the juice of Egypt's grape shall moist this lip') in order to become most herself, wearing her crown and attiring royally:

> Give me my robe, put on my crown, I have
> Immortal longings in me.
> . . . . .
> I am fire and air; my other elements
> I give to baser life.
> (5.2.280-81, 289-90)

She aspires to be etherealized, or, in more neoplatonic terms, to leave the material world for the sphere of ideas which is only perceivable by the infinite mind. Similarly neoplatonic is the final scene of *Telfth Night*. Here, the reunion of the twins, Sebastian and Viola, takes place, and unmistakably the theme of the neoplatonic idea of *Das Ein*, finds an exquisitely graphic and vividly dramatic illustration in the stage space of the Globe Theatre:

> One face, one voice, one habit, and two persons,
> A natural perspective, that is and is not.
> (5.1.216-7)

A stage spectator, Antonio, questioningly gives a surprised remark:

> How have you made division of yourself?
> An apple, cleft into two, is not more twin
> Than these two creatures.
> (5.1.222-4)

What the audience has seen in this finale is an emblematic stage tableau illustrating, quite dramatically, an essentially mysterious philosophical theme, and in this dramatized stage picture the unified twins, through the admiration of the spectators (as another stage spectator, Olivia, remarks 'Most wonderful!') (225) grow more mystically sublimated than life-sized humanity. In the spectators' eye this stage tableau looks the more unmistakably sublimated, as in David's tableau, by the subsidiary support of the two (stage) columns having their origin in classical antiquity.

Starting with the audience's interest in Viola's transvestism, the classical framework of the amphitheatre seems to have developed the theme of cross-dressing into a starkly solid philosophical issue. Similarly, in *As You Like It,* the theme of spiritual union is emphasized, this time not in a stage tableau but in a pageant-like ritual: 'Then is there mirth in heaven,/ When earthly things made even/ Atone together.' (5.4.108-10) And this comedy, presumably presented on the stage of the newly-built Globe in 1600, certainly refers to the idea of the Globe Theatre as the 'theatre of the world' in Jaques's speech beginning with 'All the world's a stage.' The word 'world' is inclusive of the meaning of the (spherical) universe, and the idea of the amphitheatre in classical antiquity is hinted at here, and the theatre, as a whole, in commemoration of the construction of the new circular theatre (the Globe), is representative of the Renaissance neo-Platonic philosophy. Because of the fundamental nature of the architectural lineament of the theatre, the pair of classical pillars standing on both sides of he platform stage must have made themselves felt the more strongly by the audience, and the final pageant-like ceremonial scene of this comedy must have been the more full of 'mirth' when 'earthly things' are made at one or 'atone'. Rosalind's transvestism, after passing through the comical process of the play, ends in a sublimation of hymeneal pageant ceremony, and Hymen says: ''Tis I must make conclusion/ Of these most strange events', and a song follows: 'Wedding is great Juno's crown,/ O blessed bond of board and bed!' (5.4.125-6, 141-2).

In Shakespeare's dramatic imagination and in the earliest audience of the newly-built Globe playhouse, the heroine ought to have come to assume a more ennobled and magnified aspect according as the final ritual 'pageants' proceeded. The initial audience of this comedy must have felt this the more strongly in this new theatre milieu of 'This wide and universal theatre' with its fundamental spiritual nature of the *theatrum mundi* emphasized by the framework afforded by the architectural design of the amphitheatre and by the imposing presence of the pair of classical columns on its stage.

Here it seems pertinent to refer to the remark made by a dististinguished scholar of Japanese drama, Earle Ernst, who, by way of suggesting the way in which drama in the West can get out of the 'cul-de-sac of realism', proposes that 'the techniques of Japanese theatre. . . may be helpful in suggesting how the Western theatre can get on with its somewhat neglected but requisite business of being larger than life'. (Quoted from *Theatre East and West*, 139.) Obviously, Shakespeare as a Renaissance dramatist instinctively knew what 'being larger than life' means, since his dramatic texts repeatedly remind us that his heroes and heroines can easily traverse between realism and stylization of performance. Since certain boy actors did belong to his theatre group either of the Lord Chamberlain's Men or of the King's Men, he could anticipate what Japanese onnagata would produce on the kabuki stage years later in the Farthest East. In the London Globe today, it is Mark Rylance that is going to materialize on his stage what the boy actors in the Elizabethan antiquity seem to have created on the original Globe stage. In this connection, it is certainly worth our while to quote here a passage from an article concerning the 2002 production of *Twelfth Night*:

> But then it is Mark Rylance's Olivia that lingers in the memory altogether. He succeeded in transforming the part not only into the star performance but, more improbably, into the absolute protagonist of the play, rather than the weak-willed but spoiled and bossy prima donna we are often given. More than a countess, Rylance looked like a perennially embalmed Elizabeth I, complete with white facial mask and coronet, slid effortlessly but somewhat rigidly across the stage and delivered his lines with an intriguing mixture of artfulness and ingenuousness, in a tone that is feminine without camp falsetto.
> (Keir Elam, from *Around the Globe*, Issue 22, Autumn 2002)

As a matter of fact, in kabuki, onnagata means more than male actors impersonating female roles, since onnagata often occupies the more crucial meaning in the whole theatre business than is usually imagined. Presumably, Mark Rylance could do more than he had originally expected to do as an onnagata actor. Of course, it is the graceful femininity that is most appealing to Japanese kabuki connoisseurs, but a female impersonator, when he performs most successfully, can acquire a deeper understanding of the play itself and a more superb knowledge and judgement of the quality of the performance onstage. What Keir Elam added is interesting enough: 'Olivia also became the comedy's true comedian, and here Rylance played unashamed to the bigger Globe audience, turning the relative refinement of his Temple performance into outright slapstick.' Female impersonators in the new Globe are sure to have become instinctively aware what tradition means in kabuki drama. Certainly, there are infinite amounts of fixed forms and patterns of performance handed down from actor to actor throughout the last few hundred years, and only through the guiding principle of this passing down of the patterns and forms of performance and by strict practice, have Japanese onnagata actors maintained the refinement and profundity of the expressiveness of the art of performance in their own traditional stage space including *hanamichi*. Future Globe audience can expect female impersonators to give a more intensified expression of Shakespearean heroines in their performance which takes place in front of the traditional 'universal' and classical background of the Globe stage.

10

Shakespeare and Kabuki in Maurice Béjart: His *King Lear: La mort de Cordelia*

Yumiko Yamada

With all of our high-tech devices for theatrical improvement, *King Lear* has remained still the most difficult of Shakespeare's plays to be represented on stage. Too huge, too heavy and too complex to handle with whimsical ideas or improvisational manoeuvres, directors' experimental exploits rarely seem to have succeeded in arousing sensations other than gross horror or nihilistic absurdity. Its productions have seldom been free from complaints, and we can hardly blame a critic who lost his temper and declared that 'a mediocre production of *King Lear* is, for some reason, much more dispiriting than the equivalent of *Macbeth* or *Hamlet*.[1] This, I suppose, may be largely due to the limits of realistic, one-dimensional acting styles; what are we to expect from that which is nothing but the faithful, sometimes even servile reproduction of the original text, when there are far more things between Shakespeare's words and their meanings than are dreamt of by the director's philosophy?

In this sense it is noteworthy that, at the 1991 World Shakespeare Congress in Tokyo, Dieter Mehl reminded us of the brilliant success of Aribert Reimann's opera version of *King Lear* (1978), which has drawn enthusiastic applause both at home and abroad.[2] From Reimann's opera two-thirds of Shakespeare's lines are absent and the remaining third has been translated into German, yet it did not fail to have a great impact on the audience of Shakespeare's homeland, with the 1989 premier in London impressing itself as 'an opera of shattering theatrical power'.[3] Mehl claimed that it is: 'in many ways closer to Shakespeare than many a thoughtless or deliberately alienating production of the original, in a new combination of words, music and spectacle, attaining the consolation of formal pathos and lament, not the depressing nihilism of absurd drama'.[4]

The primary point of Mehl's argument lay in that 'a great deal of what Shakespeare expresses in rhetoric and poetry had to be conveyed non-verbally'.[5] My purpose here is to show that the same claim can be made for Maurice Béjart's ballet *La mort de Cordelia*, composed on the same tragedy and performed in Tokyo on 24 and 25 May 1994. I am going to introduce it as nothing less than an 'illuminating instance' of producing Shakespeare's tragedy on stage.

But the present task seems to involve, for several reasons, even more complicated procedures than the case of Reimann's opera. First comes the problem that the ballet is virtually non-verbal; an opera in any form can depend largely on recited words, whatever emphasis is laid on its non-verbality. Next is the scarcity of time and characters; it was a piece of no longer than eighteen minutes, prepared as one of the nineteen *pas de deuxs* of the day's programme, and allowing only three characters plus two *kokens* or stagehands to appear on stage. And the third factor to overshadow any choreographic attempt is, again, an aesthetic problem inherent in *King Lear*.

Strangely enough, the first problem of non-verbality in itself has scarcely handicapped well-composed ballets. In order to realize this, we have only to recall a few choreographic versions of *Romeo and Juliet*, which have established it as a standard classic, almost equal to *Swan Lake* or *Giselle*; even *Othello*, which seems more difficult, has been rendered more 'eloquent' than the ordinary verbal production through the amazing art of Chaboukiani. It is the second and the third that bear hard on us, each imposing a heavier and the heaviest burden.

A ballet version of *King Lear* had been long considered next to impossible, primarily because of its aesthetic problems. Indeed you may compose whatever dances you like, but the raving squirm of a half-naked old man would make a least welcome spectacle, even to the post-modern dance audience. For this very reason Verdi, the creator of *Macbeth* and *Otello,* became frustrated in his 'ambition' for an opera version of *King Lear.* The storm scenes are said to have caused his defeat, and the blinding of Gloucester and Lear's entry with the murdered Cordelia was absent from his libretto.[6]

According to Mehl, it was all due to the comparatively narrow and rigid conventions which were imposed upon composers of his day, and Reimann overcame the problem with twentieth-century music that was capable of expressing the agonies and radical exposures of the play.[7] This is affirmed by Malcolm Hayes's report to the *Sunday Telegraph* that in Reimann's storm scenes 'the chord-clusters build up and spread in huge, roaring, opaque columns of sound . . . obliterating the last traces of rationality of Lear's mind'.[8]

Maurice Béjart also adopted contemporary music for his ballet, yet it was only in part and without any tempestuous uproar. The main composers he selected antedate Verdi: Henry Purcell, one and a half centuries earlier, and Vincenzo Bellini, older than Verdi by twelve years. And as was mentioned, we see nothing but three persons on a dark and vacant stage: Lear, Cordelia and the Fool, with two stagehands dressed in black.

Here most people may be sceptical as to what degree Béjart could attain the depth and the gravity of Shakespeare's most difficult tragedy, with such old-fashioned music, with so few characters, in such a short time, and virtually without words. The strategy he used against these disadvantages is what you may call transcendental: utterly disregarding an obsessive reproduction of minute details, he rather singled out the traditional Japanese theatrical recourses, which are ritualistic, symbolic and sometimes time saving.

*   *   *

Before going into further detail, some remarks on Béjart's literary and artistic background are in order, lest he should be mixed up with half-baked Japanophiliac foreigners or avant-garde performers in their whimsical pursuit of provocative novelty devoid of technique.

The first thing to be noticed is that Béjart is in no way beneath Shakespearean scholars in his love and reading of Shakespeare. His keen theatrical sense was first cultivated through reading Shakespeare in his father's study during his childhood, and was to be deepened by his later custom of keeping a copy of the complete works always at hand. With the exception of Homer, he declares, Shakespeare is the only author who allows the reader a direct encounter with his characters without intruding personally into his own work.[9] The Shakespearean inspiration is everywhere, including a number of pieces composed directly from Shakespeare – *Antony and Cleopatra*,[10] *The Taming of the Shrew*,[11] *Hamlet, Macbeth, Othello*,[12] and *Romeo and Juliet*,[13] to name but a few. The son of the French philosopher Gaston Berger, Béjart's concern is not limited to Shakespeare but covers nearly all regions and ages from ancient Egypt to contemporary Japan, the ample harvest of which has continued to satisfy his audience both in quality and in quantity.

Secondly, his ballets should be interpreted first and foremost as dramatic works, not as mere dancing. This was proved by the three successive victories of his ballet company at the Avignon Festival from 1967 to 1969; until that time dance had been considered unsuitable due to its non-verbality. Jean Vilar, the director of the Théatre National Populaire and originator of the outdoor summer theatre festival, declared Béjart a pioneer in transforming dance into popular drama. Today the dance programme occupies the greater part of the festival. Béjart blames Western people for having discontinued efforts to heighten the artistic value of dance when the *petit bourgeois* came to power in the nineteenth century; adorned with the sugar-coated stories of second- or third-rate writers or with stage sets reminiscent of chocolate boxes, and accompanied by a series of third- or fourth-rate melodies.[14] A conscious successor to Diaghilev's Ballets Russes (1909), his concern was always for the revitalization of dance from its critical condition, by transforming it into a new form of the total theatre with a combination of movements, sound, fantasy and colour, thus heightening its artistic value to the level of any other kind of verbal art.[15] He actually carried out his plan of bringing up 'all-round actors', and founded training schools for his company, MUDRA (1970) in Brussels and RUDRA (1992) in Lausanne.

The third thing to remember is Béjart's surprising 'conservatism' in his technique. Although he was strongly opposed to the nineteenth-century ballet and even despised it, he could not dismiss its rigid academic method that contributed to polishing dancers' bodies and movements towards perfection. Having a strong belief that those who aim at baroque styles have to control themselves more strictly than classicists, he devised his new movements from the academically-based system. Thus Béjart's ballet has acquired a 'universal language' whose vocabulary is now common to dancers all over the world.

A brief survey of Béjart's artistic background thus far promises us a full-length ballet on any story by any author, yet still it does not seem enough to realize an eighteen-minute *King Lear*. To this we have to add his encounter with Japanese theatrical arts, which, as was mentioned above, allow for a ritually or symbolically condensed production. We can see almost all its traditions introduced into Béjart's ballets: *Bugaku*, *Noh*, *Bunraku* puppet theatre, and kabuki, into which the former three are merged.[16]

Here we cannot overlook his nationality, since it was the French people that first discovered Japanese culture at the Paris Exposition in 1867, only fourteen years after Japan opened herself to the world.[17] An ardent lover of Katsushika Hokusai, he reminds Japanese readers, who generally take little interest in their own culture, that without the discovery of Japanese woodprints, Toulouse-Lautrec, van Gogh, and even the impressionist school would not have been brought into the world, in the preface specially affixed to the Japanese version of *Béjart: le tournant*.[18] Then he goes further to advise his young readers not to reject their own culture and art as stale and antiquated, for in fact, they have never lost their modernistic novelty. No doubt the previous knowledge of the theatrical synthesis of Diaghilev's Ballets Russes made the Frenchman still more sensitive to the artistry of kabuki, where three accomplishments, singing (*ka*), dancing (*bu*) and acting (*ki*) are miraculously integrated in each actor.[19] In 1986 Béjart composed a full-length ballet *Kabuki* of nine acts, adapted for his contemporaries from *Kanadehon Chushingura* or *The Faithful Forty-Seven* with its

notorious length of eleven acts – a Herculean exploit that native
Japanese choreographers had never even challenged.

In his *Kabuki*, Béjart arouses our attention to the ritual or
religious effect of kabuki, claiming that it frees the audience from
their existential anxiety through the mediating art of the actor who
enacts myths and symbols that transcend our daily life.[20] This, he
affirms, is precisely what had been long lost to the West, where
young people know no better than to haunt discotheques in pursuit
of alternative catharsis.[21] Like the masterless samurais in *Kanadehon
Chushingura*, they are all orphans of time.

In composing his ballet version of *King Lear: La mort de Cordelia*,
Béjart concentrated upon this ritual effect he discovered in the
Japanese theatrical tradition. Instead of putting Lear's sound and
fury on stage, which might well have evoked nothing but a
nauseating sensation, Béjart chose to present the root reason he had
seen behind it: it all stems from Lear's disappointed yearning for the
immaculacy of women without which, as will be discussed below, he
cannot attain any kind of spiritual salvation. This *beau ideal* cherished
in the heart of the aged king is reflected in the person of Cordelia,
and the one who is to play the part is required to transcend a
physical being and enact the very essence of spiritual beauty. For
this, Béjart singled out one of the most gifted kabuki female
impersonators, Bando Tamasaburo, who astounded him with his
prodigious ability to represent the inherent features of women
better than any other real woman he came across in the street. [22]

*   *   *

La mort de Cordelia focuses on the catastrophe of the tragedy, the
brief period from Lear's entry with the murdered Cordelia till his
heart-breaking death, comprising nearly fifty lines in all. It consists
largely of three parts, according to the pieces of music used in each
dance of the ballet.

Accompanied by Henry Purcell's plaint 'O Let Me Weep', Béjart-
Lear enters from the right, in a golden robe with a crown on his
head; he is pulling a cart loaded with the body of Cordelia. Lear's
entrance symbolizes his long-afflicted journey after retirement, and
the cart he is pulling seems to signify what Edgar calls 'the weight of
this sad time' (*King Lear* 5.3.324).[23] Lear stops on his way and looks

back, only to make sure that Cordelia is 'dead as earth' (5.3.262).

When the entrance is over, the two *kokens* or stagehands, who act like the puppet manipulators of Bunraku, raise Cordelia's body horizontally into the air and keep her there a while, displaying the ample drape of her white loose-fitting dress with long kimono-like sleeves. After her body is put down on the floor, Lear tries to hold and support it in every attempt to make it stand firmly, yet its pliable inertness in each posture makes us feel, more acutely than spoken words, that 'she's gone forever' (5.3.260).

Purcell's song continues, and Lear takes off his robe, revealing a black shirt and trousers. In the meantime Cordelia stands up before him, her arms *en haut*, while Béjart-Lear kneels down as if in prayer. The Cordelia we see from this time on is one in a flashback recollection of Lear which starts at the moment he recognizes her death. Lear also takes off his crown and hands it over to Cordelia, who puts it down on the ground. Then Cordelia begins to dance together with Lear, in a kind of *pas de deux*. Moving slowly hand in hand, with knees almost bent down, their steps look very similar to those of the kabuki *michiyuki*, the lovers' journey to their double-suicide. Of course they are not lovers, but these *michiyuki*-like steps imply the spiritual reunion of father and daughter that was long prevented by an unhappy misunderstanding; at the same time their steps presage the coming deaths. This part corresponds to Lear's imprisonment with Cordelia in the last act, short-lived but the most blissful moment in Lear's prolonged life. The *pas de deux* reminds us of Lear's lines beginning with 'Come, let's away to prison':

> We two alone will sing like birds i'th'cage;
> When thou dost ask me blessing, I'll kneel down
> And ask of thee forgiveness. So we'll live,
> And pray, and sing, and tell of old tales . . .   (5.3.8-12.)

By now we remember with conviction that the statue-like posture of Cordelia with Lear kneeling down before her is meant to represent the Virgin Mary, the archetype of immaculacy. Delicate and brittle like Parmigianino's 'Madonna with the long Neck',[24] Tamasaburo-Cordelia there highlighted his tall slenderness by keeping his arms up in an *en haut* position; we are almost brought to believe, along with the gentleman who reports it, that tears of pearls dropped from her diamond eyes (4.3.21-22). We can also realize that the horizontal lifting of her body in the air at the beginning signified the principal image of the Holy Mary brought into a temple newly set in the prison.

No sooner have we started to indulge in a fancy than Lear brings us back to the opening scene of the tragedy where he tries to measure his daughter's sincerity in terms of the size of his kingdom; at the end of Purcell's song Lear picks up his crown from the ground and places it back on his head, while Cordelia gazes upon him with a sad look.

Lear cries in Japanese, 'Doke wa dokoda?' (Where's the Fool?) Here enters his Fool, Stanislas de Nussac, with a saxophone in his mouth, tearing the father and daughter apart. The Fool continues playing the saxophone for several minutes, producing an impromptu dissonance of irregular rhythm. Lear and Cordelia, now standing to his right and left, make awkward, nonsensical and schizophrenic movements by fits and starts, to the noisy discord of the saxophone. After displaying motions incongruous with each other, Lear and Cordelia each make a brief stop in a symmetrical posture, the one angular and the other curvaceous. Then Lear goes up to Cordelia and waves his hand before her face, but she refuses to show any sign of response.

Through this dumb show Béjart reminds us of Shakespeare's distrust of language, which is the very origin of the tragedy. Then what can possibly be more absurd, Béjart seems to challenge us, than to show that by using words? The Fool's mental deficiency and Lear's spiritual decay, and the cacophony of his saxophone implies that the world swayed by him is irretrievably out of order. Shakespeare aptly makes the hero of his next tragedy compare man's life to 'a tale told by an idiot' (5.5). Deprived of the means to communicate with Cordelia, Lear kicks the Fool away in irritation. Lear tries one approach after another to make Cordelia dance with him again in happy harmony, but her reaction is worse than dead. Finally Lear sinks into his chair, his hands covering his face in desperation.

The next phase of Béjart's ballet is Cordelia's solo, accompanied by Bellini's aria from the second act of *I puritani*, 'O rendetemi la speme;/ O lasciantemi morir (Restore my hope, or let me die)' sung by Elvira who has lost her wits, finding herself rejected by her fiancé Arturo. We find Lear's senses have already been restored by driving the Fool away; the Cordelia he sees here is no longer 'the barbarous Scythian' (1.1.116) in his distorted imagination, but her real self discovered only after her death. For the first time Lear realizes that Cordelia kept lamenting the hard times awaiting her father, whose hope is no larger than that of a common old man:

> To shake all cares and business from our age,
> Conferring them on younger strengths, while we
> Unburthen'd crawl toward death.   (1.1.39-41)

In Lear's restored senses Cordelia is infinitely embellished, and Tamasaburo-Cordelia embodies a paragon of Mercy temporarily descended from high above. Yet the time comes when this ethereal being is to leave the earth; she has to die, as Bellini's song goes, since there is no place to nourish her hope. Her last moment by strangulation is to be enacted by adopting the postures of the kabuki dance *Sagi Musume* (*The Heron Maiden*), whose movements have in turn been influenced by Anna Pavlova's *Dying Swan*.[25] The dance shows not so much a physical agony as a spiritual one caused by the anxiety of leaving her old father behind.

Here again the Fool appears and makes an intruding noise with his saxophone. The father and daughter stand apart from each other, this time separated by the stagehands. We are brought back to the opening scene to review the outset of the tragedy after all our theatrical experience of its outcome. Lear calls, 'Cordelia!'; Cordelia answers, 'Iie, nani mo' (Nothing, my Lord). Again Lear calls her name, and her answer is the same, even more resolute than before.

Cordelia is sure that her love is more ponderous than her tongue (1.1.77), we are as sure that her love asks nothing in return, and Lear, who now is surer than anyone else after the reunion with Cordelia, recalls in deep remorse his former self that obstinately believed 'Nothing will come of nothing' (1.1.77-78,90). The old creature we see on stage fails to understand what the youngest daughter means, because he has forgotten God created the world *ex nihilo*,[26] and begins to grovel about on the ground like a beast in distress. As a substitute for the hoped-for love that says nothing, he reaches for the crown on the ground, and grasps what is nothing but 'polish'd perturbation' or 'golden care'. Holding the coronal calamity high above his head, 'the oldest [that] hath borne most' (5.3.326) falls back upon the cart and breathes his prolonged last. Together with the remorseful dreamer the vision of Cordelia dies, and returns to her original state of death, which worked as the heaviest weight upon her aged father.

What strikes us most in Béjart's Lear is the quiet resignation to his fate. We are not forced to share the successive agonies of the protagonists, but allowed to ruminate on them in a kind of cathartic liberation. This style of reproduction derives from the convention of *Noh* plays introduced into kabuki dances, where a ghost lingering in a particular place of some tragedy in the remote past re-enacts it in an introspective way. The music used there is lyrical rather than narrative, and the focus is on unfulfilled loves or defeated dreams rather than bloody actions.

In the same way the songs in Béjart's ballet reveal to us the secret yearning for the harmonious beauty hidden beneath the uproarious mess on the surface of Shakespeare's original. Rather than Lear's howling, which might crack heaven's vault, we hear Purcell's song that makes a modest request of letting him weep and sigh his soul away. Rather than Lear's reprobating rage in the opening scene, we hear Bellini's aria conveying Cordelia's suppressed sorrow. Even the fool's saxophone, which is to signify universal disorder, does not pierce our ears like a thunderstorm.

The comparative quietness may deprive the tragedy of dynamic violence, yet it does increase its depth almost endlessly in the choicest combination of music and choreography. For Purcell's complaint Béjart chose Alfred Deller's counter-tenor,[27] and for Elvira's aria Maria Callas's soprano.[28] Both were his favourites, and Béjart expects his audience to pay more attention and taste the tone of the voices of singers or actors than to the meaning of the words sung or spoken.[29] Besides the masterful skill Béjart demanded of the singer or the speaker 'imagination all compact' to fetch the audience 'from heaven to earth, from earth to heaven'.[30]

Deller was the right person to sing Lear's plaint; the ethereal quality of his matchless voice inspired Benjamin Britten to compose the part of Oberon the fairy prince in his opera, *A Midsummer Night's*

Dream,[31] and Béjart himself has selected Deller's *Agnus Dei* in Bach's
B minor Mass for his *Notre Faust* (1975) to convince the audience of
its power to atone for the sins accumulated by the hero. Deller's
'she's gone, she's gone', 'for ever, for ever', or 'never, never, never,
never, never', are not mere echoes of Lear's last words; it resounds
with his desperation *de profundi* and at the same time with the ' flight
of angels' that sing his afflicted soul to its rest.[32] Nor can we neglect
Callas's *soprano drammatico* in her best days, which can be *mater
dolorosa* and *Regina Coeli* at once; it 'sighs her soul away' and drives
the audience into the depth of despair, yet contains the mysterious
power to liberate herself from thence, together with those who
listen to her voice.

*   *   *

It is worthy of note that Shakespeare's main tragedies have a
common cause – the protagonists' frustrated hope of finding an
image of Madonna in the women who are closest to them.[33] Hamlet
yearns for it in his affectionate mother, Othello in his constant wife,
and Lear in his honest daughter. Their strong faith in their beloved
ones is almost equivalent to that in the Virgin Most Merciful,
Glorious and Powerful, through which they are to be saved from
their present state of depravity. Othello aptly describes it as:

> where I have garner'd up my heart,
> Where either I must live or bear no life;
> The fountain from the which my current runs,
> Or else dries up . . .   (4.2.58-60)

Hamlet loses his wit to find the place turned into 'an unweeded
garden/ That grows to seed', and possessed with 'things rank and
gross in nature' (1.2.135-37), through Gertrude's carnal 'frailty'.
Othello is driven to destroy it with his own hands when he believes
himself to have been 'discarded from thence . . . for foul toads / To
knot and gender in' (4.2.60-62). In the same way, all the bloody
incidents – Goneril and Regan's cruelty, Gloucester's blindness, and
Edgar's vagrancy – stem from Lear's failure to trust Cordelia's
sincerity. Here we may add that Lady Macbeth's unfailing constancy
simply helps Shakespeare's next hero to his ruin.

It cannot be overlooked that Lear is the only person among them to find such an image on earth and be allowed a reconciliation with it while he lives, however momentary it may be. Re-evaluated and revived for its existential heaviness by the survivors of the Second World War, the post-war productions of *King Lear* have paid little attention to this point.

Béjart's ballet is above all to be esteemed for offering us a cathartic effect and spiritual salvation, which many a director failed to read in Shakespeare's original. It has been accomplished, as we have observed, through the ritual or religious tradition of kabuki that is claimed to free the audience from their existential anxiety. With its origin in Shinto-related rites, kabuki dance still retains its religious characteristics when mediating between this world and the other, through the art of the actor-dancer who acts as a spiritualistic medium by enacting myths and symbols that transcend our daily life.

*   *   *

As Béjart aptly points out, both kabuki and ballet depend more largely on the actor or the dancer than on the director or the choreographer, since it is the former that gives material form to the idea of the latter. In this sense *La mort de Cordelia* owes its greater share of success to Tamasaburo, one of the most gifted actors in the world. Never confined within the small field of kabuki, his repertoire ranges from the ancient to the modern, from East to West, and between both sexes. As regards Shakespeare, he has played Lady Macbeth (1976) and Desdemona (1977), and directed *Romeo and Juliet* (1986). And in 1988 he began to dance Béjart's ballet as a special guest, with leading dancers such as Jorge Donn, Gil Roman and Patric Dupond, not to mention Béjart himself. Deeply impressed with the mysterious grace of Greta Garbo, Hollywood's first major romantic idol, his style of female impersonation is not restricted to the Japanese tradition.

Interestingly, this theatrical impact was not one-way but reciprocal; in her last years Garbo in fact went backstage for the first time, eager to see Utaemon VI, whose female role she declared 'the greatest single theatrical experience of her life'.[34] It is no wonder that female impersonators out-female the female, if we consider their centuries-long tradition of training to represent women as they should be, not as they are. Among the numerous heirs to this artistic legacy, Tamasaburo is estimated as second to none in enacting the fantasy of legendary myths and in making it believable with his graceful beauty.[35] No other actor or dancer would meet the demands for the part of Béjart's Cordelia so perfectly. Sanctified and idolized in Lear's vision, the performer must be ephemeral, ethereal and sorrowful, but at the same time as 'Merciful, Glorious and Powerful' and as tall.[36]

Béjart's bold challenge to extract the eighteen-minute essence from that monstrous colossus of Shakespeare was to be materialized through the ingenious movements of the unparalleled impersonator, who made an invaluable contribution to the aesthetic heightening and the philosophical deepening of the tragedy. The English Shakespeare and the Japanese kabuki – each born on a secluded island and which would have remained too local and foreign to each other – were to be incorporated into an organic whole, through the mediating art of a French choreographer, who has been a great lover of both, yet whose nationality and philosophy have kept him free from either conventions of intolerance.

Yet his ballet may not be utterly without problems; it may be that only a limited number of connoisseurs can fully appreciate its value, because its ritualistic symbolism requires some knowledge of both traditions. Béjart was probably well aware of this fact and of the need to compose a more elucidative performance for the wider multitude. Two months after the performance of *La mort de Cordelia*, he presented his new version of *King Lear*, at the dance festival of Montperrier. This is a full length ballet, danced and acted by as many persons as in Shakespeare's original, and has been combined with *The Tempest*, under the title of *King Lear-Prospero*. Here Béjart counterpoises the two old disposed father-princes and their dear daughters, Cordelia and Miranda,[37] in a way to persuade us to review the tragedy of the former as the painful labour necessary to give birth to the hopeful ending of the latter.[38] From here we may look back on *La mort de Cordelia* to realize with admiration that it could narrate no less of the tragedy, with so few characters, in such a short time, and virtually without words, yet through a transcendental mixture of East and West.

NOTES

1   Mark Ford, *Times Literary Supplement*, 1 April 1994.

2   Dieter Mehl, '*King Lear* in the Opera House' (*Shakespeare Cultural Traditions: The Selected Proceedings of the International Shakespeare Association World Congress, Tokyo, 1991*, Tetsuo Kishi et al. (eds), Newark: U of Delaware P, 1994, pp. 295-303.

3   Malcolm Hayes, *Sunday Telegraph*, 29 January 1989, 17, qtd. Jay L. Halio (ed.), *The Tragedy of King Lear*, The New Cambridge Shakespeare; Cambridge: Cambridge UP, 1992, 53.

4   Mehl 300.

5   Mehl 299.

6   Mehl 295-6.

7   Mehl 295.

8   Malcolm Hayes, *Sunday Telegraph*, 29 January 1989.

9   Béjart, *Un instant dans la vie d'autrui*, Tadashi Maeda (trans.), Paris: Flammarion, 1979; Tokyo: Geki Shobo, 1982, p. 76.

10   *Le songe d'une nuit d'hiver*: mus. Chopin, Paris, 1953.

11   *La mégère apprivoisée*: mus. O. Scarlatti, Paris, 1954.

12   *La douceur du tonnerre (Such Sweet Thunder)*: mus. Duke Ellington, télévision allemande, 1960.

13   *Roméo et Juliet*, mus. Berlioz, Brussels, 1966.

14   Béjart, *Un instant dans la vie*, p. 173.

15   See Béjart, *Un instant dans la vie*, pp. 168, 173.

16   Bugaku: *Bugaku* (mus. Mayuzumi) Tokyo ballet, Tokyo, 1989; Noh: *Leda* (mus. Japanese) Ballet du XXe Siècle, Brussels, 1979; Bunraku: *Le Marteau sans maître* (mus. Boulez), Ballet du XXe Siècle, Milan, 1973; Kabuki: *Kabuki* (mus. Mayuzumi) Tokyo ballet, Tokyo, 1986.

17   Leonard Pronko, *Theater East and West*.

18   Jean-Pierre Pastori, *Béjart: le tournant*, trans. Kazune Tatsumi: Pierre-Marcel Favre, Lausanne, 1987; Tokyo Ongakusha, 1990.

19   As to the similarity between the Ballets Russes and kabuki, see Leonard Pronko, *Theater East and West: Perspectives toward Total Theatre*, Berkeley: University of California Press, 1967.

20   Tokyo Ballet (ed.), *The Kabuki*, Tokyo: Shinshokan, 1986, p. 6.

21   Tokyo Ballet, *The Kabuki*, p. 6.

22   Béjart, *Un instant dans la vie*, p. 247.

23   All the quotations from Shakespeare are taken from *The Riverside Shakespeare*, Boston: Houghton Mifflin, 1974.

24   See Georges Banu, 'Tamasaburo or the Victory of Mannerism', *The Universe of Bando Tamasaburo*, Tokyo: Shinshokan, 1986, pp. 112-15.

25   Masaki Domoto, '*Sagi Musume*: Universal Myth of a Bird in Love's Inferno', *Engekikai (The Theatrical World)*, Tokyo: Engeki Shuppansha, October 1994, 52: 11, pp. 122-5. He points out that Kikugoro VI, deeply impressed with Pavlova's dance, introduced her technique into *Sagi Musume*, the spiritual attitude of which has been inherited by Tamasaburo.

26   Frank Kermode, *Riverside Shakespeare*, p. 1253.

27   Collected in *Music for a While*, Saint-Michel de Provence: harmonia mundi, 1979.

28   Recorded 24-30 March 1953, at the age of twenty-nine: cond. Tullio Serafin, with orchestra and chorus of La Scala, Milan.

29   Béjart, *Un instant dans la vie*, pp. 103-10.

30   See *A Midsummer Night's Dream*, 5.1.7-13.

31   *A Midsummer Night's Dream*, 1960.

32   See *Hamlet*, 5.2.360.

33   Dennis Kay, *Shakespeare: His Life, Work, Era*, London: Sidgwick, 1991, p. 19, is not decisive about his father's nonconformity, i.e. whether he was Puritan or Catholic. But Shakespeare's subconscious cult of the Holy Mary found in his plays strongly suggests the latter.

34   In 1960, when Utaemon made a highly successful tour of the United States in the troupe from Tokyo's Kabuki-za. See Pronko, pp. 128-9.

35   Watanabe, *The Fate of Female Impersonators*, Tokyo: Chikuma Shobo, 1991.

36   Here we would have to abandon the possibility of female actresses or dancers.

37   Béjart, *Le ballet des mots*, Archimbaud: Les Belles Lettres, 1994, pp. 474-5.

38   Critics have found a similarity between Cordelia and the heroines of Shakespeare's last plays, such as Marina, Perdita and Miranda, but almost exclusively regarded her sudden death pessimistically. See Robert S. Miola, *Shakespeare's and Classical Comedy: The Influence of Plautus and Terence*, Oxford: Clarendon Press, 1994, pp. 196-7.

11

FORUM: GENDER IN SHAKESPEARE AND KABUKI

CHAIRED BY TETSUO KISHI

Kishi: The phenomenon of the onnagata, wherein a man plays a woman's role, exists both in kabuki and in Shakespearean, or more broadly Elizabethan, theatre. Of course Elizabethan boy actors and kabuki onnagata are not necessarily identical Boy actors were just that – young boys – who played women's roles. In contrast, in the case of kabuki we have grown men playing women's roles. Also, and I think you will all agree, there are many other points of similarity between these two types of theatre apart from the fact that each uses men attired as women

Today we have invited scholars from Japan and abroad who are deeply versed in these and other types of theatre, so that they will freely discuss this phenomenon of male actors playing female roles. The members of the panel are Watanabe Tamotsu, Michael Shapiro, Hirata Mitsuo, Leonard Pronko and Anzai Tetsuo, and I will first ask each of them to speak freely about this topic for 15-20 minutes. Then I will ask Ann Thompson, who has agreed to join the panel at a later stage to comment on the topic.

Watanabe: I wish to lay out four points which I hope you will keep in mind when comparing kabuki with Shakespearean theatre. The first is that although many people may think of the onnagata as something belonging specifically to kabuki, such a view is incorrect. In modern Europe as well as in Japan, until the establishment of female actresses, men playing women's roles was the general rule. Such was certainly the case in Japan, where men played women's roles not only in kabuki, but in all classical theatre. This is true of both *nō* and *kyōgen*, as well as of the chanters and doll-handlers in *jōruri* puppet theatre. Kabuki as well was performed only by men, and I think there were religious reasons for this, because as an art form – as in many cultures – it was something dedicated to the gods, and therefore, it was necessary to make do with males only. It is but circumstantial that the onnagata as a specific art form still remains only in genres such as kabuki, the Beijing Opera and Koodiyattam in India. In principle, although we might go too far if we say that the onnagata is something universally shared by all human kind, it certainly is something that has existed all over the world. Consequently, I think we are being somewhat narrow if we extract the notion of onnagata only from kabuki and Shakespeare in order to make our comparison. It is also rather dangerous to discuss the onnagata in kabuki without looking at how woman's roles were performed in *nō*, or how they were recited in the puppet theatre – even though of course the term onnagata was not applied to these arts.

My second point is related to my own experience of watching kabuki. I first saw kabuki in 1941, and watched it passionately throughout the 1940s and 1950s. In those days, the women's roles were mostly played by wrinkly old men. In Japanese, we say that they were *ninsan bakéshichi*, three parts human and seven parts monster – that's how nasty they looked. For example, Sawamura Sōjurō VII, Nakamura Baigyoku III, and Kikugorō V, when they played onnagata in addition to their usual *tachiyaku* (male roles), were all quite grotesque – it was impossible to believe that they were really women. However, as one watched them, they actually became quite beautiful. A woman's spirit was reflected in them, and I think this spirit is the secret of the onnagata. Another example is the contemporary *nō* actor Tomoeda Kikuo, who is now in his eighties and cannot see well enough to get around by himself. However, when this man picks up a fan, stands on stage and does a woman's dance, he becomes a truly beautiful woman. If we cannot believe this, the very notion of the onnagata is meaningless.

Nevertheless, in the past fifty years since the Second World War, a big change has occurred, wherein onnagata like Baikō, Utaemon

Jyakuemon and Tamasaburō have come to look more and more like actresses. My point is that we must not overlook this change. It is not that pre-war onnagata were simply grotesque, but in the cases of actors like Utaemon V, Baikō VI, and Gennosuke IV, they were *men*. You watched their acting on the premise that it was a man playing the part. Today however, the fact that it is a man playing the part has been erased, deleted. This is the change in premises that has occurred over the past fifty years, and we ought to keep this in mind.

My third point is that we must understand that through all the wrinkles, onnagata acting is not a matter of mimicking women but one of semiotics. We have to regard it in terms of the semiotics of womanhood. It was something made into a detailed system of signifiers. Of course, the Genroku period (1688-1703) onnagata Yoshizawa Ayame said that if one did not live everyday life as a woman one could not produce feminine sensuality. Well, at least he is reported to have said such a thing. In any case the point is that the onnagata possesses an essentially semiotic nature, and that is a rather modern view. Here lies the essence of the onnagata, and not at all in the mimicking of women.

My fourth point is that if we do not grasp this semiotic nature, that wrinkly old man on stage can never become miraculously beautiful. We must understand the *gei* by which this occurs. Today, *gei* is usually translated as 'acting technique', but the two are not exactly the same. Whereas *engi* is a kind of technique, *gei* includes the actor's whole life, wherein one takes up a certain stance on stage and acts out a woman's role. It's like in the case of the recently deceased Onoe Baikō, who offstage played baseball and golf and drove a car. When he stepped on stage he became a woman. He held a certain stance, and moreover when on stage, Baikō's life shone through. This is the particular nature of *gei*, and without understanding its structure, we will end up viewing the onnagata merely as a matter of technique and fail to grasp what it truly is: a type of *gei*.

In order to arrive at a better understanding, then, I hope that you will use these four points as a reference when comparing kabuki to Shakespearean theatre.

Shapiro: There are several advantages of the comparison that we have been doing these last few days and for some years. For many of us who were brought up with the Shakespearean tradition, as I was, kabuki is a jolt. It really liberates the imagination. It takes us into a form that is much more presentational than most forms of theatre we are used to in the West, and while we cannot say that it is the same as the way things were done in Shakespeare's day, it certainly frees up our imagination and our thinking about the theatre. As there is only so much we can learn from the records, and, of course, no one has ever seen an Elizabethan play by boys, it is quite true, so I think, that it helps us in reconstructing Elizabethan theatre to encounter a tradition where female impersonation is different and still vital. One of the things that struck me in the course of this meeting is how many more dimensions there are to kabuki than I realized. That is, it is not one thing. It has evolved over time and it is different in different places because there are local traditions. And I gather that there is probably a lot to be learned about the older forms from the study of local traditions where those older forms are preserved.

One of the things that I learned and saw again is the importance of the appreciation of virtuosity. When people go to the theatre, they go for lots of reasons, and one of the reasons in many cases is to see their favourite performers, performers whom they have admired, whose work they know, and whose lives they may know something about too. Of course, the other reason to go is to immerse ourselves in the passionate story that is being unfolded before our eyes. Now these two modes, virtuosity and, let us say story-telling, are both very compelling, and what I like to see in kabuki performances is that there's no embarrassment about the appreciation of virtuosity. We are invited to applaud; we cannot help ourselves, because it is so interesting at several points. I think that's quite helpful, and at the same time we do not lose our interest and engagement in what is being depicted, and that's one issue that I think could be explored not only with regard to female impersonation but also in many other ways with respect to our two traditions.

The other point I wanted to raise has to do with the relation of cross-gender attire onstage and offstage. These are of course very different things, and, I think, it's not fully appreciated just how complicated this is. For example, women regularly cross-dress in Elizabethan drama. Shakespeare should, I think, be considered in all of our discussions as a shorthand for all the Elizabethan drama. There are about seventy heroines who cross-dress and become men, and it is done for wonderful reasons and usually with very benevolent happy results. Any women who tried to do this in the streets of London risked being arrested. There are some cases that have recently come to light. The magistrates of London periodically sentenced women who were found wearing male attire to Bridewell prison and treated them as if they were prostitutes, whether there was any other evidence of prostitution or not. In one interesting case, a woman was meeting her lover who never showed up, and was hauled off to the court and sentenced to a whipping. So I think the attitudes offstage to cross-dressing were quite different, and the playhouse is a magic space where things can be suspended.

This is not quite the same for men. It is is very asymmetrical. When men in the Elizabethan society cross-dressed, as in various sorts of rural festivities, the important thing to be remembered was that it was always for a time, it was always limited in duration. The man who was caught cross-dressing by the Bridewell magistrates was simply slapped on the wrist and told to get a job, get a master, or get out of the town and stop his folly. That is, he wasn't sentenced to Bridewell to be whipped. So he was treated rather differently than a cross-dressing woman. Of course onstage it was perfectly acceptable, because we were told over and over again that this is only for a time. What I find quite interesting is that there seems to be a change at some point in the way onnagata saw themselves, and several of us have quoted the similar passages from Ayame, who instructs the onnagata to live his life as a woman and then immerse himself in the role. So it is first imitating a woman, who was then playing the role, but that seems not to be the case today, and one wonders what difference that has made in performance and style. So I think there is much more to explore here, and I think kabuki scholars, too, perhaps could tell us more about offstage cross-dressing. I assume this has been studied by Japanese scholars, because it is a hot topic everywhere in the world. Again, the relationship between the rather restricted legalistic view of the social world and the more permissive or playful view on the stage, if that is the case in the Japanese theatre, would also be very interesting to explore.

One more word if I may. Before I came, I read an early book on kabuki by Faubion Bowers. He dealt with the question of whether there was any moment when it would have been possible to introduce women. Three onnagata were asked, 'Could they, could women enter kabuki?' One said: 'That's totally absurd, they have me, and I can present women much better than women can.' The second one, who was apparently more rebellious in his view, something of a maverick, said: 'I think it would be a good idea, kabuki could use the authoritative realism of women.' And the third one said: 'It's too late. Perhaps a hundred years ago we might have done it. It might have been a good idea, but it's now too late, because kabuki has created an ideal woman, idealized woman, or stylized woman as it creates a stylized man, and that system now can't be changed.' So it seems to me that there's more fluidity in the kabuki tradition than I was aware of. That's been interesting to me.

Hirata: It seemed to me that throughout the conference to this point, many people were thinking of the onnagata as a rather unique form. Others seem simply to be thinking that if a man takes the form of a woman, then that is an onnagata. In England, though really in all of Europe, women were of course not used in the drama of the Middle Ages, which was the primary dramatic current leading up to Shakespeare. The oldest surviving religious play is *The Visit to the Sepulchre* dated about 970, dealing with the three women named Maria (Mary Magdalene, Mary the Mother of James, and Mary Salome) who go searching for the crucified Christ in his tomb. A play such as this was enacted inside monasteries, and thus these three Marys were of course played by men. There is an Angel who calls out when the women approach, and this too is played by a man. My point is that from the beginning, women were played by men. We can say it was this way because these were religious plays, but this tradition continued in various forms down into Shakespeare's time.

This is not simply a problem of using men in women's roles; it relates to the very meaning of theatre, to the question of what we can achieve with theatre. Religious theatre, after all, tries in various ways to grasp the meaning of living human beings existing on earth between Heaven and Hell, and the influence of such religious theatre is clearly seen in Shakespeare. There are numerous portions of Shakespeare's plays that cannot be fully understood realistically – they are not that kind of play. To give one example that is well-known even by those who haven't studied much in English literature, let us recall the courthouse scene in *The Merchant of Venice*.

In this scene, Portia urges Shylock, who intends to stay his bond, to be merciful. He refuses, and insists on taking a pound of flesh from Antonio's bosom. This quite excites Shylock, and as he bares Antonio's chest, he flourishes his knife and makes as if to kill him. At this point Portia tells him to wait, and tells him that for such-and-such reasons his bond cannot be executed, that his fortune will be confiscated, that he must become a Christian. Performing this kind of scene is really rather strange when you try it. What's strange is that Portia knows from the beginning that if she follows such a course of action she can dupe Shylock and win the trial. Nevertheless, she allows Antonio's chest to be bared, and lets Shylock flourish his knife. Only at this point does she tell him to wait. Portia is an extremely clever woman who understands what's going on, so why must she wait so long?

Of course, here a boy actor is playing the part of Portia. When acting out this scene, the actor playing Portia has to carefully move the action along without revealing the fact that the whole thing is a lie, and if this is not done correctly, the fact that it is all a lie stands out, and the scene is ruined. What I am saying is that if an actress was to play this scene following the psychology of a real woman, it would not work at all. Portia is here a symbol of Grace or God's forgiveness, standing opposed to the Devil Shylock who is attempting to persecute Christians. She thus transcends realistic womanhood and expresses the principles of God. Portia is therefore not really a woman. She is neither woman nor man. The Portia of the trial scene exists on an altogether different level. In that way she can contest Shylock on his level. It was the boy actor that was used to portray this otherworldly, out-of-the-ordinary role and I think the result was quite different than the realism that would be brought by a woman actress.

If we look for similar examples in kabuki, we see that nearly all plays follow a like pattern. There are many female roles in kabuki, but most of them are not concerned with the imitation of a real woman. Many onnagata roles appear in connection to a transcendent other-world – the world of death, for instance – something apart from the everyday. One example is *The Maiden at Dojoji Temple* (*Kyokanoko musume dojoji*). In this play, a very beautiful maiden, a dancer, appears and does her dance, but this is actually the spirit of the maiden Kiyohime, whose love was refused by the Dojoji priest Anchin. And her spirit later appears in the form of a snake.

There are many other such examples. For instance, there is the dance *Shiokumi* (*The Seawater Scooper*). This is a kabuki dance wherein a woman gathers water from the sea in order to make salt, and it is performed with a bucket used for that purpose. This is of course not the realistic depiction of a labouring girl scooping water, but the dance of the spirit of the woman Matsukaze, who was jilted by her lover Ariwara Narihira long ago. This is why Matsukaze often enters through the trapdoor of the *hanamichi* runway. This *suppon-guchi* is a small hole that opens in the runway, and only beings that are not of this world enter or exit through this. No regular worldly characters ever use that entrance. This entrance is intentionally made as a passageway to other worlds. Kabuki possesses this kind of implement to allow interaction with such worlds. This of course points to the nature of kabuki as a whole, and not the onnagata in particular, but to return to that discussion, I think that Mr Watanabe put it well when he said that the onnagata is one big signifier.

I think we can say that what we have in the onnagata is one collective signifier made from strapping various other signifiers onto the male body. In relation to costume, for example, there is a code by which every wig corresponds to a certain role. Meanings are decided, so that when a certain wig is worn, or certain make-up or kimono used, we know what kind of woman is being portrayed. All these things carry their own semiotic meaning. When an onnagata wears a '*kokumochi*' kimono of yellowish green with white circles visible upon it, we know that she is a country girl. O-mitsu from *Nozaki* wears this kind of kimono. When the *kokumochi* is an auburn colour, we know the character is the wife of a masterless samurai such as Tonami in *Terakoya* (*The Temple School*). Everything is codified semiotically, so that a young girl of the town has a certain way of moving, walking and sitting, and the wife of a samurai has her own way of walking, sitting, using her sleeves. When these various codes or signifiers are collected together and attached to the male body, we have the basic form of the onnagata, and this, combined with an animating *gei*, forms the onnagata technique. So the onnagata is something produced by a man employing these signifiers, something created – not an imitation of something real.

People often speak of the characteristic beauty of the onnagata, that in the case of the onnagata there is created a beauty that a woman cannot achieve. While this is certainly true in some cases, for me, the special characteristics of the onnagata, when compared to the female actress, are rather size and strength. The great *shingeki* (new drama) actress Sugimura Haruko once said something like this. In her younger days, she was doing a play – *Many Passions, Buddha Heart* (*Tajō Busshin*), I think it was – where she worked with the great *shimpa* onnagata Hanayanagi Shōtarō – there are onnagata in the *shimpa* too. During rehearsal, she said, she thought nothing much of it, but when the day of performance came, and Shōtarō appeared in the costume of the townsgirl, with make-up, wig, and kimono, Sugimura was overwhelmed. What is interesting is that she says something like 'It's just that onnagata are so large. The musculature is different. They're big. It's spectacular when something that large emerges, and I think that it's this size which forms the basis of the onnagata.' This size is transformed into strength, which is then transformed into beauty. And this beauty is different than the beauty of an actress or a woman. I think that the onnagata succeeds because of the strength he possesses.

Pronko: I want to talk mainly about a sort of comparison between onnagata and boy actors. There has been a long tradition, actually, of female impersonation in the West, as was already suggested. I would like to remind us of how in 1909 or 1910, Clyde Fitch, a very famous American playwright of his day was described by one of his actresses in this way: 'Not a woman among us could approach him in look, manner, and above all, voice.' Because he impersonated women so well, he taught the women he was directing in his own plays how to perform women. A hundred years earlier

Goethe saw men performing as women, in Rome, and was very charmed and satisfied by them. Of course, it goes back much further, but what I mainly want to talk about, of course, is the boy actors and how they differ from and how they are the same, perhaps, as the onnagata. Of course, as you know, we know very little about them, so I am talking in the empty air perhaps. One way in which the results of these traditions in the West and the East have been very different has been that while in the West there have been, we might say, no results, in the East, in Japan for example, there was the establishment of a tradition. There was a transmission from generation to generation, finally ending up in a tradition, a tradition of patterns, highly codified patterns. In the West that did not exist.

Today, we might say there are two kinds of onnagata. Two kinds, at any rate, in their daily lives. There are onnagata who live offstage virtually as women. Not entirely – it's very difficult to do that, I think – but virtually. They speak women's language, they prefer the company of men, as a woman probably would, and so forth. They virtually are living as women, you might say and are perhaps projecting some of that in their roles on the stage. There are others like Onoe Baikō, one of the very top onnagata of the twentieth century who, as I believe Mr Watanabe described, drove his own car, played baseball and was very interested in sports, and that sort of thing. He was a regular man offstage, but onstage he was the perfect embodiment of womanhood of many different kinds because the onnagata of course includes a vast range. So what these two kinds of onnagata share is this code; they all use similar patterns. I am being careful, so I am not going to say the same, but similar patterns. They are all patterns, highly codified and derived from reality itself.

And what about the boys? We know nothing. So we cannot say anything about the boy actors in the Elizabethan drama. What I would like to look at a little is the conditions that might influence our way of assuming how these people played. One main condition that prevailed among the boys is that their art of performing as women was temporary. It lasted five or six years, ten years at the most, I should think. It was also brief in the sense that it only lasted until 1642 when boys were outlawed in women's roles when the theatres were closed. And many of them, if they continued at all in the theatre, changed to playing men's roles. So they really had a very brief history as performers of women's roles. And of course they were playing when they were very very young. This age suggests that they were using their natural charm, their natural femininity what was natural to a boy of thirteen, fourteen or fifteen, their natural voice, their natural sexuality. So they were in what you could even call 'feminine adolescence'. They had not yet become men, so they did not need to devise a code.

Therefore, I'm suggesting that women were performed by the boys in a much more natural way than the onnagata. The onnagata, on the other hand, it seems to me, embodies high artifice through these codes, these very complex codes. The authors of the Elizabethan theatre were very confident in the skill of the boys. To have written the role of Cleopatra or the role of the Duchess of Malfi for a fourteen- or fifteen-year-old boy certainly suggests that these young men or these boys were capable of very skilful acting. And for Cleopatra to have said, 'Some squeaking Cleopatra will boy my greatness', she expresses that here. For the boy playing Cleopatra to dare to say such a thing, which will remind the audience automatically that he was a boy playing Cleopatra, shows the skill that Shakespeare counted on in that boy. Because that boy was so convincing as Cleopatra, no doubt, that people could hear that and say 'Yes' and immediately forget that it was a boy speaking those lines and go on believing in the reality of Cleopatra. I think this arises from the fact not only of their skill but because the audiences have always been able – well perhaps not the twentieth-century Western audience who has been bred on television and films which are by and large very realistic, so they believe that the actor is the role – but with anybody else who has gone to the theatre and has been brought up in the theatre and in any age in which the theatre has dominated before film and television, I think that audiences must have enjoyed this double quality, this double awareness of the actor and the character at the same time, and revelled in it. It is what Gary Schmidgall, in a magnificent book called *Shakespeare and Opera*, calls the Gemini factor. That is, I say, this doubleness, that it always exists. He speaks of the inescapable twinning of the role and the performer. Consistency of the effect is out of the question because the two dramaturgies – he is speaking of Opera and Shakespeare, but I think it applies to kabuki as well – because the two dramaturgies are magnificently inconsistent and unnatural in their pressure on performers to run against utterly prosaic normalcy to the heights of purple patch, blank verse, coloratura, and fireworks. So there was presentational acting that appeared natural and perhaps sometimes outrageous.

The boys had a training that might have reminded us of something similar to kabuki. Robertson Davies speaks of the boys' training, including dance, song, costume wear, how to put on the luxurious costumes they wore, fencing, and so forth, but if you compare this to the kind of complex training kabuki actors receive, it rather dwindles, it seems to me. A second, totally different way of viewing these two things is the social context, the sexual context as a matter of fact. Sexuality in England at that time, it seems to me, and in the West by and large recognized no sexual categories. People never thought of defining themselves by what their sexual attitudes were, it wasn't part of a personal identity. So moralists and others accused these boys of being beautiful and of being convincing, which makes me think that they may have been very convincing. One traveller in Italy expressed some surprise that women in Italy actually performed as well as the boys did. So that is rather convincing too. But this, along with their youth, points to a rather realistic portrayal: would the thirteen-year-old boys try to create an androgynous character? I don't think so. Whereas in Japan, the climate was very different. In Japan at that time there was actually the recognition of homosexuality. It may not have had a name but the whole way of life, the *paederastaia* of the Greeks, was replicated, you might say, in Japan in the *wakashūdō* or the *shūdō*, the 'way of male love'. Paul Schalow has brilliantly written of this in his introduction to a translation of Saikaku's *The Great Mirror of Male Love*. This makes us realize that the young boys who began in the kabuki tradition by playing women, in the *wakashū* period, came into kabuki as catamites. They came from brothels by and large, and even though authorities may have forbidden such actors in 1642, they continued to feed in through the brothels, and they continued to practise both their offstage art and beyond-stage art. I don't see how they could have developed beyond-stage art without having some sort of influence from their life offstage. What would the difference have been? The difference would have been that these young men were engaging in sexual activities in which they were playing the woman's role, and therefore they were able to identify with the woman because they were on the bottom. At the same time they realized that biologically they were male, and therefore it seems to me they might have brought into the kabuki this androgyny, this mingling of both the male and the female. Indeed, what we see in the creation of the kabuki onnagata is something that is almost other-worldly And one of the reasons, I think, as so many people say, the reason why women simply cannot perform the women's roles in kabuki is that we are so used to that other-worldly character, that something strange, something sometimes grotesque, but something different about the onnagata. If you lose that, you lose an important part, I think, of the flavour of kabuki.

So the boy actor knew women as the other, whereas the kabuki catamite discovered himself as the woman and was able to work that into his impersonation or his recreation of the woman. What I'm finally saying is that the boy actor was perhaps more natural than the *wakashū*, and that the tradition that developed out of that, because that role continued despite the fact that it was separated from the brothel traditions. Still, the tradition was born then and it has continued to develop. It is more artificial, I would say. But whenever we say that a performance is artificial or a performance is natural, we are obviously oversimplifying, because the audiences, as I suggested in the beginning of this little ramble, can take in both the ying and the yang. As Eric Bentley has reminded us many times, acting is both natural and artificial, but to the extent that it is good, it is notably neither.

Kishi: The discussion has become a bit technical, so I would like to explain a few points. As I'm sure many of you know, theatre troupes in Elizabethan England could broadly he divided into two types. The first, which included Shakespeare's company, was basically one made up of adult men, but where boys played the female roles. The second type was made up solely of boy actors, and in that case they played both female roles and adult male roles. So I think a different semiotic problem arises depending on whether we are considering adult and boy actors working together, or a boys' troupe wherein the actors play both men's and women's roles. If time permits, it would be good to have a clarification of this difference. On to Professor Anzai.

Anzai: I have been forced into a corner, in terms of time as well the scope of problems to address, but I will try to tie some things together. At the beginning, we began with the idea that onnagata and boy actors were in some sense unique, but we've come to see that men playing women's roles is not really very unique, but rather something universal. Historically speaking, it is actresses who are really the exception. Nowadays, we think it only natural for actresses to play women's roles, but that is a prejudice of modern theatrical theory. Seen in the context of the long history of theatre considered as a whole, since ancient Greece, or even from the very birth of the theatre, it is rather this that is exceptional, even abnormal. The background of the notion that actresses should play female roles is a view of theatre as representational, as the representation of reality as realism. I think we can say that this is one of the conventions of theatre that was produced by bourgeois civil society. In order to put the entire history of theatre in proper perspective, however, we should understand *this* view as being unique.

What I mean with the term 'representational' in relation to the actress is the premise that a real woman should be represented on stage through the raw material of the female body. Of course, it is not at all the case that a great actress necessarily uses her technique to expose her real, living self, but the premise here is that of the representation of reality through the use of the actor's living, physiological or physical flesh. But if not in modern theatre, at least in kabuki, and in other kinds of traditional theatre, the acting body is by no means the raw material of the physiological or physical flesh. The latter has no theatrical meaning. We can only begin to speak of the acting body once the physical body becomes a vessel or mediator that channels something beyond the everyday. From this point of view, it is not even necessary that the actor be a human being. There's no reason at all why it must be a person. Think of the puppet theatre, as in the *jōruri*, or as in earlier theatres, in which masks were employed. Masks were employed in Greek tragedy, in the *nō*, and in other types of classical theatre as well – in fact, their use was nearly universal, although, of course, usually only certain types of characters wore them. The wearing of masks was a device to sublimate the physical body into an artistic or fictional body. Take this idea to its extreme and you have puppet theatre, such as the *jōruri* or the shadow puppets of Bali, wherein the raw material is a figure carved out of wood. They may be adapted in various ways to look like humans, but at bottom they aren't human, they are just wooden figures, *things*. Nevertheless, at the right moment these become something not to *represent*, but to *present*, out-of-the-ordinary existence. It is in that moment, I think, that the actor is born.

At least in the case of Japanese *jōruri* there is this kind of religious background. The doll is a medium to channel spirits from beyond, spirits that descend and take possession of it. The puppet is a tool or apparatus by which to channel spirits. I see *jōruri* as an art that arose out of such a shamanistic background, and I think that basically the same transformation is taking place in the physical body of an actor. The actor is not the physical body. It is the medium which brings into itself an other-worldly existence, being of a wholly different level. Therefore, either wooden figures or humans can suffice. To put it another way, when the body of the actor comes to take on the same qualifications as the puppet, such a transformation can take place, and it is through such a transformation that the actor becomes truly human, or that the human becomes actor. Therefore, maybe we should say that the basis of acting technique is metamorphosis, transformation, or even transubstantiation. At least in the case of Japan, the phenomenon of shamanistic possession existed as a prototype, and it was through the repetition, imitation, and recreation of this prototype that the dramatic arts were born. I think that this appears in a much more direct form in the *nō* than in kabuki, as in the play *Izutsu*.

The main point is hence that the fundamental moment wherein the theatre was established had metamorphosis or transformation as its guiding principle. This is not just something that lay at the roots of theatre, but rather something that is still now actually working in the creation of actual plays. This is repeated in the creation of drama. That is to say, it constitutes the plays themselves, or to put it more clearly, is written into their texts in a meta-theatrical sense. To give simple examples, in the case of kabuki, there are transfiguration motifs such as *miarawashi*, wherein the true identity of a character is revealed, *modori*, wherein a character who seems to be evil reveals his true, original, good nature, and *yatsushi*, when a person of wealth or noble family appears in humble disguise. It is really from the layering up of such transformations that kabuki plays are composed, as with the changes in costume that express, say, that the true form of a certain character is in fact a fox. I believe that theatre is a passageway between this world and the world beyond and in this sense the actor's physical or physiological body is merely the material existing at a stage prior to theatre, and by passing through this basic transformation, the living material body of the actor becomes the true acting body. If we understand the matter in this way, the onnagata, wherein a man is transformed into a woman, becomes but one very stark, obvious example of this fundamental premise of transformation.

Kishi: I think that Professor Anzai's discussion had several points in common with that of Professor Watanabe earlier. Although he did not use the word himself, I think we can interpret his comments as saying that it is *imagination* that is the essence of the theatre, and that the onnagata can be seen as one extreme form of that. Our first round is now completed, and I would like to turn to Professor Thompson for her comments.

Thompson: Thank you. Since I am, as you will be aware, a last-minute addition to this panel I will briefly introduce myself. My name is Ann Thompson. I was at the World Congress in Tokyo in 1991, but I did not get to the session on Shakespeare and kabuki. I'm primarily here as a feminist critic, and this presents me with a problem. What exactly is the point of entry for a feminist critic into the theatrical traditions we have been discussing? We have heard several times over the last two or three days that only men can understand femininity, only men can enact women. We did notice in Professor Pronko's workshop yesterday that women have to be taught to walk like women. And a good thing too, I think, in that to walk like a woman in the way that was being demonstrated, the way of kabuki drama, is to accept a degree of self-effacement and physical restriction that is totally appalling to a modern woman. So there are problems, I think, about approaching all this as a woman.

Something else we have been told that emerges from kabuki is that in kabuki men can manage without women, and that this is apparently all right. That is also the message of some of Shakespeare's plays. I think it is also the message of the *As You Like It* epilogue. That epilogue, if it is a man who is speaking that epilogue performing as Rosalind, puts women in their place. Women are all right in the audience, but, the performer shows, there are no women on the stage. We are all right if we are sitting down and paying our money. We are not all right if we are up here performing. So, I feel, I have just about marginally got onto the stage. This is a difficult position.

I was asked to comment on the other speaker's comments, so I just want to raise a few issues which for me have emerged from the conference as a whole but also from the presentation this afternoon. I have been very struck by the differences between what goes on in Shakespeare in terms of cross-gender casting and cross-dressing and what goes on in kabuki. I suppose we have all looked for common ground. Those of us who knew very little about kabuki when we were invited to come here have read up on kabuki and we have looked for points in common to be able to compare. But actually it occurs to me that there are enormous differences and that we might want to think about those as well. We've been looking at various sorts of asymmetries. That's the first thing that struck me.

There are asymmetries between what happens when a man dresses as a woman and what happens when a woman dresses as a man. They are not equivalent activities in terms of status, gender hierarchy, and so forth. They are not equivalent actions in real life, as Professor Shapiro has just said that it is not taken very seriously in the case of a man. It was taken very seriously in Jacobean England in the case of women, and this is precisely because of status. Women of that time dressing as men were threatening a hierarchy, they were threatening to get out of place. For a man to dress as a woman does not threaten anything. So that is an issue, and there are all sorts of other isssues to do with asymmetry, to do with things that are not the same in the theatrical tradition, not the same according to whether you are thinking about men or thinking about women.

I am interested also in the religious origins of drama, to which we keep coming back, and the extent to which that is operating as a common denominator between East and West and as a kind of reason why men should be performing. That came up in the presentations just given by Professor Watanabe, Professor Hirata, and Professor Anzai. I am slightly puzzled by this as to why it is assumed that it is appropriate for men to perform within drama if drama is seen as a religious activity, particularly within Eastern religions where it is not necessarily the case that all the gods are male. There ought surely to be room for a female religious drama in a context in which there are goddesses as well as gods. I don't think we should simply take it for granted that it is perfectly natural for religious drama to be performed only by men.

Another major issue that has come up all the time is this question of symbolism versus naturalism. How far is it the case that the Elizabethan and Jacobean theatre is striving towards naturalism in using boys for women whereas the kabuki tradition is striving towards contrivance, towards a kind of very elaborate impersonation which is not naturalism but which is something else, which is striving to get at some kind of essence of femininity, which we are told is not something possessed or capable of being performed by women. Professor Pronko was talking about the natural femininity of the boy and the way that the Shakespearean theatre exploits what is seen as a natural femininity on the part of an adolescent boy. I think it is slightly odd to say that somehow adolescent boys are naturally feminine and somehow have to be taught to become men. He then contrasted that with the contrivance of the onnagata, but in that side of the onnagata tradition whereby performers are encouraged to behave as women offstage, it was being maintained that femininity therefore precedes the role, and that somehow the onnagata also is naturally feminine and is therefore capable of enacting a woman on stage, but it is happening offstage as well. I found that a curious sort of parallel, something that began to look like a contrast but turns out to be a similarity

Finally, the final point here that I would like to make regards the defence, I suppose, of these traditions in terms of history. We are told that in most world dramas there has been a period, perhaps quite a long period, when drama has been exclusively something that men do. The assumption seems to be that this makes it all right, and I think that as a feminist, it is my role in this context to say I am not sure if it does. The appeal to history is a pretty problematic one for me, because it is also the case that in most real life societies women have been oppressed by men, and that, I think we would all now agree, does not make it all right. There is a problem about the preservation of these theatrical traditions. When I saw an all-male production of Shakespeare's *As You Like It*, I found it very exciting. I found it had another level to which it would not get with a mixed cast. But does that mean I would want to say, 'Well, women should stop acting Shakespeare?' I think there is a problem in terms of modern equal opportunities legislation about that and there is another problem about one's position as a feminist about that. Equally, I can see of course that a skill would be lost if men stopped acting as women in the kabuki tradition, but I do not see why you could not also have all-women kabuki. I do not see why you could not reverse the genders the other way. I do not see why we cannot have, similarly, all-women productions of Shakespeare. So I do not want to seem that I am being totally negative about the whole thing, but I have my doubts about some of the arguments we heard.

Kishi: Thank you. Professor Thompson's remarks both functioned as commentary and also raised several new problems. As to the question of whether there exists a female kabuki, there is an art form in Japan called the Takarazuka Revue, and though it is not exactly kabuki, in it, all of the players are women. They are not just any women actresses, but I think they enter the troupe at high school age. It includes women from their late teens up to rather great ages, and they also sometimes perform kabuki-based plays. I mention this just as a reference.

From now, the discussants will have an opportunity to add to their previous remarks or to comment on what the others have said. Professor Thompson asked just now why it is that the three Japanese panellists here have claimed that, because of the religious foundations of theatre, it is natural that only men appear in it. Would any of you like to respond? Professor Hirata?

Hirata: I would not exactly say that it is natural. In the case of European theatre, of Shakespeare, the religious drama at its roots emerged from the church. The Christian church, that is, which was presided over by men. That is the point, I think. In the case of kabuki, the main reason is that, while it was originally performed by women, that was outlawed, and so next came *yaro* kabuki, performed by male actors.

Pronko: Yes. I would like to give a sort of an answer to Professor Thompson based on something Professor Shapiro said. He was quoting a book by Faubion Bowers in which he quoted three kabuki actors, one of whom said that if a hundred years ago we had tried to bring women into kabuki it might have been possible but that it was no longer possible today. And that book was written in 1955 or so, I guess. So that would mean that in the 1850s, before Meiji in other words, if they had wanted to do that it might have been all right, and perhaps it would have been. In fact maybe it was moving in that direction, I do not know. But the truth of the matter is that in Meiji, in contact with the West the Japanese finally turned kabuki into what many people would now agree is a kind of museum art. In other words it coagulated. It froze. And it lost the freedom to constantly develop because what had been characteristic of kabuki from the very beginning up until the beginning of Meiji was that it constantly changed. It never stayed the same. It always took advantage of whatever traditions, whatever new popular music, whatever kind of popular dance, whatever trend was in the air, because it depended on popular support and so it grew constantly by change. If you look at kabuki in 1830 it is quite different from kabuki in 1750, and that is quite different from kabuki in 1700 which is radically different from kabuki in 1650. So while kabuki was still pliable and plastic and open and alive, then possibly it could have changed, just as, I suppose you might say, a painter, while he is alive might have been convinced to use some other colours, but once he is dead you would not say 'Well, we don't like the colours. We think it's not fair that he never used red, so we are going to paint this red into these pictures.' Something like that. Now that is radical, I agree, as a comparison, but it is very difficult to change kabuki now because it has reached a shape that is more or less definitive.

Fortunately, there are people who are trying to change it. Ennosuke is one of them. I am not sure he is always going in the right direction, but sometimes he is, I am sure. So it still might be made pliable enough that one day it could be opened to that, because Ennosuke has opened it to other things that people had thought perhaps impossible. I would also like to mention women's kabuki. We know that women were outlawed in 1629, but what most people do not remember is that women's troupes continued. They were not allowed to perform publicly, but they were allowed to perform in private, in the mansions of nobles and other places. I do not know enough about it to speak definitively on it, but I do know that it continued for some time, and I do know that before the war in this country, before the Second World War in the twentieth century there were still women's kabuki troupes somewhere. Now whether there was a tradition that had continued from 1629 until then, I am not sure. It might have been broken and then started again separately.

There are also women's kabuki troops in the United States and in Hawaii. One woman, Fujima Kantsuma, from whom I learned kabuki dance first in the United States, was a magnificent dancer. She was studying under Kikuguro VI, was a member of one of those troupes, and played men as well as any men I have ever seen on the stage. So there is that tradition too. It is still alive. I was also going to mention the Takarazuka, but Professor Kishi brought it up. When he mentioned it there was quite a bit of laughter in the room. I am wondering whether the laughter derived from the same feelings that I have, that although it is at a totally different level from kabuki somehow, I like the Takarazuka. I would not go every month, but I do enjoy going once every time that I am in Japan. I think that it is a very highly refined, in many ways, art, especially in the revues. But when I compare the women who play the men's roles in Takarazuka with the men who play the women's roles in kabuki, I don't find the women very convincing. But then I ask myself maybe they are not intended to be. I think they are playing more on the line between the sexes, even more than the kabuki onnagata is.

Kishi: Thank you. I previously mentioned the Takarazuka Revue, and while listening to these last statements I recalled the Ichikawa Girls Kabuki. Mr Watanabe, does that still exist?

Watanabe: I think there are still a few people left but before going on to that discussion, I think we ought to review the historical facts surrounding this problem. Female kabuki certainly has existed. Kabuki performed by prostitutes existed long before even the Genroku period, but this was basically a promotion by brothels in order to sell their women. At the time it was not illegal, but was open to the general public. However, while this was certainly kabuki, it was performed on the premise that after it was over men could purchase the services of the actresses. Therefore, I think it is a stretch to discuss this on the same level as contemporary kabuki. It is held that the originator of kabuki was Okuni from Izumo, and while she was certainly a woman, it is important to note that on stage she played male roles. There were not women who played female roles in the theatre.

Also, the Fujima Kantsuma who was just mentioned was not a kabuki actor, but a dancer. It is a fact that there were women dance masters in Edo. They would go to the homes of the feudal lords and perform kabuki there, and were known as 'Kyogen Masters'. These performances were not public, and were kind of an extension of the dance. They were a different thing than the actual kabuki. These facts have to be made clear.

As for the problem of religion which we have been discussing, this is an important matter in the history of theatre, and is not a matter of gender discrimination. Such discrimination may have existed in the past, but this is not a matter of discrimination against women in the present day This should be understood. The religious reason that woman could not appear on stage was that the dramas were offerings to the gods, and in Buddhism, while discrimination may or may not be the correct term to refer to this, there was the notion that unless women were first reborn as men they could not achieve enlightenment. For this reason women were excluded not only from kabuki but also from sumo and all the other dramatic arts. These are historical facts which should not be confused with the present situation. and in referring to them I intend no discrimination.

Also, I think for time's sake, we ought to confine our discussion to onnagata on the stage, and refrain from discussing whether onnagata cross-dress in the dressing-room or out on the town. If we consider the notion of the onnagata as a life-style, the matter will be much harder to settle.

Kishi: Thank you. I certainly agree with your last point. The social existence of cross-dressing and the onnagata on stage are two different matters. I think some of you might have various opinions about this matter, but because time is limited, let us focus on the matter of the onnagata as a stage phenomenon. Professor Thompson, do you have anything to add to Professor Watanabe's comments'?

Thompson: Yes, I want to ask Professor Shapiro about the origins of the male-dominated English drama, in that certainly there is an element of it being a religious drama, but there is also an element of it being a guild drama. His paper talked about the economic reasons for excluding women from the stage, for keeping the stage as an all-male area of employment. It is the case in the history of the guilds in medieval England that, while women in the earlier middle ages could be members of guilds, they were gradually excluded. When the guilds performed medieval mystery plays they had to be performed solely by guild members, therefore they had to be performed by men. So I think that the church and the economy in a way collude in the exclusion of women, and that the economic reasons are at least as important as religious reasons. I'd like to hear what Professor Shapiro has to say.

Shapiro: I think the religious origins of Elizabethan drama have been a little bit over-emphasized here. It is true that such troupes used to be mentioned in the textbooks as a sort of seedbed of Western drama, but I think that has really been called into question in recent years, and much greater emphasis is put on the sort of proto-professional entertainers who travelled all over the place, all over Europe, and played under the church auspices. Guild members were not religious people. It was a religious occasion, but it was also a civic occasion. By the time we get to the establishment of the playhouses of London, these are really commercial enterprises put together by very shrewd entrepreneurs whose purpose was to make money, and many were very successful at it. I would feel a little uncomfortable about looking at these female impersonations as some vestige of religious androgyny and I would be very uncomfortable about reading *The Merchant of Venice* that way myself. So I think we have a very secularized theatre by the time we get to Shakespeare's day. They are capable of invoking religious resonances but I do not think they are automatically there by any means.

I would also like to say something about the boy companies. As you know, there were companies made up of, well, they called them 'boys', but they got older and older. From about 1599 to 1608 they were two or three very fashionable companies in Elizabethan London. They started out as Queen's Chapel Choir and St Paul's Choristers, and eventually they stopped replacing the members, so they seemed to get older and older. But if you think about female impersonation in that theatrical situation it would look a little bit like the distinction between men and women is really not very pronounced. Whereas if you think of a female impersonation with an adult company like Shakespeare's, you have actors that were, I would say, aged eighteen, nineteen or even twenty by the time they played these major roles, but nevertheless playing opposite a fully developed adult male like Richard Burbage would definitely sharpen the differentiation between genders, whereas we get a kind of blurry one perhaps in children's companies.

Pronko: A lot of the research that I have done had suggested that the young men stopped acting when they were eighteen or nineteen, and I just wanted to ask Mr Shapiro if that is true. Then of course a lot of people do not really seem to know this date. They might have gone on. The absolute cut-off date seems to have been twenty-one. But if they were indeed playing roles like Cleopatra and the Duchess of Malfi when they were eighteen or nineteen, that would suggest something entirely different. They had developed, over a ten-year span perhaps, very specialized techniques which would have to include perhaps a use of the voice to compensate for the deepening of the voice.

Shapiro: Well, the issue of voice is interesting. Apparently, people who have studied this argue that puberty came later then than in the early modern period by a couple of years, and that even the change of voice can be delayed not by castration, as in other countries, but through vocal technique. But I do agree with you that the advanced age, eighteen, nineteen, twenty, twenty-one, does suggest a longer apprenticeship during which a very rigorous training could take place. We are all guessing about this, but I don't think that what we are thinking about here is exploitation of some kind of pre-adult male adolescent femininity. There are children's roles for young boys, but I think as they get confident of their training and confident of their craft, they can be assigned to those roles, like you mentioned – Cleopatra, the Duchess of Malfi, Lady Macbeth – very demanding roles indeed that call for a great deal of craft.

Let us go one small step further with this idea. Obviously, onnagata work is highly trained. They probably spend much longer time in training because they can look forward to a longer time playing those roles. It sounds to me like perhaps the onnagata are closer to the shamanistic transformations than the Elizabethan female impersonators are to their religious tradition. Maybe that accounts for some of the differences that we have been talking about, particularly the more mercurial way women are sometimes presented on the Elizabethan stage, that is, where the illusion may be broken more utterly. There are lots of illusion-breaking, wonderful things in kabuki, but perhaps they do not involve the onnagata quite as often as illusion-breaking involves the heroine. I wonder if perhaps not only the overlay of the enormous art of contrivance, heavy costumes and so on, but lots more training, and shamanistic origins perhaps closer to the surface, make it less desirable to dislodge, to call into question, even for the purpose of appreciating virtuosity. Whereas in the Elizabethan theatre, perhaps it is a convenient meta-theatrical button to press, and it is very easy to do. You can remind the audience that for the moment Cleopatra is a boy. I would read it that way and then go on with the play. But the meta-theatrical trigger seems to be available where female impersonation is concerned more so than in kabuki. So I think.

Kishi: Professor Watanabe previously used the term *kayaku* when speaking about Kikugoro VI, This literally means 'adding another role'. In my understanding, this is when an actor who specializes in male roles plays a woman. In such a case, would such an actor not only not attempt to hide his masculinity but actually try to emphasize it?

Watanabe: No, not at all.

Kishi: No? Would he then perform in the same way as an onnagata?

Watanabe: *Kayaku* is a matter of how an actor is ranked and billed. It is unrelated to what happens on the stage.

Kishi: When I watched Kataoka Takao in *Sendai hagi*, I felt he gave a very masculine impression. Don't you agree?

Watanabe: That's because that role of Yashio is not an onnagata role but a *katakiyaku* or villain role. The roles played by onnagata are all roles of the good woman. If they were not, their beauty would be lost. In the role of an evil woman, as a rule, an actor specializing in male roles appears. I think this is the same in the Beijing Opera, if I am not mistaken.

Hirata: In the case of kabuki, actors are trained from a very young age. They debut on stage in male roles, but after that they learn both male and onnagata dances. So it is not the case that an actor gets training to be an onnagata right from the start. They play both male and female roles. Kōshirō and Kichiemon are examples of actors who were given girl parts when young. I've seen such cases many times. So the image of the onnagata as someone who receives special training from a young age and is always treated as an onnagata, lives as an onnagata, as Professors Shapiro and Pronko have inferred, is quite mistaken. Even if we restrict our discussion to the stage, Utaemon, for example, plays male roles as well. I thought of this when Professor Kishi mentioned the *kayaku*. There's really a lot of freedom involved. However, just because each actor has one specialization, it does not mean that some are onnagata right from the start to end. The best example we have heard so far is that of Baikō, who, though a great onnagata, also has played numerous wonderful male parts, from young boys without their forelocks shaved, to Enya-Hangan the magistrate. So I think that you make a mistake by looking at onnagata in the same light as boy actors.

Kishi: This may be a little bit off the point, but I would like to ask Professor Thompson who is English, about the uniquely English art of pantomime, which is performed at Christmas time. I do not know much about it, but I think it is a very complicated art form wherein there is a principal boy, who is actually an actress who plays roles such as Peter Pan, and a pantomime dame, a male actor who plays characters such as Cinderella's ugly step-sisters. Following the earlier discussion, this also seems to be a case where masculine strength is being emphasized. Here, we have a kind of two-layered cross-dressing: an adult man plays a woman, usually an ugly one, and an adult woman plays a male just before manhood. How does this relate to today's theme?

Thompson: Yes, it is true. Within the British pantomime tradition there is no attempt for a principal boy who is Aladdin, say, to pretend to be a man. The whole pojnt is to display the female body, her legs and so on. There is no intention for the men playing the ugly sisters and the Widow Twankey to conceal the fact that they are men. They play very stereotyped, sexist versions of women basically. I do not think it is the sort of level of cross-dressing or cross-gender casting that really can be seen in the same way as what we are talking about. Though you could put it into the context of cross-dressing within the popular tradition. In England there are lots of pubs that have drag nights with male impersonations of women as popular performances, particularly in towns that have a large military or naval presence, and the audience are often men. They are often very good. But that is slightly different from what we have been mainly talking about.

   I think something I am interested in and I would like to take up from some of what has been said is the question of the strength of the performer and the argument that the man playing female roles in kabuki has a particular kind of strength, and certainly something I read before I got here was arguing that one reason why women could not take on these roles is that the women would not be strong enough either physically to sustain the costumes, the wigs, etc., or in terms of stage presence somehow women could not be sufficiently assertive on the stage to play those roles. I would very much like to hear comments from the members of our panel who are here as specialists in kabuki on that point, if it is an important aspect of the onnagata to portray a kind of strength which is not in fact seen as feminine.

Watanabe: The question of strength really is connected to the role in question. The women played by onnagata have a very strong touch, because on the stage they must find a balance with the male characters, and this point is lost if we talk about onnagata alone. Strength is needed because a balance must be found; it has nothing to do with the fact that the costumes are too heavy for a woman. I think a woman could bear the weight of the costumes. Without that strength of touch in the balance the style of the play would collapse. I think that is the important point.

Hirata: I want to ask Professor Watanabe. As you just said, the onnagata is one part of the unified form that kabuki has taken, a form that includes male acting roles. So I think you are correct in saying that in the form of contemporary kabuki, style and harmony are based upon the premise that women's roles are played by men. Japanese women today, however, are bigger than in earlier days, and if they are trained from their young days in the way that present kabuki actors are trained, would not they be able to play onnagata roles in the manner that men now do?

Watanabe: Actually, my first book was entitled *Women into Kabuki*, so actually I am pretty much on the same side of the argument as Professor Thompson. There is one episode I know of that I think will shed light on the question.

Shirasu Masako was the first woman in Japan to dance the *nō*. There have been others since, but the reason she decided to quit was that she found that *nō* roles were carefully fitted to the male body. She as a woman did not possess the requisite suppleness. Conversely the Inoue school of Japanese dance in Kyoto will absolutely not take any male students. The Inoue style of dance is coming from *nō* and *jōruri* puppet theatre, but in this case if the dancer is not a woman, the right suppleness does not emerge. This is related to artistic balance. It is not about discrimination against either women or men. In the case of Shirasu, the female body could not produce the softness fundamentally required by *nō*. It is related to *nō*'s essence.

Anzai: I think it would be helpful to remember that onnagata play various roles, ranging from the hero Yoshitsune, a beautiful young man, to foxes. Of course, not all foxes are played by onnagata – some are played by the actors who specialize in male roles. So in the case of a fox, gender is not important at all. As I mentioned before, *nō* and also the puppet theatre are not exclusively human dramas at all. We find many animals, spirits of trees and plants, gods, ghosts of dead people, monsters and all kinds of characters in these plays. They create a world wherein foxes and other beings enter on the same level as human beings. I said that it is not even important that the actor be a human, so I think to be too concerned with the idea of gender will also lead us to miss the deeper meaning of kabuki. Kabuki, *nō*, and the puppet theatre are worlds that transcend gender and include animals, plants and the like. Certainly, there are both male and female animals, but there are aspects to these arts that cannot be fully grasped in terms of gender, and I think this touches upon the profoundest aspects of kabuki. There are even creatures which transcend the very boundary between fox and human. It is a world of creatures, of creaturism, we might say, or perhaps animism if you like, and placing too much emphasis upon gender misses much of the point.

Watanabe: I think it is just as Professor Anzai says. An actor, whether kabuki or otherwise, is one who impersonates something else, even the spirit of a plant or animal. Once you take the point of view that male or female gender is easily transcended, it does not really matter whether we are talking about an onnagata or any other actor. Rather, more important than that is the notion of *gei* which I spoke of earlier. *Gei* is a truly fantastic, illusionary or illusionistic thing through which the actor transcends his body to create an imaginary being and in discussing kabuki it is the actor's technique of expressing this *gei* that becomes most important. And what is so fantastic about *gei*, as Professor Anzai just said, is that in kabuki it does not matter that the actor is human. This is what makes kabuki seem so fresh when compared to modern theatre, why it seems just as contemporary. Kabuki does not attempt to re-present anything. Both kabuki and *nō*, when they try to communicate something, do it with methods unrelated to modern notions like facial expression, psychology or personality. All classical Japanese theatre, be it *nō*, *kyōgen*, or *gagaku*, originally used masks, so they are unconnected with human facial expression. Later, *kyōgen* ceased to use the masks, but the *jōruri* is similar in that it uses puppets, and kabuki is too in its thick make-up. Kabuki, then, has solved the great problem of modern theatre in the notion that artistic expression starts once the natural expression of humans is killed off. This is also an important element when performing Shakespeare, which is why Ninagawa Yukio uses onnagata in his Shakespeare productions. I think this is important.

Kishi: Unfortunately, we have come to the end of our time. I think many of you are familiar with Shakespeare is *A Midsummer Night's Dream*, at the end of which a play is performed by a group of amateurs. It is a terribly boring performance, and there is an exchange between two members of the audience. One of them says it is very silly. The other answers that any play will be tolerable if one supplies imagination. The first says that it must be the imagination of the audience, not the actors. The second then says that if the audience think of the actors as highly as they think of themselves, any actor will become a really accomplished one. We up here do not think that we are great actors, but once, when Noël Coward directed his own play *Hay Fever* at the National Theatre in London, he said that the cast was so good that they can even perform the London Telephone Directory. I did not act as the director today, but I am certain you are feeling that such a panel as this can perform perfectly well even without a mediator.

N.B. Forum exchanges originally in Japanese have ben translated by Mark F. Meli (Kansai University).

AFTERWORD

MICHAEL SHAPIRO

I n the late 1980s and early 1990s, I was working on a book on plays with heroines who don male disguise in the plays of Shakespeare and his contemporaries, which was later to be published under the title *Gender in Play*. Since female roles were played by male performers on the English stage, I felt I needed to broaden my thinking about the problem by looking into other traditions which used female impersonation. I did not think of kabuki right away because the only productions of kabuki I had ever seen were those on my own campus, the University of Illinois, which cast women in the female roles. Although two of these productions, under the direction of Shozo Sato, in fact, were kabuki-style versions of *Macbeth* and *Othello*, only later through reading did I understand the importance of the onnagata tradition and how, as an unbroken living performance practice, it might shed new light on our understanding of female impersonation on the early modern English stage. In order to bring kabuki and Elizabethan practices into some sort of dialogue, I organized a seminar for the World Shakespeare Conference held in Tokyo in 1991 and as there were no performances of kabuki to be seen at that time, I invited a young Japanese-American named Mark Oshima, who was studying kabuki in Tokyo, to demonstrate the art of the onnagata and to discuss his understanding of it with members of the seminar. It was an unforgettable experience: dressed in his ordinary man's street clothes and accompanied by a tape on his boom box, Mark performed a song sung by a rejected female lover, and then showed us phrase by phrase how its highly codified movements and gestures combined with the lyrics to express a rich, nuanced, and rapidly changing sequence of emotions.

Most of the participants and observers felt that they had gained valuable insights into a kind of cross-gendered performance practice that might have been close to what was practised on the English Renaissance stage. One such participant a fellow midwesterner, an Iowan named Wayne Silka, who was then teaching at Yamanashi Eiwa Junior College in Kofu, Japan, felt that the seminar had raised enough questions and generated enough interest for an entire conference on female impersonation in the two theatrical traditions. Silka and I corresponded a great deal about the feasibility of such a conference and he took some preliminary steps to organize it. He also engaged the interest of John Russell Brown, who was then embarking on his own cross-cultural studies of theatre. Brown was a major influence in these early planning stages of the project, and later was a featured speaker at the actual conference even though his work is not represented in this collection. In the end, the idea of the conference came to rest in the capable hands of Minoru Fujita, and it was he who did all the practical things which transformed it from an alluring fantasy into a well-funded, well-attended, skilfully-organized, intellectually-stimulating, graciously-appointed, international meeting. Looking again at the essays, both those that grew out of the conference and those added later, recalls the excitement of those days spent in Nishinomiya in August 1995. It is gratifying to see these papers in print, because the conference, though it took place more than a decade ago, was a seminal event in the evolution of critical thinking about female impersonation in both theatrical traditions.

My own contribution to both the conference and the present volume, addressing the introduction of actresses to the English stage, focuses on the moment when the two traditions diverge. Why the English did not introduce actresses sooner is a complex question, and my original intention in writing the essay was to rebut Stephen Orgel's argument that the English preferred female impersonation to female performers because of a cultural inclination towards male homoeroticism, and to suggest that there were historical and structural factors that played an even more significant role. That essay first appeared in another collection, *Enacting Gender on the English Renaissance Stage*, edited by Viviana

Comensoli and Anne Russell (Urbana: University of Illinois Press, 1999), but in light of its genesis it is gratifying to see it in the present volume. In this context, it seems less polemical and more attuned to the collegial spirit that animated the conference, the spirit of theatre historians and theatre artists thinking together about the aesthetic, historical, social and political issues involved in female impersonation on the kabuki and Shakespearean stage.

INDEX

Note: *Names of kabiuki performers are indexed by their stage or art names; all other Japanese names are indexed under family names.*